Outplayed

Mina Myles

Original Cover - Andra Murarasu (@andra.mdesigns)

Special Edition Cover - Fay (@whoisflattery)

Chapter Header Art - Sam, Ink and Velvet Designs

Editing - Lauren, Author's Best Friend

Alpha Reading - Kat's Literary Services

Playlist

Eliana Jasper's Playlist

Fast Car — Tracy Chapman
16 Carriages — Beyoncé
Mirrorball — Taylor Swift
You're On Your Own Kid — Taylor Swift
Teenage Dream — Olivia Rodrigo
Over My Head — The Fray
The Only Exception — Paramore

Jake Keeley's Playlist

In Bloom — Neck Deep
Young Blood — Noah Kahan
Glory and Gore — Lorde
Coffee Talk — Broadside
Forever — Noah Kahan
Late Night Talking — Harry Styles

Author's Note

Dear Lovely Reader,

Thank you so much for picking up a copy of *Outplayed!* Eliana and Jake's story is very special to me and one that completely caught me by surprise. Before you start reading please note that this book contains depictions of microaggressions, anxiety, panic attacks, and parentification of children. Characters in this book discuss their past experiences with being cheated on, emotional and verbal abuse, and feeling pressured to engage into sexual acts (brief mention). Additionally, this book contains profanity, alcohol use, and descriptions of consensual sex. As much as I want you to meet Eliana, Jake, and their loved ones, please prioritize your own well-being.

With Love,
Mina

To every eldest daughter who had to be a provider, caretaker, and parental figure before she was ever allowed to be herself— this is for you. Don't be afraid to put your own needs first. You deserve it. And more.

Chapter 1

Jake

A few weeks ago I *thought* I was fucked. Some Ds on homework assignments never made any parent proud but who the fuck looks at their kid's report cards in college? Definitely not my parents. My coaches, however, do look at my grades. And they were pissed. Now, staring at this fat F on my PSYCH101 midterm, I *know* I'm fucked. My NHL contract was all but signed at this point, but knowing Coach Jameson he'll bench me for the rest of the season for this major screw up. And without any ice time, I can sure as shit kiss my prospects goodbye.

Which is why I was currently on my way to speak with my teaching assistant to see if there was something she could do. I take a deep breath. *You can't lose hockey because of this Jake. Come hell or high water this grade needs to get fixed.* I knock on the door before walking into the office that definitely used to be a broom closet. "Are office hours still going on?"

Violet looks up from her computer and gives me a smile. "Yes! Come on in and feel free to take a seat." She gestures to the chair across from her. "What can I help you with, Jake?"

Shit. She knew my name. PSYCH101 is a pretty popular lecture with at least 100 students enrolled. If Violet knew your name, it was because you were either a kiss ass or a problem child. I definitely fell in the latter category. "I've gotten Ds on the past two homework assignments, and I was wondering if we could maybe figure something out."

I pull out two crumpled worksheets from my backpack and hand them over to her, hating the embarrassment that comes with having to admit I'm struggling. For the most part I was a solid B- student. If I wanted to, I probably could've been an A student, but hockey always comes first and takes up most of my time. Which was why I was here. My hockey eligibility was at risk as my PSYCH101 grade inched closer to a F and I would not spend my senior year on the bench. In previous classes, no one assignment was enough to tank my grade but in this class, 50% of your overall score were these write-ups. And now no matter what I tried — reading the textbook, study groups, online forums— nothing clicked for me. Which was par for the course at this point.

I took this class with the misguided idea that it would no longer make me the dumb jock in my family. So I could finally have something to contribute every time my mom or one of my sisters brought up their research.

After Violet glances over my responses she starts to lecture me about the difference between independent and dependent variables. I tried and failed to focus as my face heated from the shame of not being able to understand one of the most basic topics in the course. My sisters probably learned the difference between independent and dependent variables in middle school, and I still mix them up. The shame amplified my desperate need to get through this conversation as quickly as possible, so I cut her off.

"Coach has really been on my ass lately about my grades,

and I was hoping maybe you could just take a second look and bump me up to a C, or even a C+? I know it would probably look shady if I went from a D to a B."

She blinks at me as if I was speaking a different language. "I'm sorry?"

Grade grubbing isn't something I've ever needed to do, but I know it's how a lot of my teammates get by. The reality is that hockey players at Westchester are responsible for bringing in a large amount of donations to the school. Plus, our fan base is like 60% faculty, so we can get them free passes for games.

"I know that's not my finest work, but I'm sure if you read it again, you'll notice places where you were a little harsh with grading and give me some points back." I nod back to the papers in her hand, and flash her my patented smirk. One that has a tendency to make girls flush. Flirting to get my grade up isn't something I'm proud of, but I'm really *really* desperate. And Violet and I both know I didn't earn a C. Which means it's time to bring out the big guns.

"I'm taking a look at the answer key right now. Unfortunately, I don't see any places where you were mistakenly penalized. I am happy to walk you through these different concepts though, and answer any questions you may have." Her tone is calm, but firm.

"Are you sure? There's really *nothing* you can do?" I sprawl my arms out further exposing my Westchester Men's Ice Hockey shirt as if to say, 'C'mon miss, cut this poor hockey player a break.' Subtlety was fully out the window, but I would let any future embarrassment of this moment haunt me in my nightmares. All rational thinking left me when I realized how close I was to being benched for the rest of the season.

"You're more than welcome to take it up with the professor if you would like. However, I try to be lenient when I grade these assignments and I can't promise that Dr. Grant will do the same. You risk lowering your grade by asking her to regrade it." She hands me back the papers.

This is not going well. The stress and impending doom of losing my whole future starts to weigh down on me and the words that come out of my mouth sound irritated. "C'mon Violet. Can't you cut me a little slack? I had two big games the night before these assignments were due."

"Again, any grade changes are going to have to go through Dr. Grant. If you're worried about your grade in the class, I'm happy to talk to Dr. Grant about coming up with an assignment for you to earn extra credit. We've offered that a few times to students in the past and they've all been able to recover their grades with the additional points."

Fuck me. She really wasn't going to budge. And if all I could muster up on the homework was a D, there's no chance in hell that I could do the extra credit correctly. I studied like hell for the last midterm and I still managed to fail. Any extra time I dedicate to this class would have to be at the expense of prepping myself for games, and I can't do that. "I barely have enough time to do the homework as it is."

I crumple my assignments in my fist and throw them inside my bag next to this week's unfinished homework assignment. I could feel my frustration start to get the best of me. If I was smart I would just confess about how embarrassed I am about this whole situation and how hard it is for me to ask for help.

Unfortunately, my pride wins and I decided to keep digging myself a grave instead. "Well, if you can't change my grades, can you at least give me an extension for the next assignment? It's due the night after our game at Bolton which is honestly just unfair. The whole school is gonna be at that game."

"We don't typically grant extensions unless it's due to extenuating circumstances, and previously scheduled games that you were aware of do not count." Her lips turn into a frown.

"Whatever, this was clearly a waste of my time." I wince as the words come out of my mouth, and I rush out of her office not wanting my mouth to get me into any further trouble. It wasn't her fault I had bit off more than I could chew just to prove a point to myself. Hopefully she wouldn't hold it against me too much.

Whereas many of my teammates came from generations of hockey players, my family legacy included a long line of groundbreaking researchers. Playing hockey on a professional level starts to pale in comparison when you're sitting in a room full of people trying to figure out whether your brain's stress response is a survival mechanism or just your neurons being drama queens. I guess the good news is none of them knew I was even taking this course, which means I didn't have to admit that I was never going to fit in with my family. That didn't quite help me out of my current situation though. What a mess.

Chapter 2

Jake

Any day now Coach Jameson is going to pull me aside and read me the riot act. The fact that it hasn't happened yet puts me on edge as I enter the arena for practice. Around my teammates I've acted like my normal cocky self. No one's the wiser about how rough things have been for me. I didn't want to scare anyone. Having your alternate captain benched would definitely cause a panic amongst our players, which is not what we needed right now. I needed my teammates to have their sole attention on improving their own game, instead of worrying if I would be playing alongside them.

All of my anxieties fade as I enter the locker room. Hockey is my center of gravity, everything about it keeps me grounded. From the chill of the ice when I first skate out, the rush of scoring, to celebrating with my boys — who are more like brothers to me. Everything made sense in this locker room. In this arena. On the ice. Sometimes hockey felt like the *only* thing that made sense to me. Women, school, life — all confusing as hell. And I'll be damned if I let PSYCH 101 take that away from me.

Adam, my co-captain and roommate, gives me a nod as I walk to my locker to get ready for practice. On the outside, we couldn't be more different. He was an interesting blend of inquisitive and broody. I was the wild child who couldn't keep my mouth shut and loved having a good time. Our differences balanced us out in a way that made us perfect roommates. Plus, on the ice we were magic together. I'd never been on the same line with someone who could practically read my mind.

From the corner of my eye, I catch two of the freshmen wrestling over a roll of stick tape and I can't help but be reminded of the first time Adam and I met. I nod my head toward the freshman and nudge Adam. "Remember our first practice together? I ate your last protein bar and you nearly strangled me." It was the only time I've heard Adam raise his voice.

"You mean after you used up all of my stick tape and hid my change of clothes as a 'prank'?" He rolls his eyes.

"I made it up to you later by getting you a Costco-sized box of your favorite protein bars."

"I guess putting up with your harassment does have its benefits."

A wave of silence washes over the locker room, and I turn to see a former Westchester legend. A guy I looked up to when he made it to the NHL and won the Stanley Cup. And also felt really bad for when he had to medically retire. Coach Jameson had warned us he was coming by and I couldn't wait to pick his brain about how to tighten up my slap shot.

"Holy Shit. We got Mason Hayes back in Westchester. You back to see the new golden age of college hockey?" I couldn't help my shit-eating grin or my momentary lapse in judgment as I threw my arm around this living legend like we are old pals. I'm star stuck and handling this the best I can. "Listen man, any chance you can get me two glass seats to the next Rangers game? There's this absolute rocket in my marketing class that I've been trying to take out and—"

"Shut your big mouth Jake before you say something that will get us all skating suicides after practice," Adam hollers over me, rolling his eyes before nodding at Mason. "Adam Reed, right wing, and team captain."

"And he never lets us forget it, ," I quip which earns me a laugh from the rest of the team. Adam ignores me as he continues to get dressed.

Coach Jameson bursts into the room right after, clueing us in as to why Mason's here. "Alright everyone, listen up. We have some important announcements. As you may know the process of finding a new assistant coach after Coach Whitney retired has been a shit show. Mason will be filling in until we make our final decision."

Holy shit this is about to be fun. Not only was Mason one of the best players on his team back in the day, he had a killer reputation as a ladies' man and life of the party at Westchester. Coach Jameson had a stick up his ass and regularly called us out for our 'work hard, play hard' mentality. Now that Mason was here, I had a feeling that mentality would be more appreciated. My teammates apparently agreed as cheers echoed throughout the room.

"While I understand all the excitement, I'd like to remind everyone that Mason is here to be a Coach. And *not* your friend." I hold in a snort. Yeah, we'll see about that.

As the locker room starts to clear out for practice, Mason pulls me aside. "Hey Jake let me talk to you for a second."

He sounds a little serious. Was asking for Rangers tickets too much? "What's up coach?"

"We need to talk about your PSYCH101 grade. You know the University has a strict policy on benching players that have any active grades lower than a C-. We're going to have to take you out of the next game if you don't get your grade up." He crosses his arms over his chest — all business.

Dammit. Coach Jameson had already gotten to him. I was hoping I'd be able to impress Mason with my hockey skills before he learned I was on the brink of being benched. I hated that he already viewed me as a liability for the team. He's also playing his new hard-ass assistant coach role really well, and it feels incredibly hypocritical. While I understand that he is being forced to follow university policy, from what I heard about Mason's time on the team, he also dicked around and didn't take his classes seriously.

My irritation starts to build. "Are you serious?"

"I don't like this any more than you do," he confesses. That softened me up a bit. Coach Jameson probably put Mason up to this as his first big task. *"Go fix the problem child with the bad grades and even worse attitude."* Not exactly the first impression I wanted to have with one of my heroes. Mason gives me a sheepish look. "But the rules are the rules."

He just aged himself 10 years with that line. "We're going up against Bolton and UCONN soon. All the scouts are going to be there. I need to be on that ice. Besides, it's not even my fault I have a D in that class. The TA took off all these extra points on my assignment and when I tried to ask her to fix it, she just blew me off." I huff in frustration. A therapist would probably have something to say about how easily the lies roll off my tongue when hockey is threatened.

Mason raises an eyebrow at me. "C'mon man, be real with me here and I'll do what I can to help get you out of this."

I give him a rough recap of my meeting with the TA, editing the story to hide how much of an asshole I was. Storming out of the room and acting like an entitled brat during my conversation with Violet was definitely not something I'm proud of. But I'm in way over my head and beyond desperate to keep hockey. So whatever I have to do to keep my time on the ice, I will.

I can see Mason debate whether or not to trust me, when he finally concedes. "How about I talk to your TA? Maybe she'd be more understanding of your situation if it came from your coach."

The heaviness on my shoulders lightens a bit. "You'd honestly be saving my ass. I can send you her office hours and maybe you can drop by?"

"Yeah, that sounds like a plan. I'll let you know how it goes." The sound of the whistle signaling the beginning of practice catches our attention. "Why don't you get your ass on the ice and show me— what did you say earlier? 'The new golden age of college hockey?'" He rolls his eyes at my previous jab.

I flash a smug grin. "You got it Coach."

Chapter 3

Eliana

My Google calendar was currently lit up like a Christmas tree. Classes were in red, my lab hours as a research assistant were in purple, and nannying was in blue. Admittedly there wasn't a ton of open space left for things like eating lunch, watching TV, or sleeping, but that was to be expected. Between a full course load as a psychology and creative writing double major and my jobs, I was spread thin. *Very* thin. But I loved (most of) the things on my plate. Getting to see the babies I nanny turn into small humans with their own little personalities and opinions always warmed my heart, and being a research assistant satiated my curiosity and perpetual need to problem solve.

I also loved a challenge and was very bad at saying no to people who needed my help. On the outside, I was headstrong and scoffed at any obstacle in my way. On the inside, I was a chronic people pleaser who felt the need to take on too much to make everyone else's life easier. That was what I had always done. What I felt comfortable doing. What I was good at. Sleep be damned.

I became this people-pleasing provider as soon as there was a vacancy in the family. My dad cut contact with me, my mom, and my sister when I was 13 after finding a new wife with a bank account that could keep his gambling habits funded for as long as his heart desired. It was hard to be sad about him leaving since before he cut contact, it wasn't like he was touting a #1 Dad cup. Most weeks he was away on business trips — or at least that's what he told us. He'd send back enough money to keep us out of a community shelter. My mom never resented him for it, or let us see it if she did. She probably felt like she had to be grateful. Though my mom was now a U.S. citizen, the only reason she was able to immigrate to the U.S. was because of him — a marriage that was set up by both of their parents in Iran. Her initial years here were spent learning English and catering to my father's needs. I wasn't alive to see the tumultuous first few years of their marriage, but I've heard enough to know most nights she went to bed terrified of his temper.

The dining hall starts to flood with the lunch crowd when a calendar reminder pops up on my screen — *really, what would I do without it?* — prompting me to pack up my bag and head towards the psychology building. Entering Dr. Bethany Coleman's lab I see Violet, the graduate student who serves as my main mentor and general support system. Violet hired me to work on her projects when I was only a freshman. In addition to getting to work with MRI scanners and super cute, chunky babies, Violet and I bonded over being first generation college students, and women of color. Watching her navigate the very political land of academia was incredibly inspiring and motivating. In many ways Violet was like the older sister I never had, and her kindness towards me was something I would always be grateful for.

"How was your weekend?" Violet asks looking up from her laptop.

"The usual. Saturday was spent nannying. Little Kai has started to babble my name and it's the *cutest* thing ever. Truly love that kid. Sunday was spent working on a paper."

"You're really living the wild life aren't you? It wouldn't kill you to go out once in a while," she teases.

"True. Nothing beats dusty, overcrowded frat basements."

"Is this semester any less busy for you than the previous one?"

"That would be a negative. But such is being a student at Westchester. I'm used to it at this point."

Violet opens her mouth before hesitating. Instead of continuing she shakes her head.

"What is it?"

"I feel bad asking you, given how spread thin you already are…" She bits her lip.

"Just ask me. I can always say no." *But would you?* I ignore the voice in my head and give Violet a reassuring smile.

"I know you decided to take a break from tutoring this semester but there's a student in my class who is in desperate need of one. And you're the best."

I had initially decided to put a pause on tutoring to free up some time in my schedule for the additional courses I was taking to knock out some of my creative writing requirements. At one point my advisor suggested dropping my double major, but I couldn't imagine that. I'd chosen psychology because I loved learning about people, but also because the job prospects seemed a lot more stable than being a novelist. Despite the part of me that was a realist, I refused to fully give up on my second dream — writing murder mystery novels, with a proper dose of romance.

Which meant the tutoring gig was on the back burner, even though I loved it. I was addicted to that moment when you could *see* the lightbulb moment in your mentee's eyes. The elation when they finally see their grades improving. It never failed to make my heart overflow with joy. Thinking back on those moments makes me reconsider taking a break. "I should have room to take on one client. I can just cut back on some of my nannying hours, which should be fine since I can still get paid through the tutoring center."

"Are you sure? I'd hate to add more to your plate."

"Yup. I'll make it happen, don't worry about it." As a people pleaser herself, Violet knew hearing someone was in need was my kryptonite. It was frankly impossible for me to say no at this point.

"I have to warn you...This student is a little rough around the edges. Tutoring is his only option to stay on the hockey team, not something that he personally is choosing to do. He's already attempted to bribe three other tutors and if another one quits on him, the tutoring center will put him on probation."

I'd worked with lots of student athletes before without any issues, but as a hockey fan myself I knew the team on campus viewed themselves as celebrities. The kind that didn't need to work for their grades. I would need to keep my guard up with whoever my new tutee was.

"He's not the first athlete I've had to tutor." I shrug. "Plus, I love challenges. I do appreciate the warning though."

"If he does end up giving you any trouble, even a hint of it, let me know and I'll figure something else out."

"Will do. Don't worry Vi, I'll whip him into shape." I wink. I've dealt with cocky athletes before, and given he was at risk of being benched, he was stuck with me. Whether he liked it or not.

Chapter 4

Jake

Admittedly my initial attempt to fix my grade (demanding Violet change my grade and lying to my assistant coach about how she had been failing me for no reason) was not my brightest idea. I could've just told Mason the truth. If anyone would've understood prioritizing hockey it would've been him, but alas I couldn't keep my big mouth shut.

Which ultimately led me here— stuck in an incredibly awkward and tense meeting where my coach and TA try to figure out what to do with me. I had assumed they didn't know each other but the longer I sat in the room with them the more I felt like there is some weird history there. Mason's longing glances in her direction every 30 seconds, and Violet's attempt to barely acknowledge his presence had my hook-up-gone-wrong alarm sounding. Great. Just what I needed. One more reason for Violet to hate me.

"With the urgency of the situation, and everyone's strong desire to help Jake get back on track—" Violet emphasizes the last bit in a not-so-subtle dig at how I claimed she didn't care about her students. Alright fine. It was a dickish thing to say. But I hated it when people felt sorry for me and looked at me like I was helpless. I hated it even more when I felt pitied.

"I think we should start Jake's first tutoring session next week. I already have the perfect person lined up who has agreed to help."

Violet's words snap me back into the present. "Wait *what?* I'm not getting a tutor." It was bad enough that my coaches and Violet knew I was struggling. Now a complete stranger had to know too? "Not happening."

"Jake," Mason starts, his eyes pleading with me to listen. "There's no other option. We need to get your grades up."

I turn my attention to Violet. "Can't I just promise to study some more? And do that extra credit you offered?"

"Unfortunately, even with the extra credit assignment, if you don't start improving your homework grades significantly, and get at least a B on the final, you won't pass the class."

"This is a fucking nightmare," I groan, dragging my hands over my face.

"I promise Eliana is the best tutor we have. And she's worked with a lot of athletes in the past so she's used to accommodating busy schedules."

Violet goes on and on about how great my new tutor is, but all I can think about is how I managed to get myself into this mess. *You really thought you'd prove to your family that you're more than just some hockey player huh? Now look where you're at. You might not even be a hockey player anymore.*

"Jake?" Mason asks and I realize I'd managed to zone out again.

"Sorry. You're sure there are no other options?"

"I'm afraid not." Violet gives me a small smile. "You know Jake, there's nothing wrong with asking for some help."

Oh brother. Not this. Anything but this.

She takes a small breath before continuing. "I failed Intro to Psych during undergrad. It was a real hit to the ego. I still remember how embarrassed I felt. How I thought my whole life was over. It was hard to reach out for help. To admit that I had failed at something I wanted to make into a career, but it was the best thing I could've done for myself at the time. And I'm here now because of it."

Well I definitely wasn't expecting *that*. If tutoring was the only way to get me back on track then, "Alright fine, I'll do it. I'll do whatever I need to if it ensures I get to stay on the team."

"Good. I'll send Eliana your contact info. She'll be in touch soon about your first session." Violet closes her laptop and leaves the office before Mason can even get out the words he was opening his mouth to say. Instead, he closes his mouth and stares at the now-opened door to his office.

A few seconds later he brings his attention back to me. "This will be good for you Jake. I know it doesn't feel like it now, but it will be."

"I guess we'll find out soon enough."

* * *

"Wanna head to O'Malley's for dinner?" Adam asks after going through our fridge and realizing we have nothing left to scrape up into a meal. Adam, Ollie, and I had gotten home from practice about an hour ago, too sore to do anything but lay on the coach until our stomachs started growling.

A greasy burger sounded heavenly right now, but I had to head out soon to my own personal hell — tutoring. "I want to, but I can't."

Oliver, our team goalie and one of my best friends, scoffs in mock offense. "Why not?"

"I just have something I gotta do."

"Blowing us off for a hook-up, Keeley? I'd like to say I'm surprised but we know that would be a lie." Ollie smirks.

"It's not that." I couldn't blame him for assuming that's where I was heading. I tried not to bail on the boys too much, but the moments I did it was to scratch an itch with whatever sorority girl was free that night.

Ollie raises an eyebrow at me. "What's going on man? You've been cagey about plans for the past few weeks."

"I'm fine I just have a lot on my plate."

"Like what?"

I wish I could forget about the fact that I messed up so badly that I now needed weekly meetings with someone who would constantly remind me how incompetent I was. Tutoring was all I could think about these past couple of days. If I could go back in time and talk myself out of taking this class, I would. No amount of praise on my psych knowledge from my family was worth losing hockey.

For as quiet as Adam was, he was also incredibly perceptive, "Dude, you're normally an open book. You're freaking me out by dodging all our questions."

"My psych grade is bad enough that I might get benched if I don't fix it. I start tutoring today." I mumble the words that feel like acid in my mouth.

Ollie clicks his tongue. "Why didn't you tell us sooner? We could have tried to help."

"I didn't want to worry anyone...and I didn't realize how bad it was."

"Well. Shit."

"My sentiments exactly. I should probably get going." I give them both a nod before walking out of our house, which is in a neighborhood right next to campus where a bunch of Greek life and athlete houses are located. I make it halfway down the street when I hear my name being called.

I give the familiar blonde a nod. "Mandy. You coming to Hockey House this weekend?"

"Absolutely. I miss seeing you around." She closes the distance between us, clutching my bicep with her hand. She licks her lips, dragging her eyes down my body." It's been a while since you've come over. My feelings are hurt." She pouts, giving me her best puppy dog eyes.

Mandy and I had an understanding that whatever went on between us was physical and only physical. I had no interest (or time) in getting into a serious relationship, and neither did she, which is why things were so easy between us.

"Well, that's the last thing I'd ever want to do. Maybe I can make it up to you soon?" I offer. The suggestive tone of my voice making it very clear how I planned on making her feel better.

"What about now?" She asks tugging me off the sidewalk.

"I don't know if that's a good idea. I have to be on the other side of campus in an hour—"

"An hour is more than enough time. Or are you that out of practice?" she teases.

Taking a quick glance at my watch I do the math in my head. I'd be out in 30 minutes. 40 tops. More than enough time to make it to the library, and get settled. "Oh Mandy, you have no idea what you've just unleashed." I follow her inside the Sigma Kappa house.

Chapter 5

Eliana

I loved getting new tutoring clients. Learning their background, helping them tailor their study techniques, watching them grow from our first meeting to the last. As I sit in the library prepping for Jake, some of the tension in my shoulders starts to fade as I think back to all my previous tutoring experiences. Even my more demanding clients, who had to bring several of their grades up, always ended up making my day as I watched their confidence and knowledge grow. I imagined tutoring was a lot like co-captaining a ship— in the beginning you're battling unruly waters, but with experience and a confident crew, things become smooth sailing.

I anxiously glance at my colorful calendar. It took some shuffling around to squeeze my new tutoring client in, but his late arrival is making my tight squeeze look a little questionable. I know life happens — see the already accounted for 10-minute buffers in my calendar for people showing up late to meetings — but Jake was now 30 minutes late and I was starting to get antsy.

He had responded to my email yesterday confirming he

could make it so he definitely knew our appointment was coming up. Maybe I should just leave and reschedule? I don't want to be late for my study session with Nicole...Ugh, I can't. This was a favor I was doing for Violet, someone I really cared about and respected. And after putting off nannying, I really needed the money that came with a steady tutoring client. So here I sat, anxiously checking the analog clock hung up on the library wall as all this precious time went by. Wasted. *Maybe I should start working on my own homework while I wait...*

"Hey are you Eliana?"

My attention shifts from the clock to the sound of a deep male voice. I have to crane my neck to take in the 6'4 blonde rocking a Westchester U Men's Ice Hockey hoodie.

"You're late." The words come out much harsher than my normal greeting, but Violet had warned me that he had an attitude and a bad habit of being disrespectful. Which wasn't in the least bit surprising. Westchester's hockey team all viewed themselves like God's gift to Earth, or at least God's gift to hockey.

As an avid hockey fan myself, I couldn't say I blamed them for their massive egos. Being born and raised in New England, rooting for the Boston Bruins was expected of me from birth. And given the Bruins had a solid track record of signing players from local universities, I often found myself keeping tabs on the star players in the Hockey East conference. Lack of punctuality and poor grades aside, Jake Keeley was incredible on the ice. And if rumors were true, in a few years he'd be rocking a spoked B and playing for the Bruins. Unfortunately for Jake, it appeared he had forgotten his future in hockey was tied to maintaining his GPA. I won't deny that there's a part of me that's geeking out over the fact that I'm tutoring one of the NHL's biggest prospects, but I'd already told myself I wouldn't treat him differently than any of my previous clients.

Despite my current snippiness, I had no issues with hockey or student athletes. If anything, the previous athletes I had tutored had shown me how many of them got a bad rap for not caring enough about school. My best friend Nicole fell into this category. In addition to being the current captain of Westchester's D1 softball team, she was also premed.

"In the future could let me know if you're running late? Just so I'm in the loop." I try not to sound super annoyed. Just because I lived my life maximizing every second of every day didn't mean he had to.

"Sorry I thought I gave myself enough time to get here but...let's just say I didn't account for the traffic." Jake shrugs, taking a seat in the chair across from mine. "I came over as fast as I could."

"I understand. Life happens. Let's get started. I put together a study guide—"

DING! His phone goes off in his pocket and pause. He waves me on to continue.

"That outlines the main concepts of the chapters. It looks like your midterm covered observational psych to—"

DING! Jake sighs heavily, pulling his phone out. His eyebrows knit in concern as he rapidly texts.

My concern for whatever is happening is mixed with the slight irritation I feel bubbling up in my chest. "Everything alright?"

Jake's eyebrows pinch together as he shakes his head. "No. Defusing a big disaster."

"Sorry to hear that. Is there anything I can do to hel—"

"Ollie is freaking out right now. He forgot to let the Tri Delts and most of the Sigma Kappa's know about the party we're throwing this Saturday so now we're stuck trying to coordinate something with the Gamma Phi's instead."

I blink once. Then twice. "Excuse me?"

He glances up at me and likely catches my annoyed expression. "Shit sorry, where are my manners? You're totally welcome to come and bring any friends. Preferably girls since our guy-to-girl ratio is kinda off already. Feel free to drop by Hockey House after 10 p.m."

Despite being a hockey fan, you wouldn't catch me dead in the cesspool that was Hockey House. I am almost certain if the CDC did a full swipe of that place, they'd probably discover three new STDs among other atrocities. "Do you think we could get back to the reason why we're both here?" I shove the study guide back into his view.

"Shit sorry, yes." He finally places his phone back into his pocket. "Go ahead."

"Since you need to diffuse a…crisis…maybe it's best that for our session today I show you the general schedule I came up with for our tutoring sessions and then next session we can dive into content. I've added some practice worksheets you should try to complete before we meet." I pull out the color-coded document detailing the remaining weeks of the semester and slide it over to him, while annotating my own copy. "I already have all your games, home and away, accounted for but if there are other events or conflicts I missed—"

"Yeah this all looks great." Jake barely even skims it over before haphazardly folding the schedule into his bag and pulling out a crumpled paper to show me. "So, I have some questions on the homework that I'm struggling to wrap my brain around."

Through the crinkles I recognize this week's homework assignment, which he's half completed. "Sure, I can take a look at the answers you have so far. And then we can go over the rest next week when we meet again…." I trail off taking a second to actually look at the worksheet in front of me. "This is due tonight."

He winces in response, "I know. I'm sorry. I tried my best to finish it, but I just couldn't figure out the answers. My notes and the textbook were no help."

My heart tugs. So many of my past tutoring clients had said the same. Shared that defeated look on their faces. My sympathy dissolves a moment later when he opens his mouth.

"Given the tight deadline, I was hoping you could help me out. Just this once. Then next week you can walk me through how you got all the answers." He worries his bottom lip between his teeth, looking like a child that got caught sneaking a cookie before dinner.

I grit my teeth, then let out a deep breath and manage to say, "I don't think it would be appropriate for me to give you the answers without you first trying."

"I understand. But I promise I'll go back and review my notes later." Jake bats his eyelashes at me, and for some reason that sets me off the edge.

Did he really think he could flirt his way into getting these answers out of me? Sure I may be a people pleaser, but I'm not a complete pushover. I glance at the time on my laptop, mentally calculating how far behind I would fall on my work if I continued to entertain this. "You know what? Unfortunately, I don't think this is going to work out." I pack up my bag and stand up from the table. "But I will be sure to get you connected with another tutor ASAP."

A pit in my stomach starts to form. As much as I wanted to quit right now, I definitely needed the money from tutoring especially since I'd stopped my nannying job. It's fine, I'd figure something else out.

That seems to catch Jake's attention as he collects his things and follows me out of the library. "Wait what?"

I don't make it far before he cuts in front of me and blocks me from going any further. "I feel like my schedule and my tutoring style just aren't aligned with your needs. So I think it's best if I help you find someone else—"

He shakes his head vehemently. "You can't quit, you're my tutor."

I think back to my conversation with Violet. Jake had already had several tutors quit on him, one more quitting would put him on probation. As annoyed as I was in this moment I didn't want to leave him hanging. "Don't worry I'll tell the tutoring center that I couldn't make things work with my schedule. You won't be penalized, so they'll be able to get a new tutor lined up by tomorrow. There's usually a lot of tutors who have extra availability in their calendar—"

"I don't want someone else. I want you."

My stupid heart skips at his words, because yes, even though I'm enraged who wouldn't have at least some reaction to a declaration like that?

"I'm really not that special."

"That's not true." He shakes his head vehemently. "You're the best tutor in the psychology department. Maybe even in the whole school. And that's what I need."

"I just don't think this is going to work out."

"It will. I need it to. Please." He pinches the bridge of his nose, takes a deep breath, and then continues. "Listen, I made a lot of mistakes recently. Including showing up late today. My coach gave me an ultimatum about my grade in this class. Either I take tutoring seriously or I can expect to ride the bench for the rest of the season. I can't do that. I *can't* lose hockey. I won't."

"I get that. I just don't see why *I* have to be your tutor."

"If my coach finds out I chased off another tutor after the first session, I'll be screwed. He's already mad at me for how I've handled this whole situation. This is basically my fourth chance. You quitting would be a surefire sign that I blew it." A look of shame and self-doubt spreads over his face. "I can't mess up again. I'm out of chances."

Flirty comments and smoldering looks did not affect me. Begging for my help however... "Fine." I watch as his face perks up, back to its normal cocky state. "But we do things my way. On my schedule. And you promise to never ask me for answers to your homework again." He gives me a small nod. "Great. I'll email you a new time to meet, and what to have prepared ahead of time."

"Yes, Sergeant." Jake gives me a mock salute, that I roll my eyes at.

I walk away wondering if I just made a colossal mistake agreeing to be his tutor.

Chapter 6

Jake

I was going to get *another* shitty grade for this week's homework assignment. I should've known better than to take Mandy up on her offer for a quick hook-up. I also should've known better than to ask my tutor to give me the homework answers. But I was feeling really desperate. Whenever I felt desperate or stuck in a corner I tended to make some really stupid decisions. *This fucking blows.*

After Eliana left, I decided to head back home. Our triple-decker building, lovingly dubbed 'Hockey House' decades ago by some former Westchester players who were too drunk to think of anything more creative. From the outside, it looked normal and blended in with all the other apartment buildings on the street. The inside was what I liked to refer to as 'controlled chaos.' With nearly half of the team living in one house, there was no better term for it. The basement had fully been converted into a home gym/man cave although some could argue our entire house was just one large man cave.

With a bunch of college hockey players left to their own devices on how to decorate three stories, it should come to no one's surprise that our living room was decked out with various forms of hockey and sports memorabilia. Thanks to Adam being especially anal about cleanliness —that man had somehow got us to agree to a regular chore schedule— we had actually managed to keep this place in pretty great shape over the years. I wish I could say that was the case when we inherited the house. Did I still have nightmares about the fact that we had found used condoms in places where used condoms should never see the light of day? Yes. Yes, I did. But after the hellish deep cleaning, we all agreed to be better than our predecessors and never let anything like that happen on our watch.

Before I make it upstairs to my room and sleep away the long day I had, Adam waves me over to the kitchen where he's currently reheating emergency lasagna I made and stashed in the freezer for nights we I am too lazy to cook. My father's love for cooking was very much passed down to me. Growing up, food was always a solace in my house. Which means even if I wanted to walk away, I couldn't. The smell of tomato sauce provide a level of comfort and make my stomach grumble. Between practice and Mandy, I was drained. The smell carries through the kitchen as I walk in. Adam slides over a plate and nods for me to pull up a seat on the bar. "So how did tutoring go?"

"Fine. My tutor seems super organized. The girl's tiny, but works like a drill sergeant...She'll hopefully be able to get me back on track." I shrug, painting a slightly more optimistic picture of my session.

"Well hopefully this tutor will pull through." Adam shoves his face with more lasagna.

"This'll work. I promise."

Adam nods his head in response without making eye contact with me. "You know we're all here for you if you need us, right? We can host group study sessions as often as you need them."

"I appreciate it. I'll let you know if I need extra support. For now, I'm going to hope this tutor is as much of a miracle worker as they say she is."

"And she had the *audacity* to say that I should have analyzed my data using multilevel modeling, instead of ANOVAs." Charlotte screams into the phone as if I was the cause of all her problems. Such is the glory of being the middle child. You get to be your older sibling's punching bag while getting none of the perks of being the youngest. "Can you believe that, Jake?"

What I couldn't believe was that Charlotte thought I knew the difference between multilevel modeling and ANOVAs, but I'd come to learn when she academically rambled like this, she really just wanted someone to vent to more than anything else.

"Damn that's wild. I can't understand why she would say that to you." Like I literally didn't understand. We had started to get into some basic statistics in PSYCH101 the past three weeks, not that I had retained much from lectures. Lucky for me, I had spent most of my life learning how to provide a comment here and there that would show I was insightful instead of utterly clueless about whatever the hell my mom and sisters were talking about.

"I. KNOW. It gets worse. After she dumps that little nugget of information on me, she THEN says I should rerun *all* of my stats, for projects that are already completed, before I have to defend my dissertation. Which, by the way, is in two days. Does she not understand how stressed I already am? Why couldn't she have just been like 'Looks great Char, I'm so proud of all you've accomplished'?"

"Because she's Mom. And Mom will compromise on many things but her thoughts when it comes to research isn't one of them. Why did you even send her your proposal anyway? It's not like she's your advisor or even on your dissertation committee."

Deep down I knew the answer. No matter how much me and my siblings wanted to and tried to deny it, we all wanted our mother's approval more than anything. Even though she was one of the most supportive moms out there, we always felt like we had to prove ourselves to her. Just the aura world renowned neuroscientist Katherine Fisher has when you're in the room with her makes you feel unworthy. Even as her children.

"Because even though I'm nearly 30 I still crave some validation from her. It's the price you pay be an academic. You give away your best years hoping a few people will give your work enough praise and support to keep you going for the foreseeable future while you continue to seek that same validation. Rinse and repeat. Unfortunately, one of the most prominent researchers in my field also happens to be my mom. So that just comes with its own extra fun baggage."

"I bet your therapy sessions are super fun."

That manages to get a laugh out of her. "Oh you have nooo idea."

"I can't judge, mine wouldn't be any better." If anything, they'd probably be worse. At least Charlotte understood what mom was doing and knew enough that they could argue about it. I could barely even keep up when it came to the basics.

"Well if you ever want to talk to Cheryl, let me know. She's been a real rock these last few years."

"I'll keep you posted." Given how it was hard enough already for me to talk about my academic problems with my best friend, I didn't see me opening up about other insecurities to a complete stranger.

"So how are things going with the team? Sienna and I did a little watch party last weekend and streamed your last game against Quinnipiac. Nice goal by the way."

It was moments like these where I felt a bit silly for being insecure about being the only nonacademic in my family. Both of my sisters kept up with my season, which included streaming my away games together on the weekends.

"Yeah we had a rough start, but I think things are slowly starting to mesh. We have a new assistant coach too, Mason Hayes. He used to play for Westchester before going to the NHL. And now he's back." No one really talked about Mason's early retirement due to a rough history of concussions during his time in the pros. It was clearly still a sore subject for him.

"How exciting. I bet you've already picked his brain about your pending NHL contract."

That had been the plan initially, until the only thing Mason wanted to talk to me about was how I planned on fixing my grades so I wouldn't get benched for the rest of the season. My odds of getting an NHL contract were solid up until the threat of being benched. Hard to convince teams you're not a liability when you're not getting any ice time. "Yeah, I haven't gotten to it yet, but I definitely will soon."

"Well keep me posted on any updates. I want to be the first to know when my baby brother makes it to the big leagues."

"Ah still upset that I told Sienna about signing with Westchester before I told you, huh?" I snicker.

"I just don't understand why you would choose to tell her before you told your older sister. Who — in case you forgot — made sure you were fed, clothed, and bathed when mom was finishing up her dissertation and dad was too busy managing a newborn. A little appreciation would have been nice," she teases.

"Hmm maybe I blocked that out because I was still scarred from when you would make me wear princess dresses and play tea time."

"I plead the fifth...and also need to go figure out what the hell to do with my proposal." Charlotte groans and I can feel her irritation through the phone. "Wish me luck."

"Don't overthink it, and don't let mom get in your head. You got this Char."

"Thanks Jake. Love you. Let me know if you need anything."

She hangs up before I get the courage to ask her for help with my psychology homework, which is probably for the best. As badly as I didn't want to mess up on another assignment, the idea of her knowing I was struggling with the one thing that connected my mom and sisters the most felt even worse.

Chapter 7

Eliana

"What are the odds I convince you to be my wing woman this weekend?" Nicole walks into my room with an excited look on her face. "I'm thinking we start at Club Café and end at Dani's."

"Hmm that depends. Will I be playing the role of your jealous ex-girlfriend to get you out of painful conversations?" I snicker.

"You only had to do that *once*," she protests.

"And I ended up getting kicked out of the bar because the girl flirting with you thought I was a crazy stalker who couldn't let you go!" The worst part was I had been tossed out before I could grab my coat. If not for the shots I had taken forming an invisible liquor jacket I would've frozen my ass off.

"Don't act like you didn't have fun. I even got you on the dance floor!"

"I honestly don't remember the last time I've gotten that drunk." I remembered the hangover, though. It was not pretty.

"Sounds like the perfect reason to say yes then." Nicole

throws my closet door open and pulls out a hanger. "You still haven't worn out this cute little black dress you thrifted?"

"Ugh I know it's practically screaming at me to be worn out."

"Perfect. So then Saturday's a date?"

"Yes! Absolutely. Let me just double-check my calendar..." Ah shit. "Dammit. I'm already booked. I'm watching Kai."

Nicole's eyebrows scrunch together. "I thought you had weekends off from nannying?"

"Normally yes, but they're going to an anniversary dinner and their backup babysitter dropped out last minute. I couldn't say no." I mean I probably could've, but I loved seeing little Kai babble new words and getting his bearings running around the apartment.

"Well at least you ended up dropping that tutoring gig. You were spreading yourself way too thin."

"About that..." I wince, preparing for Nicole's scolding. That was the thing about living with your best friend: they look you in the eye and tell you the cold, hard truth whether you want to hear it or not. Or at least that's how Nicole and I operated.

"I have a bad feeling I'm not going to like this." Nicole sits on my bed, crossing her arms.

"Violet, didn't he show up thirty minutes late and ask you to do his homework for him?"

"Yes...except I may have left out the part where I still agreed to be his tutor despite all of that." I give Nicole a sheepish smile, hoping she'll go easy on me.

"I'm sorry, say that again. I must have misheard you."

"I said I'm Jake's tutor."

"Well Jake is a very common name. This simply must be a different Jake than the one you ranted about for three hours—"

"Two hours—"

"For *three hours* to me a few days ago. It has to be someone else. A different Jake. Either that or you managed to give yourself a minor concussion that also comes with amnesia. Or maybe you're really sick and hallucinating. That could also be it." She shakes her head before walking over to me, pretending to check my vitals. "Don't worry, if you're coming down with something, I can take you to the hospital."

"Are you done now?" I roll my eyes, batting her hand away.

"I am satisfied for the moment, yes. Please continue."

"It's the same Jake I spent three hours venting to you about. And before you give me too much shit for it, you should've seen his face when he realized I was serious.He just looked so helpless and I...I just caved, okay?" I drag my hands over my face, too embarrassed to face Nicole, who I know was trying her best not to look at me with pity. She never had any issues telling people no or actually keeping the boundaries she put in place. Me, on the other hand..."I'm an absolute sucker, aren't I?"

"No, you're not. You just have a soft heart for anyone who's had it rough and a tendency to spread yourself too thin to try help everyone you think needs saving instead of imposing boundaries for yourself."

"Damn. You sound a lot like my therapist."

"Well maybe you should listen to both of us and give yourself a break. Starting with pulling out of this tutoring gig. Seriously, I don't know how you're managing to stay afloat with all the different things you're juggling right now."

"Lots of coffee. And spite." It's amazing how caffeine and an immense desire to prove people wrong can really drive a person.

"I'm serious, Ellie. I'm worried you're going to burn yourself out if you keep going like this."

I shrug. "I'll be fine, don't worry. It's not the first time I've had to juggle working several jobs and a bunch of different classes in my life, and it probably won't be the last."

Nicole shoots me an empathetic look. "And I'm guessing you still have to send money to your mom?"

Attending one of the most elite (and expensive) private universities in Boston has only been made possible due to a combination of scholarships, loans, and work study appointments. Finances were tight but manageable if I was only worried about myself. The main issue was also having to worry about my family.

Once my dad left, my mom picked up as many odd jobs as she could find. That left me to take care of my baby sister, Josie. Where I was quiet and often too scared to speak up for myself, Josie was loud, defiant, and a force to be reckoned with. She was also the best listener, despite being ten years old. I think she realized early on that since our mom was stretched to thinn to handle our finaces, that I would the primary caregiver emotionally. I may have been too young to pay the bills, but I was the one who made sure Josie was fed, got to school on time, and completed her homework. As soon as I was old enough to get a job and contribute to our family I did. While my mom still worked wherever she could, most of the gigs she found were part-time, or paid so poorly she was living paycheck to paycheck.

After my first semester at Westchester, I realized the only way I could afford to pay my own bills while still helping my mom was to pick up extra side jobs. Anything I made from nannying or tutoring was sent to my mom, while the work-study money I earned as a research assistant was mine. Most days it felt like the only thing that was mine was my research. The first place where I ever felt fully listened to and supported unconditionally.

"Of course I'm still sending money home. I want to help out and have the means to, so why shouldn't I?" I felt a sense of responsibility to help make my mom's life easier. Make Josie's life easier.

"Do you think you could tell your mom that money is tight right now? "

My stomach drops at the thought. My relationship with my mom was a bit more complex than some, though very common amongst other second-generation immigrants. I was your classic angsty teenager grappling with the identity crisis that came with being raised by a Middle Eastern parent while growing up in American culture. As a kid, I would get annoyed having to translate my school documents for her or explain common phrases, jokes, and pop culture moments most other parents seemed to know. But the older I got, the more I understood the magnitude of all she had sacrificed in her life for me and my sister — immigrating to America, barely knowing the man she was marrying, and unable to speak any English when she first arrived. It was exceptionally difficult for her to land a job or even make friends. She was all alone and yet she persevered. The years after my dad had left my mom was like a candle that had been left on overnight — melted to the core with nothing much left of herself. Which is why I still sent money home to tide them over. And also called them every night to check in.

"I could....in theory tell my mom I can't send money anymore. Maybe."

Except it wasn't just my mom I had to think about, it was also Josie. Leaving my little sister for college was one of the hardest things I'd ever done, but I knew I needed to do it. I had never done anything for myself until I decided to go to Westchester. When it was time for me to start college, she assured me she was fine on her own. I wasn't entirely convinced.

Nicole sighs, "I get it. It's hard to feel like you'll ever be able to pay her back for all she's had to sacrifice. It's not just the money we have to think about."

And this is why I loved Nicole. She understood me as a person, and she knew what it was like to feel the same pressures that I did. Nicole's parents immigrated from Cuba when she was seven years old. I'd been assigned to show her around the school and the rest was history. Initially we bonded over our love for The Lion King and over time we connected over experiences other kids in our grade knew nothing about. Like the way we would translate bills and school documents as best as we could for our parents every night. Or how they would ask us to proofread any emails they had to send to their coworkers to make sure there weren't any major typos. The way you would feel everyone's eyes on you in the grocery store whenever your parents spoke to you in their native language.

Our parents may not have been raised in the same country, but there's a shared bond and understanding between most immigrants who left everything they had in hopes of making their children's lives a little better. And a shared understanding among children of immigrants that our successes weren't just made on our own— they were made off the sacrifices of our parents. We knew that one day we would be able to thank them for allowing us to have access to more opportunities than we could have ever imagined. One day their sacrifices would be worth it. One day they would pay off. Which is why it was so hard for me to tell my mother no. How could I when deep down I knew I wouldn't have anything in my life if it wasn't for her?

Nicole ends the silence that's consumed our apartment. "Well if not this weekend, maybe we can have a girls night out next week? You and me are gonna paint the town red."

"That sounds like a plan, but until then..." I trail off, my eyes catching on the stack of books and half-completed homework assignments.

"Until then, we figure out how to make it to the end of this week alive."

"How many all-nighters do you think we're going to have to pull?"

"Too many, Eliana. Too many."

Chapter 8

Jake

"Are you feeling alright man? You were all over the ice today." Adam pulls me aside after practice. Why he couldn't have done this when we were still *inside* the building as opposed to now having to stand in the frigid fall wind is anyone's guess. But I suppose also shouldn't complain too much about my friend wanting to check in on me.

"Yeah I'm fine. I think I'm just a bit nervous about bringing my grade up so I don't get benched." I whisper the final bit under my breath. Only he and Ollie knew how close I was to the chopping block and I didn't want it to become a whole thing. Last thing the new kids on the team needed to hear was how one of their captains may be out for the rest of the season. "I have my first, or I guess a redo, of my first session today and it's all I can think about."

"You'll be fine. I know things seem scary now, but your tutor will be able to help you get back on track and in a couple of months we'll be holding up the NCAA championship trophy over our heads." Adam gives me a small reassuring smile and I wish I had half of the confidence in myself that he had in me. Maybe then I wouldn't feel so nervous.

"You keep wishing that for us while I head out and make sure I'm not late this time." I give him a small wave before I head toward the parking lot at the back of the arena.

Normally I walk to practice but after staying up all night trying to make sense of my homework, I decided to reward myself by sleeping in a bit today. By the time I make it to my car I see the only car left here belongs to Ollie. Judging from the very flat tire on the front of his car I can take a guess on how his day's been going. "You need help changing out the spare? I have a toolkit in my trunk."

Ollie looks up from his tire at the sound of my voice, his face in a tight grimace. "I'm afraid you're looking at the spare." He nods to the half-deflated tire. "I've been pushing off getting another one because money's been a little tight lately and it looks like that decision finally bit me in the ass today."

"Don't worry about it. I'll give you a ride back to Hockey House and we can call triple A to come fix this." I unlock my G-Wagon and gesture for him to get in the passenger seat.

"I was actually on my way to the airport. I decided to go home for a few days since we don't have a game this weekend. My grandpa's getting older now and well..." He shrugs to release the tension in his shoulders. "I'll just call an Uber."

"An Uber's gonna cost you like sixty bucks. Get in, I'll drop you off at the airport."

"You sure you have time?"

"Yeah it should only take me like thirty minutes there and back." Which should leave me with more than enough time to drop my car off at home and walk over to the library for tutoring. "No biggie."

"You're the best captain I've ever had Jake, I mean it." Ollie pulls his bags out of the trunk of his car and throws them into mine, and a few minutes later we're pulling out of the parking lot.

"Make sure you let Adam know that. His ego's been getting a little big lately." That was the farthest thing from the truth, but a solid part of our relationship was me busting Adam's balls while he rolled his eyes in response.

"Seriously man, you're really saving my ass. I was scared I was gonna miss my flight."

"Don't worry Ollie, we'll get you there in no time."

Getting Oliver to the airport with enough time for him to make it through security? Check. Getting myself back to campus in time for tutoring? Big fucking fail. I was sitting in bumper-to-bumper traffic moving less than a hundred feet every five minutes. Eliana was going to kill me.

And to think this time I actually worked my ass off to finish the homework and was even going to arrive early if not for the emergency detour I had to take to help.Ollie. What an absolute nightmare.

It's fine, everything's fine. I'd just skip the trip home and head straight to the library. I still had a solid fifteen minutes until I had to be there and I was only two miles from campus. No need to freak out yet. Except with every minute that ticked by I realized how absolutely screwed I was.

There was no way I was going to be on time which meant I had to cross my fingers and hope that Eliana hated last minute rescheduling much less than she hated me showing up late. I reach for my phone to send Eliana an email when I realize it;s dead. This has to be a joke. There's no way that I'm stuck in traffic AND my phone is dead. I reach over to the glove box, digging through it like a mad man and sending all of its contents onto the floor. I send a silent prayer out for a charger. No such luck.

This was bad. Really, really bad. I bang my head against the steering wheel. With every minute that passed by, I felt the hopes of me playing hockey this season fade.

Chapter 9

Eliana

Unlike last time, when I sat alone in the library fuming waiting for Jake to show up, this time, I came fully prepared with my own agenda of things I needed to get done this week. I'm not sure whether I should thank him for giving me the extra time to submit my research paper for my Childhood Adversity and Resilience seminar but it was one less thing I had to worry about for this week. I check the time on my computer and can't help but snort. Of course he's over thirty minutes late. Again. And of course he couldn't be bothered to send me an email.

I composed a quick email to the tutoring center informing them that I can longer commit to being Jake's tutor and request that they find someone else willing to tolerate his bullshit. Well, I don't use that exact phrasing, but the message is clear. I'm free of Jake Keeley.

I close my laptop and head into the lab a few minutes early. A part of me hoped Violet wouldn't be in today, because I didn't want to tell her I had quit. She probably wouldn't even be surprised given she did warn me that Jake had a bit of an ego. Still, I had worked with some pretty difficult clients in the past and this was the first time I wasn't able to make something work. Tomorrow. I will tell her tomorrow.

I'm two feet away from the entrance to my lab when I hear someone running down the hall. From his frantic expression and the way he keeps glancing down at his very fancy and likely expensive watch, Jake's definitely piecing together how much trouble he's in. I feel my heart twinge a bit and for a second, I debate how bad it would be if I give a third chance.

My therapist's voice starts to play in my head from our last session. *"I get that helping people can be very aligned with your values, but burning yourself out is not a solution. Sometimes the best way we can care for others is by taking care of ourselves. And also not enabling their behaviors."* Stephanie was right. I would just have to stick to my decision to no longer be his tutor.

I keep my head down hoping Jake won't notice me. Maybe it's a bit cowardly to hide but telling him I quit was going to be really hard. Setting boundaries was still very new for me, and if he poked my wall hard enough, the wall and my resolution would definitely cave. I hear him call my name. Shit. I guess we're doing this now then.

I turn around and get a face full of his chest, craning my neck up to look at him. "Jake."

"Listen I know you're pissed—" He takes a moment to catch his breath.

"Honestly I'm not." It was the truth. The reality is I never should have taken on an extra client this semester. I had tried to make it work, but clearly he wasn't going to put in the same amount of effort so all I can do at this point is move on.

His eyebrows knit together. "Oh um...well that's good. So should we head back to the library?"

"Unfortunately, I can't. I realized I may not be the best fit as your tutor so I emailed the main office asking them to reassign you with someone who can meet your needs." Easy. Polite but firm. I give myself a mental high-five for not immediately caving into his request.

His eyes widen. "Please don't quit on me. I had to drop a friend off at the airport. It was an emergency. I got stuck in traffic on the way back."

"I understand that emergencies come up, but you could've told me you were running late. Or that you needed to reschedule."

"I tried to, but my phone was dead." The sincerity in his voice, paired with the mix of panic and guilt in his eyes, made my heart squeeze. My stupid bleeding heart.

"I see. Well I appreciate the transparency, but I've already emailed the tutoring center asking for you to be reassigned. I just don't think our schedules and my tutoring style are compatible with what you need. But I'm sure they'll connect you with someone new soon."

"Wait, are you serious?"

"You should hear from one of the admins at the center soon about my replacement. Feel free to reach out to them if you haven't heard anything in 3-5 business days."

I needed to get out of this conversation. Quick. Jamming my key into the lock, I can't stop myself from glancing up at Jake's panicked face, which also holds a hint of guilt and downright hopelessness. I slam the door shut behind me before he can even respond and spend the next three hours burying myself in my work so I don't have to think about the desperate look in his eyes as I walked away.

Chapter 10

Jake

The middle-aged receptionist looks up at me with such pity I may just crumple over and die at this very moment. "Unfortunately, Mr. Keeley, it doesn't look like any of our tutors are available right now to take on a new student. We've reached the busiest point in the semester and all of our tutors booked up weeks ago."

This couldn't be happening. "Are you sure there's no one else who can help me out? Even if I have to pay extra for it." I don't like to flash my trust fund around. My parents worked their asses off to earn that money, and I hated the perception that came with being a trust fund kid. That I was just a brat who didn't know the meaning of hard work. However, my hockey career is worth everything to me, so if Daddy's credit card gets me a passing grade, so be it.

"I'm afraid not. The only tutor who has an opening now is...." She trails off, and I can fill in the blank myself. The only person who is available right now is the same one who quit on me. Fantastic. "We do provide free study materials for most courses in the library that you can check out. Beyond that, I'm afraid my hands are tied."

"Well, thanks anyway. I appreciate it." I pinch the bridge of my nose between my fingers, feeling a headache coming on as I walk into the hall where Ollie is waiting for me. When I emailed the tutoring center and found out they were booked, Ollie kept me from finding the nearest bridge and jumping off and suggested we come in person to "wave my charm around."

"Another dead end."

"Are you serious?" This might be the first time I've ever seen Ollie look nervous.

"Yup. All their tutors are fully booked. Well all except..."

"Shit."

"My sentiments exactly."

"What are you gonna do?"

"I have no idea," I groan, dragging a hand over my face. "I need Eliana." Never in a million years would I have imagined my fate would be so strongly tied to a random person I barely even knew, and yet here I was.

Ollie winces. "Yeah good luck with that one."

"Do you have any other brilliant ideas?"

He thinks hard for a few minutes before shaking his head. "I guess not. So what's the plan? Can you complain to your TA about how your tutor just up and quit? There has to be some rule against that."

"Probably. I doubt complaining would win me any favors, though. My TA kinda hates me and it's not like my tutor didn't quit without a solid reason..." Though she did seem pretty close to caving when she realized how desperate I was. "I just need to find a way to show her that I'm serious about this and that I'm willing to do whatever it takes."

"Okay, sure. How exactly do you plan on doing that?"

"I have a crazy idea, but it just might work out."

"That sounds moderately concerning."

"Trust the process, Ollie. Trust the process."

* * *

This plan was either incredibly genius or would end up getting me arrested. I realized there was a zero percent chance that Eliana would simply take my word that I had changed and would never be late again. That ship had sailed, sunk, and was currently in the bottom of the ocean with the Titanic. Which is why I came to the conclusion that I had to *show her* I was different. While I may not know much about her, I did know she worked in research. Though I still didn't entirely understand all the intricacies of what my mom and sisters did, one thing I did know was the importance of collecting multiple points of data before drawing any conclusions. Currently, the only data Eliana had was that I was an asshole hockey player who couldn't figure out how to work a clock. I was determined to change that.

Which is why I was currently sitting on a bench directly across from her lab reading my psych textbook while trying to decipher my latest homework assignment. I wasn't entirely sure what her work schedule was yet, but I had nowhere else to be today, so I planned on camping out here until I either saw Eliana or someone who could tell me when she'd be in. I'd sit on this bench as long as I needed to, day after day, to show her that I was very serious about fixing my grade. At least, I hoped that would be her takeaway message. The last thing I needed was for her to think I was stalking her.

The next hour featured a series of people shuffling in and out of the building, most of whom gave me weird or confused looks. It's not until 2 p.m. when Eliana finally enters the building. And pretends not to see me. Lucky for me she struggles to find her keys, leaving me with an opening.

"Get up to anything fun this weekend?"

She freezes for a moment at the sound of my voice, then continues on, shaking her head.

"*I* for one spent a majority of the time trying to memorize which regions of the brain interact to control our emotional processes. I think I got most of them down, but maybe you can help me with the res—"

"I'm sorry. I can't talk right now." She rushes into her lab and gently shuts the door.

Okay cool. She had work to do. I respected that.

By the time she comes back out again, my ass is incredibly sore from sitting on this bench and the sun has fully set. I managed to finish my homework, which was a step in the right direction, though I couldn't say whether any of the answers were right. I haphazardly throw my belongings in my back-pack and follow her out of the building, holding the door open.

She looks up at me, startled as if she didn't expect me to trail behind her. "Jake? What are you doing?"

"Well you see, I was wondering if you knew any tutors who were willing to take a struggling student on."

"I told you to reach out to the tutoring center if you didn't hear back from them soon." Eliana shifts into a brisk walk, likely in an attempt to ditch me. Unfortunately for her, I had a solid foot on her which made it easy to catch up.

"Ah you see, I did that. It seems as though all of the current staff are fully booked for the rest of the semester. Well everyone except for—"

She turns to look at me and misses the lip in the sidewalk, causing her to spiral forward. My arms are out in an instant to stop her from hitting the concrete. She's still a little wobbly, so I tuck her firmly into my side and give her a moment to gain her composure.

It takes her a few seconds to catch her breath and release the vice-like grip that's clutching onto the back of my coat. "Thanks for catching me."

"No big deal. You alright?" My eyes lock with hers and for the first time since we met, I notice the small smattering of freckles dusted along her cheeks.

"Y-Yeah, thanks for not letting me eat shit." She gives me a sheepish grin, slowly pulling away from me, and it's only then that I realize I still have one of my arms wrapped around her waist. I remove it quickly before she misreads my good intentions.

We continue walking, Eliana clearly on a mission to get somewhere. "So back to the tutoring situation." She keeps her head forward, but I can tell she's listening to me. Or at least I hope she is. "Any chance I can get you to reconsider taking me on?"

"I can't."

"Listen, I know I messed up. But I'm really desperate here. I tried to find someone else, but you're it."

"I wish I could help, but I made a promise to myself not to rush to help everyone else before I take care of my own needs. I hope you can understand."

Shit. I definitely understood and respected her for setting boundaries, but without a tutor, I had no chance of getting my grade back up. We come to a halt in front of one of the student housing buildings, and I realize I've followed her all the way back to her apartment. I may have gotten nothing out of this, but at least I know she got home safe.

"I hear you." *I just need you to change your mind, and I'm not planning on backing down without a fight.* For as headstrong as she's coming off right now, I can already see the cracks in her armor. She feels bad for me, and all I need to do is keep that going for a little while longer. A rush of shame fills my gut at that thought. I'm not particularly proud of the fact that I'm trying to guilt-trip Eliana into this. But my hockey career was dangling by a thread, and the level of desperation overrode the shame I felt. "Well I guess I'll see you around then."

She gives me a small nod before heading inside.

Chapter 11

Eliana

I had resorted to sneaking in through the back entrance of the psychology building to avoid seeing Jake. It wasn't a perfect plan, seeing as he beat me inside the building a few times and I ran into him camped outside my lab door. He had spent the past few days "working" outside my lab for the better part of the morning. The first day he had tried to play it off casually, like he was surprised to see me at his new study spot, then he'd shifted the conversation back to whether I would reconsider being his tutor. I slammed the door in his face.

On the fourth day, he came armed with one of my greatest weaknesses — a mocha Frappuccino with extra whipped cream from the Beanery, one of the best coffee shops on campus. It nearly killed me to push past him without taking the bribe. The night before I was woken up at 3 a.m. to the sound of the fire alarm in my building going off so the sweet treat would've definitely perked up my morning. But I cannot be bought. I'll buy my own damned coffee.

When I entered the lab, I saw April, fellow research

assistant, happily sipping on her own drink from the cafe. She confessed that Jake had offered to buy her a drink if she told him what my order was. I called her a traitor and spent the next three hours silently coding participant data while trying to ignore the small voice in my head that begged for caffeine.

After 2 hours of staring at my screen wide-eyed, I decided to take a break before I needed a trip to the ophthalmologist. I left the lab to use the restroom and on my way back, I couldn't help myself. I stopped around the corner and dared to glance at Jake. His eyebrows were pinched together as he nervously ran his hands through his hair, biting his bottom lip. I watched him scan the same textbook page three times before pulling out his worksheet, reading the page again, and letting out a frustrated noise. He slammed the book shut and leaned back against the wall, rubbing his temples with his fingers as he let out a heavy sigh. I look down and see my forgotten coffee, likely melted by now. I shake my head. *What a travesty.*

Aside from being the recipient of his determination, I knew nothing about my new stalker. I'm not entirely sure what possesses me, probably my drive to understand the human psyche, but I walk over to the bench and sit down next to him. "Hey."

He startles slightly at the sound of my voice, opening his eyes to look at me. "Hi."

"How's it going?"

"Oh. Super. It's really starting to click, and I might even consider changing majors. Me and psychology are like this now." Jake crosses his fingers.

"That's...great. Glad your little stalker study sessions in the hall are paying off."

"Eliana?" My name is barely a whisper from his lips.

"Yeah?"

"What if things aren't going well? What if things are really, really bad? Even though I'm trying really hard to fix them."

It sounds more like a confession than another attempt at bribery. "I'm sorry to hear that. I really hate seeing people struggle with school. That's why I became a tutor in the first place. I'm sorry I can't offer the help you need."

He drags a hand over his face, "No I'm sorry. I put all my eggs in your basket and then shit all over it. Or whatever the saying is. My headspace is a mess right now and feel like I'm in a hole I can't dig out of. I also can't talk to anyone about how hopeless I feel because my teammates are all relying on me and I don't want to freak them out."

Jake's uncharacteristic vulnerability intrigues me more. There appears to be a lot more to the hockey captain than I've gotten to see, "Well, if you ever need a friend, just someone to talk to or be around to help the weight of life not feel so heavy, you can call me. Just because our tutoring relationship didn't work out doesn't mean we can't be friends."

"Thanks. My friend hours are before practice from the hours of 6 am to 8am. Beyond that you're officially invited to all the keggers at hockey house."

I snort "Not sure if I have the upper body strength to do a keg stand but, if you bring the mocha fraps, you can always come by at 6am. It's my quiet time in the morning to prep for the day. I'm not committing to looking over your homework but if you happen to have a psych question, I might happen to have an answer."

His eyes fill with hope, "Holy shit. Yeah. I'm down. Should we plan to meet at the library?"

"It's not open that early. We could meet at my place?"

"Sounds good to me."

"Cool. I'll email you my address. I guess I should probably get going." I nod my head towards the lab.

"I appreciate this. More than you know. Friend." He winks, sliding off the bench and bringing me in for a small hug and the scent of mint and soap consumes me. "See you Thursday, bright and early."

"Looking forward to it." I pull back and finally enter the lab.

The first person I see is April. "So you finally caved huh?"

"Yeah, yeah. I'm a pushover who can be bribed with sweet treats. What's new?"

"I can't say I blame you. Who wouldn't want to spend time with Jake Keeley? He's sooo hot."

"We're just friends." Or at least we would be soon.

"Sure, sure Ellie. You say that now." She giggles to herself and I let it be. Jake and I had only started our friendship all of a few second ago, we were a very long way from being anything more than that.

Chapter 12

Eliana

I was half awake and half delirious when I opened the front door to find Jake Keeley standing on the other side of my door holding a large mocha frap with extra whipped cream in one hand and a regular coffee in another. "You're early."

"I figured I'd make up for all the times I was late. Nice pants by the way." He smirks and I look down at my pajama bottoms, which have sleeping koalas all over them. At least I had thrown on a bra before I opened the door.

"In the interest of being honest I'm a little surprised you're here. The library at 6 p.m. was too inconvenient, but I guess 6 a.m. in my apartment does the trick?"

"I guess I never knew how lonely I was in the mornings, until I was up at 5 a.m. looking forward to seeing you in an hour."

My heart warms at his words, not expecting him to be so sweet. "Have a seat at the table. I'll go grab my laptop." I take the coffee from his hand and chug it down like it's my lifeline. The sugary concoction hits my tongue and I can't help but let out a small moan of delight. *Coffee gods, thank you for this sweet blessing. Please let this caffeine carry me through another hellish day.*

When I come back to reality, I catch Jake's eyes focused on my mouth as I lick away the bit of whipped cream left over on my lip. A wave of unfamiliar heat comes over me, and I realize I'm blushing. Since when do I blush like a schoolgirl when a guy looks at me? It's been a while since I dated a guy, but I didn't think I was this starved for attention.

Whereas I'm still learning about Jake, I'm surprised to find he's quite chipper in the mornings. He seems completely comfortable as he unpacks his bag and prepares to start a friendship(?) in a strangers home.

I head into my room and grab my laptop along with some of the psych study materials I prepped for him for our first study session. I'm still not tutoring him, but good boys who make an effort get treats. When I return to the kitchen, he's already reviewing what looks like a homework assignment.

I casually slide over the forms before plopping myself across from him and getting to work on my to do list for the day.

He thumbs through the forms before looking at me with a sly grin. "What's this?"

I give him a casual shrug. "Don't get too excited. I prepped those before I even met you. It's a schedule detailing the material you should focus on over the next few weeks to prepare for your final two exams. There are also some practice quizzes in there. I may not be tutoring you but I refuse to let good practice quizzes go to waste."

"Thanks Eliana. You may be the most thoughtful *friend* I've ever had."

I roll my eyes, and continue responding to emails.

Jake lets out a groan as he flips through his homework,

mumbling to himself, "Of course this week is focused on research..."

"Do you have a problem with that?" I bristle, his words clearly hitting a sour spot for me. He wasn't the first person to tell me they didn't get why I found research so interesting or wanted to make a career out of it. Normally I would let it go, but something about Jake made me want to push back. Or maybe it was the fact that being up this early messed with my ability to be polite. It was probably that. "Because research is a super important part of our field and is a big reason why we know so much about how humans think, function, and process the world."

"I know."

The words come out of my mouth before I can even stop them. Unfortunately for Jake my filter is nonexistent at 6am, "Granted some the early pioneers in the field pushed theories that were either racist, sexist, homophobic or combination of all three, but there are so many incredible researchers today doing groundbreaking work or even sharing small findings can help us make important foreground."

I expect him to make a snarky comment or roll his eyes at my mini rant but instead the side of his mouth lifts up into a half smile, "I'm very aware about both the shitty history of research and also how important it is. I didn't mean anything bad by my comments, and I'm sorry if it came off that way."

"Oh." Oops. "My bad. I'm a bit crabby before 10 a.m."

That draws a genuine laugh from him, "Most people are. I'm only used to it because we have some early morning practices. I take it that working at a research assistant is more than just a work-study opportunity for you?"

"Yeah. Don't get me wrong, I love tutoring and nannying too. But being a research assistant, getting to work with Violet on projects, that feels different. Feels like it's a space where I can bring all my questions and ideas to life."

"So you're a full-time student who works as a tutor, nanny, and a research assistant?" He sounds equally impressed and surprised.

"Yup. I squeeze in being a human sometimes too," I joke. Sort of. I sleep. Not anywhere near the recommended 8 hours a night you were supposed to get but enough to constitute more human and less zombie status.

"Have you ever considered taking on less so you're not over-stretching yourself?"

I repeat the same words I've said to countless others over the years, words that have basically become my life motto. "It's nothing I can't handle."

He opens his mouth to rebuttal, but I redirect us back to the task at hand— him homework, me life prepping.

For a second it seems as if he's going to fight me on it, but instead he takes the paper from my hand and starts working. At least initially. "We're not done talking about *your* issues, by the way." He keeps his eyes locked on the worksheet in front of him.

"*My* issues?"

"Yeah, your problem with not letting yourself have a little fun now and then. You don't always have to put yourself last."

"That's like friendship level 6 stuff. We are still on, 'So how many siblings do you have?'"

"Two. Now, why no fun?"

"I traded in fun for an A in PSYCH101. Now focus."

He chuckles to himself and thankfully returns to his work.

Chapter 13

Eliana

"**A**re you sure there's nothing else I missed?" I stare at the Word document in front of me, waiting for some glaringly obvious mistake to jump out at me.

"I'm positive, Ellie. I've looked over your drafts multiple times, and it's perfect. It's strong. You're ready," Violet reassures me.

"You don't think I need to buff out my skills section more? Or add another few sentences about my career goals and how this summer internship would get me there?" I feel a tension headache starting to build and I try my best to unclench my jaw.

"Nope. It's perfect as is. You sent this to Bethany, right?"

"Yes."

"And what did she say?"

"That it was a super impressive application and Kathrine Fisher will be dying to have me," I whisper.

"So what are you waiting for? Go ahead and submit it."

"My CV font is currently in Georgia. Should I change it to Times New Roman? Or maybe Calibri?" I frantically pull up the document while also doing a quick google search for fonts that are accepted by the American Psychological Association. *Calibri, Arial, Lucida Sans Unicode, Times New Roman, Georgia, or Computer Modern.* Okay. We were fine. Everything's fine.

"I don't think I've ever seen you so tense before. And that is saying something." Violet gives me a sympathetic look.

"Sorry. Getting this internship would just be so perfect. It's not every day that you get to work with one of the most renowned researchers in developmental neuroscience. And I'm thinking of applying to grad school next year, so my anxiety is just all over the place right now." I take a deep breath, trying to slow my heartbeat down.

"One, as I've stated before, you're an absolute shoo-in for this program. You've worked so hard the last three years, and they'd be more than lucky to have you. And two, you put a lot of pressure on yourself. I get it, I do. But I hope you realize how amazing you are and give yourself some grace."

The tension in my shoulders relaxes a bit. "You're right. You're right. Okay, I'm going to submit it." I hold my breath as I scan through the application portal one more time before pressing submit. "Welp, it's done. All we can do now is cross our fingers and hope for the best."

"It'll all work out, trust me. Do you know when you'll hear back?"

"The application portal closes tonight, and they said interview invites should go out about two weeks after that. Which means I should probably start doing prep for that just in case."

I couldn't help but overprepare for almost every major thing in my life. If there's one thing I hate, it's not having control over things, so naturally, anything I could control I tried my damndest, even if sometimes I went a bit overboard when planning out my life.

"Feel free to throw something in my calendar if you want to do a mock interview with me."

"Has anyone ever told you how amazing you are?" I meant every single word.

Before I enrolled at Westchester, I had no idea what research even looked like or that I could have a career doing it. Being the first in my family to go to college, I felt like I was already behind compared to my classmates. So many of them already knew what they wanted to do or had already started working towards the career paths they were seeking while I was trying to figure out how to register for all the right classes and that my work-study checks were coming through. I met Violet in my freshman year of college after taking a class she was a teaching assistant for. On day one she announced she was looking for a research assistant to work in her lab. I applied without a second thought. Despite my lack of experience, she decided to take a chance on me. I don't think I'd ever be able to thank her enough for it.

"Ditto. I really couldn't imagine how behind I'd be on my dissertation if you weren't helping me run MRI sessions. And not to mention how you stepped up to tutor one of my students. I don't know how you're juggling so much at once."

"Eh aren't we all juggling a hundred things at once? Just part of life." I shrug.

"Life will definitely throw some curve balls at you when you least expect it. Which is why it's important to take care of yourself as much as you can."

"Absolutely. I agree 100%."

"Do you, though?" Violet asks, looking skeptical.

The vibe in the room shifts and I get the sense there's something she wants to say but isn't quite sure how I'll react. "Whatever's on your mind, you can go ahead and say it. I promise I won't take it personally."

"I think you need to make more time for yourself. And not just time to do work or school-related things. Time where you can start a new hobby, write that murder mystery you've been trying to start for years now, or even just relax and take a breath."

"I appreciate you looking out for me. And you're right. I should be better about making time for myself.".

"When is that going to be? I can promise you it won't be in grad school. Or when you're trying to secure a faculty position. And not when you're first starting out as a professor."

"Well I guess I'll just sleep when I'm dead then." I attempt to make a joke, but the unimpressed look on Violet's face tells me it falls flat.

"I'm serious Ellie. I say this from my own experience when I say no one is ever going to force you to take a break. You have to be able to set those boundaries yourself and stick to them. Or else you're going to burn out before you even make it to grad school."

Even if I wanted to argue with Violet, I couldn't. Not when I knew she was right. "I hear you. Honestly. I'll work on saying no to things. And taking time for myself. I promise."

* * *

"Hockey House is hosting a party this weekend. Tutors are invited." Jake winks at me from across the table. It's Thursday morning and just as he did two days ago, he showed up at 5:45 with a coffee and a smile. When I criticized his 15-minute early arrival, he explained to me that if he didn't leave "Hockey House" (the house he shares with his 10 roommates, I learned) by 5:30, he'd get roped into extra morning workouts.

"I'm your emotional support friend, not your drinking buddy. And *definitely* not your tutor. "

He raises an eyebrow. "I didn't realize there were friend categories. And I think it could be good for you to let your hair down for once."

Ouch. Between Violet and Jake calling me a workaholic, maybe I could use a weekend off. Didn't mean I had to spend it getting drunk though. Weekends off were for relaxing, and beer pong and groping didn't sound relaxing to me. "Pass."

"C'mon Ellie. It could be fun."

I blink, not realizing we had reached the level of friendship that included nicknames. "I'm busy Saturday night."

"You're going clubbing instead?" He cocks his head at me, a glimmer in his eye.

"Nope." Though I did love dancing.

"Dive bar?"

"Definitely more my speed. But also no."

"So...girl's night? Your friends are welcome to come too."

"I have a paper I need to finish, which will happen on Saturday."

Jake's jaw drops. "What do you mean you have a paper to write? *That's* your idea of fun?" He scoffs.

His mocking tone pisses me off. Friends don't judge other friends for trying to be successful. "I never said I don't have any plans. I said my plans don't involve being stuck in a dingy frat basement or getting so drunk I can't function for the rest of the weekend," I snap. "Now if we can get back to our respective tasks, that would be great."

Jake was a little rude, but the fact that I hadn't eaten an actual meal since lunch the day before was the main contributor to my attitude. I had been way too busy this week to find time to buy groceries. Plus, my mom called two days ago lamenting about the cost of Josie's field trip which I offered to cover, effectively wiping out my bank account. My direct deposit went through today, which meant the second I was done here, I would treat myself to a bacon, egg, and cheese from the Beanery, followed by a trip to the grocery store. My current task was making a cost-efficient shopping list.

"You're in a mood today," Jake notes.

"And you're nosey."

"True. But Tuesday Ellie would've just rolled her eyes and kept it moving. But today, you're looking for a fight. Why's that?" He raises an eyebrow.

"Maybe it's because you're being particularly insufferable today. Have you considered that?"

He taps his index finger on his chin a few times, contemplating. "Nope. I don't think that's it. I think you're upset I—"

His words are cut off by the embarrassingly loud sound of my stomach growling. My eyes widen as I clear my throat, attempting to cover the noise.

I expected him to tease me about it or, at the very least, look smug about the fact that he figured out my bad mood, but instead, he just looks concerned. "Maybe you should take a break and make some breakfast? I promise to do my homework for this week while you do."

"Do your homework or don't. I'm not your tutor, remember?"

"I'm serious. I don't want you skipping meals to entertain me."

"I'll just eat something after." My stomach conveniently grumbles obnoxiously.

Jake pushes himself away from the table and walks towards my kitchen, a determined look on his face. He throws open my fridge and grunts at the sheer emptiness of it. He turns his attention to my cabinets next, also extremely empty, which draws another irritated noise. "Is all your food hidden somewhere or?"

"I'm all out. I've been too busy this week to go to the grocery store. My plan was to go after our session."

"When's the last time you had something to eat?"

"Um, I had a pretty big lunch yesterday..."

He looks aghast. "Are you being serious?"

"Not everyone needs 6 eggs and a pack of bacon a day for breakfast, okay? Us non-athletes can survive on granola bars and coffee. We actually prefer it that way. What are you doing?" I watch as he throws on his coat and grabs his wallet, leaving the rest of his belongings.

"Going to grab us some breakfast. Any specific requests?"

"Jake sit down. Let's just finish this and then I can head to the grocery store."

"Actually, I'm *starving*. I only had 4 eggs and half a pack of bacon. This is more for me than for you."

My eyes narrow at his obvious deflection. "I can take care of myself just fine."

"Never said you couldn't. Now, what will it be? Chocolate croissant? Breakfast sandwich?"

"Jake, I—"

My words die as he leaves me and my weak excuses behind.

Chapter 14

Jake

Eliana missing two meals really bothered me. Her stomach continuing to grumble, her empty fridge, and the way she looked more tired than usual this morning worried me just enough to storm out of her apartment and make a beeline to the Beanery. I don't know much about being friends with girls, but I do know I'd never let one of my boys go hungry. I still wasn't sure what she wanted, or if she had any dietary restrictions, which meant I ordered three breakfast sandwiches and hoped one of them would be edible.

While I'm waiting in line, I send a quick text to, Sienna, my younger sister, who's an undergrad student at MIT.

The next thing I know she's calling me. "Hello?"

"Sorry, currently getting ready and thought it'd be easier to talk on the phone. Why are you suddenly invested in the eating habits of women?"

"I have a new friend; she does psych research like you. She

just told me that last time she ate a meal was lunch yesterday. Isn't that crazy? Her stomach was grumbling the whole time we were together too." Unsure why Eliana's eating habits had become a problem I had to solve but here we were.

Sienna clicks her tongue, "Well if she is an academic there's a super strong possibility she's struggling a lot financially. Even really established academics tend not to make a ton of money. You have to remember mom inherited *a lot* of money from grandma and grandpa."

Shit. Yet another thing I wasn't aware about when in comes to psych lifestyle.

"You're right. I'm being a dick. Hopefully the breakfast sandwiches I'm about to bring her will make up for it."

"It would certainly cheer up my day— wait. My brain is finally putting this together....since when do care about what your random hookups do?"

"First of all we have not hooked up. We're *just* friends."

She snorts, "You just friends with a girl? As if."

"Why is that so hard to believe?

"Jake. Be for real for a minute."

"I am!" I exclaim.

She refuses to listen, "So who's the girl that's finally gotten my brother to settle down."

This was definitely my worst nightmare. The last time my sisters and mom thought I was seeing someone, they had uncovered her Instagram, Twitter, and LinkedIn in a matter of minutes. Not that what was going on between Eliana and I was even remotely romantic. Unfortunately, the only thing worse than Sienna thinking I was seeing someone was her finding out how much I was struggling.

"Again we are just friends."

"Friends who hang out at 6 a.m.?"

"I ran into her on my way to practice." I lie. Easier than

coming up for an excuse as to why I was in Eliana's apartment before the sun was fully out.

"No you didn't. You have practices Mondays and Wednesdays. Thursdays are your rot-in-bed day in preparation for weekend games. You sent your schedule to me so I can keep track of when you're busy, remember?"

Dammit. For once I wished she wasn't so damn supportive.

"So tell me all about her, don't leave out any juicy details. Well, actually maybe not *all* the juicy details. There are some things I should never know as your sister."

I snag the food from the counter and start walking back to the apartment. "I'm hanging up now."

"Hang up on me and I'll text Mom and Charlotte right now. The Keeley woman will be on your ass and have your secret lover's astrological birth chart in two hours. Tops."

"I'm going to change my name and move to a different country when I graduate. You'll never hear from me again." I groan.

"Just give me one small detail, and I'll leave you alone forever." A promise even she knew she couldn't keep. "Or at least I'll try minding my business until you decide to tell me more."

I sigh deeply. "Her name is Eliana, and we're friends. That's it. That's all. Now I have to go. Goodbye." I hear a squeal before I hang up the phone.

I knock on Eliana's apartment door and when it opens, I find her roommate holding it open. She shoots me an unimpressed and downright irritated look before moving out of the way. Okay so roommate is clearly not a fan. When I reenter the living room, I see Eliana seated at the table. Well, slumped over the table. Fast asleep.

She looks fully at peace, and I get the urge to leave the food and let her get some sleep. Ultimately she makes the decision for me as her eyes flutter open to meet mine.

"Hey. Sorry, I told myself I would put my head down for just a second and then..." She shrugs, then winces, rubbing her neck .

I hand her the bag of breakfast sandwiches and settle back into my seat as she inspects each one and then proceeds to inhale all of them. I guess that's a no to the food allergies.

After 20 minutes of honest concentration, I get stuck. I give Eliana a sheepish look, and she smiles, spinning my textbook around so she can read the question.

"Alright, so t-tests are basically statistics we can run to test whether there are differences between groups. More specifically, we compare the mean, or average, of each group to each other to see if there's a difference," Eliana starts.

My eyebrows knit together as I read over the section she's underlining with her finger.. "So there are dependent and independent t-tests. How do you know which one to use?"

I pause for her to roll her eyes or scoff at how basic my question is. Instead, she gives me a soft smile and starts drawing on the small white board next to her.

"That's a great question! So *independent* t-tests are for when you're comparing two separate groups that have nothing to do with each other. For example if you wanted to see if there was a statistically significant difference in shooting accuracy between forwards and defensemen. Does that make sense?" She looks up at me for confirmation.

I quirk an eyebrow and feel myself smile. She reminds me of Ollie, using the one thing he knows I understand to communicate with me. "Yeah it does. Or if you wanted to compare how many goals were scored between two teams?" I offer.

"Yes exactly!" Eliana's eyes light up as she nods enthusiastically.

"So what about dependent t-tests?" I ask.

"Dependent t-tests are used when you only have one group and you're trying to compare them before and after a certain outcome. So if you test how fast you can skate before and after a training program—"

"Or if you want to test whether getting a new coach impacts how many games a team wins?"

"Yup. That's another great example."

Damn, all it took was relating things back to hockey and suddenly things became a lot less confusing. I guess I shouldn't be surprised.. "You just might make a statistician out of me." I let out a self-deprecating snort.

"Hey, you never know. Why don't you try figuring out what tests to run using some examples from class?"

I worry my lip over as Eliana reviews my answers on the sheet she gave me on Tuesday. I find myself waiting for her to shake her head or tell me I'm "close, but not quite" but instead, she looks up at me and smiles. "You got four out of five right! And the last one was a bit of a trick question. You technically need to do an ANOVA, which Dr. Grant only started to cover toward the end of last class. This is great progress, Jake."

Holy shit. "Really?"

"Really." She nods. I may be overanalyzing, but I swear she looks proud of me. Then she lets out a huge yawn. Damn, I even brought her a large coffee today. Girl metabolizes caffeine like nobody I've ever seen.

"Have you been sleeping?" I wince as soon as the words come out of my mouth. She's clearly over me digging into her personal life this morning.

All I get is a small shrug. "This semester's really busy for me. Extra class load, nannying and working in a research lab, and suddenly almost all of my time to sleep, eat, or breathe is gone."

"That sounds exhausting." There were moments where the hockey season felt equally as packed, but at least we got a break during the off-season. Something told me it had been a long, long time since Eliana had gotten a real break from anything.

"That's life. You get a bunch of things thrown at you at once and do your best to juggle it all."

"I'm not sure if life is always meant to be exhausting. I think there should also be moments where it's fun and relaxing."

"Okay, fun police. You did your good dead for the day. And you nailed your homework. Time to go so I can finish my table nap."

I want to press more, but she starts cleaning up the dining room table, stacking all her textbooks, and effectively signaling this was the end of our conversation.

Chapter 15

Jake

"Why do you keep watching the door like the cops are gonna bust through any second?" Ollie screams over the loud music pouring through the speakers. I'm two beers in and currently nursing my third, but even the slight buzz from the alcohol and the pretty girl eyeing me from across the room couldn't fix my sour mood. Normally I'd be the life of the party, bouncing around between doing keg stands, doing body shots, and playing beer pong with the boys. But tonight I was sulking away on our battered old couch.

"I'm not staring at the door." I roll my eyes, taking a swig from my drink.

"Denial is a river in Europe—"

"Egypt." I correct.

"I knew that. I'm just drunk." He hiccups. "Regardless, you're definitely holding out for someone."

"I don't know what you're talking about."

"You're staring at the door like Taylor Swift when Jake Gyllenhaal didn't show up to her 21st birthday."

I nearly spit out my beer. "What the fuck?"

"Taylor Swift. She used to date—"

"Stop. Why do you know any of this?"

"First of all, All Too Well is a banger. Second of all, every girl on campus is a Swiftie. It pays me, and my dick, to know these things."

"You're an absolute nuisance."

"You're one to talk. Do you even remember the name of the girl whose tongue you were sucking on earlier tonight?"

"I will pay you twenty dollars right now to leave me alone." I pull my wallet out of my pocket. "Actually, make that a hundred."

"Wow so this is the thanks I get for coming to help a friend in need? I guess that's why they say no good deed goes unpunished."

As hard as I try not to laugh, I can't help it. Oliver was as unserious as he was a loyal friend, and I appreciated his concern for me. "I'm alright man. Maybe a little tired, but I'm still having fun."

"Jake, I think I've seen you look more alive after Coach made us skate suicides than you do now. Which is why I'm circling back to my question. Who are you waiting for? Or if you prefer you can also answer, 'What's her name?'".

"No one. And none of your business."

"Hmm how can a secret mystery woman not exist while also not being any of my business? The math isn't mathing for me, Jake."

"Where's that redhead you were talking to earlier? I'm sure she's more willing to entertain you right now than I am."

"Regina went to get me a drink. I could tell her to bring me back an extra if you want?"

"I'm good for now." I lift the red solo cup in my hand to show him. "I appreciate it, though."

Oliver clicks his tongue. "C'mon man. I planned this whole party to cheer you up after the bomb Coach Hayes dropped on you."

"Ugh don't fucking remind me." If I could go back in time and take back all the stupid things I did that made Mason hate me I would. Today he decided to switch up the team lineup, knocking me down to the second line and sticking me with two freshmen. Mason insisted this change was for the betterment of the team, that it would help bring our freshmen up to my level and prepare us for playoffs. But I couldn't help but feel like it was a personal punishment. Like he was trying to tell me, "If I can't trust you to keep your grade up, how can I trust you on the first line?".

"I really thought you were going to have an aneurysm in the locker room." Ollie snorts.

"Honestly I'm surprised I didn't. I'm still super pissed that he moved me down to the second like, but I guess I just have to trust the process. Hopefully Mason's right about this being good for the overall team. And if not maybe Coach Jameson will rewrite the wrong."

Ollie stands up abruptly. "I refuse to leave the resident party boy down in the dumps. I'm going to fix this."

Before I can tell him that I'm just having an off night he's disappeared into the crowd. How bad would it be if I hid in my room for the rest of the night? Damn I really was mopey tonight. If only I could figure out why. It definitely had nothing to do with the fact that every time I thought about doing something fun, I imagined Eliana tucked away in her bedroom stressed over whatever assignment she was working on.

If she continued the way she was going she would definitely burn herself out. And I was contributing to that. Another burden on her schedule that she had to deal with. The fact that she was so busy she didn't even have time to buy groceries was more than concerning. I wonder if she's even had dinner tonight. Or if she's so preoccupied by what she has to get done that she doesn't even realize how late it is already. I blink confused about when I suddenly became so preoccupied with my tutor that I was worried about whether or not she was eating. There was a zero percent chance she was thinking about me at that moment. Yet somehow Eliana had managed to take up my headspace without me even realizing it. Maybe Ollie was right. I needed to snap myself out of whatever weird state I was in. I head towards the kitchen to get myself another drink when I see Mandy in the corner with her sorority sisters. Just the distraction I needed. Mandy was easy, and totally fine with my no-strings-attached rule. Except I can't bring myself to get any closer to her. I'm reaching for the keg when Mandy grabs my hand and drags me down the hall into a decently secluded corner of Hockey House.

"Hey." She practically purrs as she wraps her arms around my neck.

"Hi." I give her a small smile, and then her lips are on mine. She takes a step forward, effectively pushing me against the wall as she grinds herself on me. I kiss her back, but I'm nowhere near as enthusiastic as she is. The second I close my eyes I see Mason's disappointed expression, telling me I'm being demoted. I try my best to focus my attention on Mandy, except now Mason's face is replaced with Eliana's exhausted expression. I feel a twinge in my chest. *Fuck me.* What the hell is wrong with my brain and why does hooking up with Mandy suddenly feel like such a...chore? This blows.

Mandy pulls away, looking confused. "Jake, is everything okay?"

"Yup. Definitely. Why wouldn't it be?" I shrug, shoving my hands into the back pocket of my jeans.

"Well, for one, you're not touching me at all. And your lips are giving dead fish." She scrunches her eyebrows."Did I do something wrong?"

"No. No. Definitely not. I'm just in a weird head space right now."

"You sure I did nothing wrong?" She looks down at her shoes, clearly embarrassed.

"Mandy, I promise it's not you. I'm just going through it right now." I keep things vague, not having it in me to confess the fact that I could get benched soon.

"Oh, well, I'm sorry about that."

"I appreciate it." I look around awkwardly, wanting to get out of this conversation as fast as I can without offending her. "I'm probably not too fun to hang around tonight. I just need some space."

I plop back down into my spot on the coach, eyes glued back onto the door, because *alright fine*. Maybe Ollie was right and maybe there was a part of me that was hoping Eliana would come through the door. Because she deserved a break and fun Saturday night to herself. That was the only reason why I wanted to see her tonight. For her sake. Not for mine.

"So why'd you just blow off Mandy?" Ollie shows up again, startling me. He's like my damn sleep-paralysis demon.

"I didn't blow her off. I just wasn't in the mood to hook up."

"Since. When." Oliver places a hand on my forehead like he's taking my temperature. "Are you coming down with something?"

"Fuck off." I swat his hand away.

"No, I'm serious. I'm genuinely concerned now. Maybe I should take you to the hospital."

"Alright. I'm done here." I get up from the couch and head towards the door.

"Where are you going?" Oliver calls.

"For a walk." I just need to clear my head. And some fresh air.

Chapter 16

Eliana

I've re-read this paper at least three times, and somehow, I was still finding small typos. There was nothing I hated more than editing my own papers. Other people's work? No issues. I could spot an extra space or a misplaced comma in a nanosecond. The same rules didn't apply when I was proofreading my own work but I was determined to have this paper finished by tonight.

Nicole had made me promise to not stay up too late working on this assignment, but she was also out clubbing right now which meant she would be none the wiser. The sound of my stomach growling pulls me back into reality. The last time I looked at the clock it was 7 p.m. and I convinced myself I could handle another thirty minutes of work before eating dinner. It was currently 9:45 p.m. and I had yet to eat dinner. Classic tunnel vision.

In an effort to improve my quality of work, I decide to feed my needy body. And hopefully, brain. I search through my now not-completely-empty fridge for something I can throw together quickly. Breakfast for dinner is always a solid option. I make a move to pull out the eggs and bacon when I hear a knock on my door.

"Pizza delivery." I didn't order a pizza....did I? Admittedly, I have been known to order takeout in a mid-work haze and forget about it until it showed up at my doorstep. Perhaps 7 p.m. Eliana had looked out for 10 p.m. Eliana. I love myself from 3 hours ago.

Throwing open the front door I glance up at the delivery guy. My first thought is that he's hot. My second thought is that I know him. It's crazy how the malnourished mind works. Jake Keeley is standing at my door. My nose immediately takes in the scent of melted cheese and toppings.

"I'll take a slice or two as payment. The rest is all yours." He extends the box out for me to take.

My eyebrows furrow together. "What are you doing here?"

"Bringing you pizza." He shakes the box as if to say 'Obviously.'

"Oh. Did I order this? Do you moonlight as a delivery person?"

"No? Do you have another pizza on the way?"

"No I thought maybe I had— nevermind. Weren't you having a party tonight?"

He shrugs casually. "Yeah, party got boring. I was just in the area and figured you'd want some dinner."

"Oh. That's...really nice. C'mon in." I stand back, letting him enter my apartment. He takes his shoes off by the door and heads towards the dining room table we use for our tutoring sessions.

"Wow, you weren't kidding about spending Saturday working." He nods his head to my laptop and the scattered papers surrounding it.

"Nope. I did not make up a ten-page paper just to get out of going to your party." He enters my kitchen and removes two plates from the cabinet for us. "How many slices do you want?"

Him seeing me near starvation twice in one week has me feeling defensive. Guy probably thinks I can't take care of myself. "You really don't have to share your pizza with me. I was just about to make some dinner."

"Oh. Well you're welcome to get back to cooking. But this is hot and ready now. No effort required." He winks.

I sigh because cooking sounds like work I don't have the energy for. Guess I'm letting this man feed me twice this week. Is this normal guy friend behavior? Is bromance love language feeding each other? "Thank you. I really appreciate it."

"So, two slices or three?" He's interrupted by the sound of my stomach growling. "Let's start with three and go from there."

I take the plate from his hands. "Ugh Anthony's is the best."

The second the cheesy goodness hits my tongue, I let out a small moan. My eyes close as I inhale my first slice and when they reopen, I find Jake staring at me. His eyes are fixated on my face as his tongue traces his bottom lip slowly. I feel my body heat up under his gaze. "Um, is there something on my face?" I ask, snapping him out of whatever trance he seemed to be in.

"What?" He gulps, still fixated on my lips.

"Did I get sauce on my face or something? Is that why you're staring?"

"I wasn't staring." He grabs a slice for himself, shoving it in his mouth while refusing to make eye contact with me.

Though I'm still hungry after three slices I start to feel my stomach settle along with a small boost of energy I plan on using to finish the paper. I move to bring my laptop closer to me when Jake shoots me a weird look. "What is it?" I sigh.

"Are you really going to spend your entire night working?" He asks.

"I'm almost done. Just proofreading. Or at least trying too. Editing is one of my least favorite parts of writing." He snatches my laptop from me. "What are you doing?" I reach my arms across the table in a feeble attempt to get my computer back.

"Reading over your paper."

"That's not necess—"

"I may be struggling in PSYCH101, but I'm not illiterate. I can scan for typos." He attempts to keep his tone light but I can tell I struck a nerve.

"I know you're more than capable of helping me edit."

"Then what's the problem?" He asks, clearly not convinced by my response.

"I like doing things myself. And I struggle with asking people for help."

"Ah." He laughs to himself.

"What's so funny?"

"Nothing."

I give him a look to let him know I'm not convinced.

"I guess I realized how we have a lot more in common than I thought we did and found it kinda funny."

"What do we have in common?"

"Other than the fact that we're both incredibly hot?" He teases.

"Don't deflect. Especially with a compliment that strokes your own ego."

"Fine. Fine. Your comment about how it's hard for you to ask for help." He points at his face. "Why do you think I let my grade tank for so long? Or why I chased off so many tutors?"

I'm intentional about my eye contact. "There's no shame in asking for help when you're struggling in school, Jake."

"Just like there's no shame in letting a friend read over your paper so you can start relaxing on a Saturday night." He gives me a small smirk, knowing he had me there.

"But now you're not relaxing. Seems a bit contradictory to your stance of not working on weekends, no?" I quip.

"Well you've helped me with my homework, so now I'm returning the favor. As a friend. Plus I already got to have my fun tonight at the party."

"I thought you said the party was boring."

"It was. Because you weren't there."

I bite my lip trying not to break out into a smile. *No need to blush like a schoolgirl over some nice words, Eliana.*

"See, I am capable of giving you a compliment without it being tied to me."

"Alright. Alright. Less chatter, more editing." I gesture to my laptop that's still in his hands.

"Aye, Aye Sergeant." He gives me a mock salute, turning his attention back to my laptop as he gets to work.

Chapter 17

Jake

The familiar scent of garlic, basil, and roasted tomatoes hits my nose as I enter my parent's house. You would think that with both myself and my younger sister Sienna going to college in Boston, we would have more time to visit home. But I honestly couldn't remember the last time we all came together for a family dinner. This one was particularly special as we were celebrating Charlotte's dissertation defense, we'd attended this morning. She'd spent the rest of the day celebrating with her lab mates which left the dinner plans to us. From the entrance of the house, I can hear my mom's cackling laughter, which is followed by a groan from my dad as Sienna whines, "Mom it's not funny."

Among a fit of giggles, my mom manages to get out, "I don't knooow SiSi. I think it's pretty hilarious."

I turn the corner into the kitchen to see my dad and Sienna dripping wet and my mom with a half-empty champagne bottle in her hands. "Damn, you guys started celebrating without me?"

If looks could kill, I'm sure I'd be dead already with the glowering look on Sienna's face. "Don't you start, Jake."

I have to clamp down my lips to avoid busting out into a howling laugh, which is really difficult given how ridiculous her and my dad look right now. I'm sure I would be pissed if I was in their shoes, but they looked like two cartoon characters who just got stuck in a torrential downpour. Add the fact that my mom had either accidentally, or maybe even intentionally, doused them in champagne really made this situation ten times funnier. "Can I get you a towel or something?" I snicker. "Maybe next time you'll learn not to stand in the splash zone."

"Ha. Ha. You're sooo funny." Sienna takes the half-empty champagne bottle from my mom and stalks closer to me, like a hunter closing in on their prey.

"Whatever you're thinking, I'd highly recommend you reconsider." I hold my hands up above my head in mock defeat. "We don't want a repeat of my 14th birthday now, do we?"

Sienna and Charlotte had both conspired to shove my face into my cake in front of all my teammates. Probably as payback for all the times I had forgotten to put the toilet seat down that week. Unfortunately for them, I had it spotted from the moment they stood on either side of me to sing me happy birthday. And in the end, I spent the entirety of my party clean as a whistle while they spent the rest of the night washing icing out of their hair.

"Thanks for reminding me. I owe you 7 year-old payback!" A few seconds later she's chasing me around the living room trying to douse me with the remaining contents in the bottle while my mom yells at her not to get any of her furniture wet.

There are a few close calls but I'm able to use my height to reach over and snag the bottle from her hands in sweet victory, taking a swig from the bottle in celebration.

"You're so annoying," she huffs, stomping off to her old room to clean up.

My dad follows her out a few seconds later after putting me in charge of watching over the stove. While my mom was an absolute genius when it came to research, her skills in the kitchen were lacking at best and at worst, the direct result of our entire family getting food poisoning during Thanksgiving ten years ago.

When the coast is clear, I turn my attention back to my mom who is definitely a couple of glasses of wine in. "You did that on purpose, didn't you?"

"Me? I would never?" She winks, walking over to me and giving me a big hug. "I missed having all of my kids under this roof. Charlotte should be here any second now."

"Well it's a good thing there's still some champagne left in the bottle. Maybe you could let her drink it instead of wearing it since she just defended her dissertation." *And maybe you can also avoid giving Charlotte feedback about her project because every time you do she thinks you're judging her skills as a researcher.*

"Fair enough. I also got her favorite tiramisu from Cafe Vittoria so we're all in for a treat tonight."

My stomach growls in response, and it takes everything in me not to sneak a bite of dessert. Charlotte would definitely rip off my head if I even tried it. It's almost as if just the thought of me touching her tiramisu summoned her because a few minutes later, she's strutting into the kitchen.

We immediately tackle her in a group hug, and shouts of congratulations. Charlotte tries to pretend like she didn't like the attention on her, but I can tell she's soaking it up. As she should. It's not every day you become a doctor, and Charlotte had busted her ass off to get to this stage. My mom hands us all a glass of champagne and we cheers in celebration.

It's not until Charlotte moves to top off her drink that she realizes the bottle is nearly empty. "Did you get started without me? And why is the floor so sticky?"

"Mom thought it would be funny to douse Sienna and Dad in champagne." I nod my head to the nearly empty bottle on the counter.

"Jake Keeley!" Mom mock scolds. "It was an accident I swear. I was trying to have our drinks ready for when Charlotte arrived. Why would I waste a bottle of Dom Perigon?"

Charlotte and I exchange a knowing look as if my mom hasn't done a few wild things to rile Sienna and my dad up. The two are definitely the most reserved and uptight of our family and mom was relentless in her attempts to help them "loosen up".

My mom rolls her eyes at our silence, "I purchased an extra bottle just in case. It's in the fridge right now, if you want to grab in Char."

"Will do. After I finish whatever's left in this bottle, seeing as this is my party." Charlotte ruffles my hair and gives Mom a big hug before pouring herself a drink.

"So what's for dinner?"

"Homemade cheese ravioli with your grandmother's famous tomato sauce. Your father woke up extra early today to make the pasta dough." Mom sighs dreamily as she watches Dad come back into the kitchen.

He doesn't even seem mildly upset about the prank she pulled earlier. Instead, he tucks a piece of her hair behind her ear and presses a soft kiss to her temple. When we were younger, I'd always make jokes about how utterly whipped my dad was, but as I got older, I wondered what it must feel like to be able to find peace in someone else.

"What, no fake gagging or comments for them to get a room, Jake?" Charlotte shoves me, pouring herself a drink.

"Oh, our little Jake is all grown up Char. Haven't you heard? There's a new girl in his life." Sienna sing-songs.

"You don't know what you're talking about." I bite out, knowing that if Mom got a whiff of me potentially seeing someone, she'd spend the rest of the night trying to pry every detail out of me. The worst part is I couldn't even fess up about Eliana being my friend-and-sometimes- tutor. That would open up an entirely different can of worms I didn't want to get in to.

Charlotte snorts. "When *isn't* there a girl in Jake's life? No offense bro, but you're a major slut. Just because you want him to settle down, Si, doesn't mean he's going to."

I never had any issues in the past of being called out for sleeping around, but for some reason, the words sting a bit this time. "I thought we agreed to stop slut shaming people years ago."

"Siblings always get a pass when it comes to insults," Charlotte shrugs. "If anyone else called you a slut though, I'd bite their head off."

"Thanks I guess?" I roll my eyes.

"This time is different, Charlotte. He's really serious about this girl. He even wakes up early on non-practice days to get her breakfast."

Charlotte snaps her head in my direction, eyes widening. "Holy shit. You *are* seeing someone, aren't you?"

"Is the bar really so low for me that the thought of me grabbing coffee for someone is breaking news?"

"I'm afraid so. In our defense, you were the one who told us not to freak out if we don't hear from you on Thursdays because you're dead asleep to recoup for weekend games. We're just following the rules you set."

Well, they got me there.

"Dinner's ready. Let's set the table." Hopefully food will be enough of a distraction for them to stop prying.

I grab extra glasses and cutlery while my dad transfers the hot pans filled with pasta to the table. As we sit at the dining table, my sisters sandwich me in between them and I have a feeling I'm in for a night of questioning. Fantastic.

"To celebrate defending your dissertation and officially getting your PhD, I made your favorite three-cheese ravioli. Before we get started, I want to say a few words." Dad's fingers are entwined with Mom's as he looks at Charlotte. "We are so, so proud of all you've accomplished over the years Char. And we can't wait to see all the amazing things you do next."

"Thanks Dad, Mom. Love you both. Now let's dig in."

In between stuffing our faces, we catch up on life lately.

"Jake, your win against UCONN was such a nail biter. I swear I felt my blood pressure rise every other minute." My mom places a hand on her heart as she reminisces.

"They're definitely our toughest competition this year. I thought we were done for when we ended the first period down three goals." Thankfully we managed to get our shit together.

"The goal you scored in the second was such a thing of beauty. Really changed the tone of the game." Sienna beams like a proud little sister.

"Seems like the new assistant coach is starting to get his bearings," my dad notes.

"Yeah. Admittedly we had some tense moments when he decided to take me off the first line, but now I get it. He wants a leader on each line to help elevate our freshman, and it's working. Dylan scored his first goal this season, which was really awesome to see."

"Getting to show off your skills as a captain. No wonder the Bruins are dying to sign you." Mom says gleefully.

The comfort I felt immediately vanishes as Sienna asks Charlotte and my mom about some feedback on her honors thesis. She mentions something about trying to decide which nonparametric test to run that will best fit her data, and I'm immediately lost. What happened to a good old t-test?

The three of them go back and forth for twenty minutes, and while I laugh along to the different jokes they tell, I understand none of them. The joy I felt seeing my family excited about hockey is replaced by the feeling of being an outsider again. A reminder as to why I decided to take PSYCH101 in the first place. To be able to join in on the conversation.

"Speaking of stats— Char I noticed you didn't show any of the new analyses I suggested during your defense," Mom starts.

To my left I feel Charlotte tense slightly, chewing on her bottom lip.

My mom takes a sip of her wine. "That makes sense. I did give you that advice super close to your defense. It would've been way too much to redo everything on such short notice." She gives Charlotte a warm smile and for a moment, I think we're in the clear until Mom continues. "You'll change them for your manuscript though, right?"

"I don't really see the need to. My advisor doesn't have any concerns," Charlotte counters.

"I really feel like reviewers are going to have issues with your approach. I would hate to see it rejected after all the hard work you put in."

"Rejection is a part of being an academic. *You're* the one who taught me that."

Mom's eyebrows pinch together. "I know honey. Doesn't make it any easier when it happens though. Maybe you should talk to your advisor about it again?"

Charlotte opens her mouth to retort but Sienna cuts her off. "So Jake, why don't you tell us more about this mystery girl you're dating?"

A wave of silence crashes over the table before my mom lets out a loud squeal. I turn my head to shoot daggers at Sienna and her face is covered with remorse. She subtly nods in Charlotte's direction, who is currently clenching and unclenching her hands on the table, and I get the memo. Sienna threw me under the bus as a lifeline for Charlotte. I can't even be upset about it because I knew how the conversation with Charlotte and my mom would've ended— with Charlotte storming off while Mom would be left confused and hurt because all she wanted to do was help her daughter who she loves with all her heart. Unfortunately, I don't think Mom really understood how difficult and overwhelming it was for Charlotte to always live in the shadow of one of the most prominent researchers in her field. I'm not saying Charlotte is necessarily justified for getting angry with Mom, but it's not always easy to stay calm when your insecurities are constantly being pointed out. That was definitely something Charlotte and I had in common.

"Jake. Have you been holding out on us?" Mom's smile takes up her entire face.

"Sienna's being dramatic. I'm not seeing anyone."

"Is that why you wake up every morning at 6 a.m. to bring her coffee?" Sienna challenges.

"Not every day. Just twice a week. And we're just friends."

Mom's not having any of that. "6 a.m. is quite early, Jake. She must be very special."

"It's really not that big of a deal." I shrug. "She likes to start her days morbidly early and I decided to help her out by getting her coffee. Friends buy friends coffee all the time."

"They do. Although we've never heard of you doing this for a girl before," Dad teases. Great. He's an even bigger helpless romantic than my mom is. The two of them being invested in my love life was a true nightmare scenario. "There's only one person I would've dragged myself out of bed for that early when I was in college." He brings my mom's hand, still entwined with his, up to his lips and places a soft kiss on the back of it.

"We're just friends and that's all I have to say about it. You're not getting anything else from me."

"Oh I'll get it out of you sooner or later Jake. But for now I can hang tight. Who wants dessert?" Mom exclaims, heading into the kitchen.

My dad gives me a wink followed by a knowing smirk, and I hold in a groan. I guess in their defense they were half right. Eliana was a pretty important part of my life now, just not in the way they imagined. I was finally starting to understand the material in PSYCH101, which would help get my grade back up and keep me from getting benched. Though I had to admit, regardless of the reason, I didn't really care why she had found her way into my life. I just liked the fact that she did.

Chapter 18

Eliana

Oh my god. Is this real life? I pinch my arm to ensure I'm not dreaming. Ow. Nope. Totally awake. "I can't believe I actually got it." I say to myself, continuing to stare at the personalized email from Dr. Katherine Fisher congratulating me for being accepted as a summer intern in her lab.

I had to tell Violet. And Bethany. And anyone else who was in a two-mile radius.

I rush down the hall towards Violet's office where I find her crouched over her laptop analyzing the MRI data we had collected earlier in the week from a chubby little 6-month old baby and his mom. From the corner of her eye, she notices me standing in the hall and waves me in. "How's it going?"

A massive smile takes over my face. "Oh you know..."

She matches my smile with one of her own. "Could it be that you heard some good news today?"

"Sure did. You're looking at Katherine Fisher's new summer intern," I squeal, not being able to contain myself.

Violet jumps to her feet and throws her arms around me in

a big hug. "See? I told you you nailed that interview. She absolutely adored you. And can you blame her?"

"She was so hard to read when we met. I guess that's the con of doing a virtual interview. I was convinced she hated me and thought I was stupid." I normally had a good read on how people felt about me after any interview, but Katherine Fisher had a poker face that would probably win her a ton of money in Vegas.

"Well now you can bask in the glory that you've secured one of the most competitive summer internships you could apply to. And celebrate too. The celebration is non-negotiable, by the way."

"I will, I will. I just want to accept the offer first. So it's real. Because right now, I still feel like I'm dreaming." I stare at the email from my phone, re-reading it to make sure it wasn't one of those fake-out emails like, "CONGRATULATIONS...you've earned a spot on the waitlist! We'll let you know if a spot opens up, but it probably won't. Have a nice life!"

"Well, respond to her whenever you feel ready. Then tell Bethany so she can celebrate, too. And finally plan some fun this weekend to ensure that you *do* celebrate. Wins don't come by too often in academia, so you have to make sure to appreciate it when they do." She gives me another hug. "I'm so happy for you!"

"Thank you! Okay I need to respond to this email or else I won't be able to stop thinking about it." I head back to the office and delete at least ten different versions of my reply before I finally settle on something that balances gratitude without coming off as a nerdy fangirl. Because that's definitely what I was.

To: Katherine Fisher (fisherk@bu.edu)

From: Eliana Jasper (ejasper@westchesteru.edu)

RE: Offer for Summer Internship at Boston University

. . .

Hello Dr. Fisher,

Thank you for your email! I am incredibly excited to accept this offer for the summer internship program. Please let me know if there's any additional information you need from me for the onboarding process.

Looking forward to joining your lab soon,
    Eliana

    --

    Research Assistant - Brain and Early Emotions Lab
    Westchester University

I tried to distract myself with work after I pressed send, instead of re-reading the email a bunch of times and wondering if I used too many (or too few) exclamation points. I was in a grove with recruiting participants when my phone buzzes, an email from Katherine Fisher popping on my screen. Oh god. I messed up. I should've included an extra exclamation point in the email to show how excited I was. She probably hates me now and is going to rescind her offer. *Relax Eliana. Relax. She's far too busy to be analyzing your tone over email.* Oh, rational inner monologue. Why can't you always show up in times of great panic? I take a few deep breaths before reading her email.

To: Eliana Jasper (ejasper@westchesteru.edu)
    From: Katherine Fisher (fisherk@bu.edu)

RE: RE: Offer for Summer Internship at Boston University

Eliana —

Excellent. We look forward to having you! HR will be in touch soon. Bethany invited me to give a talk at Westchester next Thursday at 4pm, in case you're free. If I don't see you there, I'm sure we'll see each other plenty in the summer.

Also, call me Katherine.

Best,
 Katherine
 --
 Professor
 Boston University

Call me Katherine?! So much for not being a nerdy fangirl because right now all I could think about was how I was on a first name basis with Katherine Fisher. That and the fact that I needed to rearrange my schedule for next week because there was absolutely no way I was missing this talk.

Chapter 19

Eliana

I was currently sitting next to Violet as Bethany introduced Katherine Fisher as the guest speaker for today. Violet scored us seats close to the front of the room; close enough to see Katherine give me a small smile from the stage.

Katherine's talk goes by in a flash and I line up behind a group of faculty who approach her, listening in to them to discuss future directions and potential collaborations. Violet comes with me for moral support, and before I know it, we get so distracted talking about the latest episode of *Selling Sunset* that neither of us realizes most of the room has cleared out. Luckily for me, Katherine has still stayed behind, leaving me with the perfect chance to speak to her without an audience. "Hi Katherine. I'm Eliana."

"Hi Eliana! I was hoping we'd get to meet in person before you started. We're so excited to have you this summer." She gives me a warm smile. "So, what do you think about the work we're doing in the lab? Any immediate interests?"

"It was amazing. I'm curious if you think a social reward

might be more enticing to adolescents, rather than the monetary ones used. Do you feel like their responses would have been different?"

"That's an interesting question. I have some initial ideas, but maybe we could talk more later about how we could test that in an experiment. Why don't you shoot me an email? Normally I'd offer to stick around and chat, but I promised my son I'd grab dinner with him."

"Of course. I'll definitely be in contact! Does your son go to Westchester?" I realize I know nothing about Katherine outside of being a researcher.

"He sure does. Though I know Westchester is a large school, so I wouldn't expect you to know him."

That's fair especially given psychology is one of the more popular majors. There was also the chance that he wasn't a psych major. That'd be surprising, given who his mom is, but I could also respect wanting to carve out your own niche. I couldn't imagine the pressure that came with being Katherine Fisher's son. "Is he in psychology?"

"Nope. My two daughters are but he's the rebel of the family. Decided to follow his own path, and I couldn't be any prouder of him for pursuing his own dreams." She beams, the unconditional love coming through on her face.

My heart clenches, "He sounds great. Maybe one day our paths will cross."

"Why don't I introduce you two? That's him right there." She walks over to the door where I see an incredibly tall blonde leaning against the wall with his back to us. That slouch looks oddly familiar.

The mass of a man turns around and I'm met with a set of piercing blue eyes and a sharp jaw that I know was toned over years of sweet talking. I blink once. Then twice. "*Jake is your son?!*" The shock flies out of my mouth before I can stop it.

"Eliana?" His eyes flash between me and his mom and widen as he realizes we've been talking to each other.

Katherine wraps around her son, giving him a big hug topped off with a kiss on his cheek. "Hi Mom." I expect him to be more embarrassed, like any other college boy being smothered by his mother, but he just returns her hug.

"Well, I was just about to introduce my new summer intern Eliana, but it seems you two have already met."

Huh. Never in a million years would I have guessed that I was tutoring Katherine Fisher's son. I figured that boy would get all of the psych support he needed, but maybe she was too busy. He confessed it's hard for him to ask for help, so maybe working with a tutor seemed easier than going to his parents.

"How do you two know each other?" Katherine asks.

Easy enough of a question. "Oh, I'm Jake's t—"

"GIRLFRIEND. She's my girlfriend."

Chapter 20

Jake

"GIRLFRIEND. She's my girlfriend." The words fall out of my mouth before I can take them back, and I immediately know I'm fucked. A few seconds ago I was shitting my pants over my mom finding out that Eliana was my friend and unofficial PSYCH101 tutor, and now I was shitting my pants that Eliana was going to blow my cover. I look to Eliana as if that will somehow help her read my mind.

Instead, she just looks at me like I'm crazy, and laughs. "He's kidding—"

I wrap my arm around her waist and bring her closer to me. The sudden movement, paired with the touching, shocked her enough to cut her off. "Oh babe, you don't have to be shy. I know you wanted to keep this lowkey, but it seems like the universe had different plans for us."

"I—uh, what?" Eliana keeps looking between me and my mom as if she's slowly starting to notice the family resemblance.

Shit. Shit. Shit. "Honestly, this is all my fault. Ellie and I started dating a few weeks ago, and we've been so focused on getting to know each other that neither of us have really talked about family stuff yet. I never got around to telling her that my mom was a psychology researcher. In hindsight I probably should have assumed your paths would cross one day, given you both work in the same field."

"Oh sweetie, is this the girl you were telling us about during family dinner?" Mom smiles.

Eliana's eyes widen even more, and I need to get her alone before she finally breaks out of her state of shock and blows my cover. Thankfully another Westchester professor swoops in to ask my mom some questions about her talk, giving me the perfect opportunity to pull Eliana into the corner of the room so my mom can't hear us.

"I promise I can explain."

"Well you better get started because I've spent the last five minutes pinching myself to wake up from the nightmare that is you telling one of my idols and *new boss*, who happens to be *your mom*, that we're dating."

"This is definitely real life."

"I just don't get it. Why did you say I'm your girlfriend? Also why didn't you tell me your mom is Katherine freaking Fisher?!"

"Saying you're my girlfriend just came out of my mouth before I could even stop it, so I just rolled with it. She doesn't know I'm struggling in psych, or that I was looking for a tutor. And honestly? I completely spaced how small academia can be. It never once crossed my mind that you two would run into each other." Which, in hindsight, was pretty short-sighted of me.

"We're past running into each other. I'm going to work for her this summer! She can't think that we're dating. That has to be against some code of ethics or something. I can't lose this internship, Jake." She runs her hands through her loose curls while gnawing on her lip.

Ugh. I had really managed to fuck this up. "You won't lose it. My mom had no idea we had any relationship — fake or otherwise — when she selected you. HR departments manage conflicts of interest all the time."

"Okay, okay. That's good. I still don't get why you couldn't just tell her I'm helping you with a class?"

I fidget with the hem of my hoodie and my throat tightens.

Eliana's voice is extremely soft as it hits my ears, like she's talking to a wild animal that's been wounded. "I'm not going to judge you. I'm just trying to understand."

"My mom is Katherine Fisher." That's all that needed to be said.

Eliana crosses her arms and gestures for me to continue. "Yeah, I gathered as much."

"She's literally one of the most famous researchers in her field. My older sister chose to follow in her footsteps. Younger sister is also probably going to end up doing the same in a couple of years. Meanwhile, I just...play hockey. And I love it. It's the one thing that's always been mine. The one thing that I always excelled at and loved doing. But when I sit down in a room with my family, I end up feeling so...small. Like I don't even exist sometimes. Like I don't even matter. That's why I chose to take PSYCH101."

"So you could prove to them that there's more to you than just hockey?" She guesses.

"Sort of. There was definitely a small part of me that wanted to prove I could also use my brains if I wanted to. But I think a bigger part of me just wanted to feel like I fit in with my family. Since research is basically the family business it's often all that gets talked about. And I wanted to be able to contribute to dinner conversations. Or at the very least, be able to keep up." A self-deprecating laugh slips out. "I probably should've known better. I still know next to nothing about psychology, but now it might also cost me hockey."

"I won't let it come to that. I promise." She sounds so sure.

"I hope you're right." I shove my hands into my pockets. "So, are we okay?"

She takes a moment to think to herself. "Honestly, I don't know. I don't like the idea of lying to your mom, and while I appreciate you trying to comfort me about not losing my internship, I don't want people to think the only reason I got this job was because I'm dating you. Especially when we're not even dating. I've worked way too hard to get to where I am today, for all of my accomplishments to be written off as favoritism."

"You're right. It was really unfair to put you in this position. I honestly wasn't thinking at all and just hit the panic button. I'll tell her the truth soon. I promise. But maybe we can wait until after my next exam so I can at least tell her I'm not at risk of being benched anymore?"

It was a selfish ask, but in my head, telling my mom I had a friend/tutor who was helping me stay on track was an easier blow to my ego than telling her I was failing and about to lose hockey.

"I don't know..." Eliana nods her head to the left, signaling my mom approaching.

"I just called the restaurant to add an extra person to our reservation. Eliana, can you join us for dinner?" My mom gives us a big smile.

Eliana sends me a look that screams, *This is really bad!* "Oh I really don't want to impose—"

"It's not an imposition at all. In fact, I insist. I would love to get to know more about the incredible researcher who will be joining my lab soon. I'm just going to clean up my things, and we can head out?" Katherine walks away before either of us can respond.

"This is bad. This is very bad." Eliana starts biting her nails. "I can't go to dinner with Katherine Fisher. Especially when she thinks I'm dating her son."

"You saw the look on her face. She's not taking no for an answer." I try my best to come off as calm and collected, but I couldn't deny I was also freaking out a little. I know very little about my supposed girlfriend.

"Fine. One night. What's our game plan?"

"I'll say you were tutoring Ollie, which is how we connected. She knows we only recently started dating so it makes sense there's still a lot we don't know about each other. Would you feel comfortable with holding my hand?"

"Whoa there, buddy. Maybe buy me a drink first." Eliana snorts, her tone laced with sarcasm.

I chuckle, then drape my arm across her shoulder and hold her hand from that position. Tucked at my side I can't help but notice that the top of her head is at the perfect height for me to rest my chin on. Huh. *This actually feels pretty nice.*

"Alright, you kids ready?" My mom's voice snaps me back into reality.

Or at least the very fake reality in which Eliana and I are pretending to date. "Ready."

Chapter 21

Eliana

When I asked the universe to give me more face time with Katherine Fisher, I should have been more specific. I never would have guessed I would be going out to dinner with one of my idols pretending to be her son's girlfriend. If I somehow managed to make it through this dinner without making a complete ass of myself — or revealing that Jake and I are, in fact, *not* dating — it would be a miracle. Jake on the other hand was calm, cool, and collected. If he ever wanted to pursue a career besides hockey, he should seriously consider acting. The performance he's giving currently is top-notch.

The second we walked out of the conference room, Jake immediately wrapped an arm around my waist like this was just a thing that we did. He didn't even flinch when I elbowed him hard in the ribs to get him off me. Instead, he looked down at me, winked, and then gave my side a small squeeze that must be a secret pressure point because I immediately melted into his arms after that. Even though I didn't want to. Or at least I didn't think I did. With him acting like a boyfriend straight out of the romance novels I loved so much I didn't know anymore.

We managed to make it to the restaurant without Katherine asking us any questions, but I could tell she was dying to pry and find out all the juicy details about the girl who had locked down her son. Because evidently that's what I had done. Locked down one of the biggest players on campus. Except our whole relationship was a lie. A lie so his mom wouldn't find out that we met because he needed a tutor. I still have no idea why I didn't protest coming to dinner more. Or come up with an excuse, like my roommate needing my help with installing a new wall-mounted TV.

We put in our orders, and Katherine slips away to the bathroom, leaving Jake and me alone. I make note of every exit sign in the vicinity and debate whether I can make it outside before she gets back. I'd never been one to run away from a tough situation, but I feel extremely out of my element in this one. Plus, Jake seemed more than capable of coming up with a quick excuse. If I bolted now, he'd probably just tell his mom I came down with the flu or something.

"I'd catch you before you even made it 100 feet," Jake whispers into my ear. His words snap me out of my escape fantasy and I realize his gaze had followed mine to the exit in the back right corner of the restaurant. He had also moved his hand from around my waist to over my shoulders, his fingers playing with my hair. *When had he gotten this close to me? And why hadn't I immediately noticed and moved away?*

"I don't know what you're talking about."

"So you weren't scanning the room for a means to escape this dinner and plotting out how you would do it?" He lifts an eyebrow.

"Nope. I was just taking in the ambiance."

"Is that so?"

"Yup. I've never been here before. It's extremely fancy. Lots to take in. I wonder how much that crystal chandelier costs."

"Eliana, c'mon. Be real with me for a second."

"Oh, so now we're being real? Funny. I thought we were still pretending to be together. I can't keep up with you."

"Alright. I get why you're upset, and you're well within your right to be. The second we get this dinner over with I'm willing to take whatever you have to give me. Whether that's a long lecture or a punch to the gut."

"You're an incredibly disturbed individual."

"You say the kindest things to me, Ellie." He jokes.

I give him a look so lethal I see him physically cringe in response. Good. At least my resting bitch face wasn't broken. Even though it seemed like every other part of me — including my rational side — was.

"You gotta loosen up or else my mom will start suspecting something's up."

"I'm sure any girl would feel nervous getting dinner with her boyfriend's mom for the first time. Now double that, given the fact that we're not even together." I whisper the last bit and look around as if our entire conversation is being eavesdropped on. What a mess.

"It's fine to come off as nervous, but right now you look like you're going to be sick."

"How are you so calm about this? You know she's going to come back and start grilling us for details. And we haven't exactly had enough time to coordinate a game plan so—"

"First off, I told her this was new, so I think she'll understand if there's still a lot we don't know about each other. But you do make a good point. We have a few minutes now, so why don't we figure it out? If she asks you what your first impression of me was, what would you say?"

"That you were an entitled hockey player whose ego

sucked all of the oxygen out of the room and nearly suffocated me." The sarcasm in my voice is heavy, though there was a part of me back then that thought he was entitled.

Jake snorts. "That's a perfect response."

"See? I told you I'm awful at this. I'm going to ruin our cover." I drop my face into my hands as I groan.

"Just stop overthinking it. My mom knows I've always been a huge flirt, and also anti-relationship. She always told me I would one day meet my match. She would get an absolute kick out of your answer and then turn to me and go, *'See Jake? I told you this would happen.'*"

"So I should just be honest?" The plan was so logical it could hopefully work. "Hopefully" being the operative word here.

He nods. "Be yourself and be honest with her. Or at least honest enough without telling her about the whole unofficial tutor thing. You've already withstood a job interview with her. What's a casual dinner?"

"Sure, sure. Easy enough." I take a deep breath as I watch Katherine approach our table. *Be normal Eliana. You can do this.*

"So what are you two kids whispering about?" Katherine beams, taking her seat across from us.

"Did you know that kangaroos are the size of a jellybean when they're born?" I blurt out. *Perfect. I've resorted to reciting facts you find on the back of Snapple Tea caps.* I try to shoot Jake a look to help me out, but he's too busy trying not to burst into a fit of laughs. Incredible.

When I finally look back at Katherine she has a confused, yet amused expression on her face. "Oh, how interesting. I can't say that I did."

"Yup. They spend the first 8 months in the mom's pouch until they can finally hop around on their own." *Stop talking*

Eliana. Please. Stop. Talking. "Sorry, sometimes my roommate leaves Jeopardy on in the background when we study, and it seems I've retained a few random facts."

"No apologies needed. I also love learning new things." She takes a sip of her wine, and I resist the urge to chug from my own glass. "Like how my son has a new girlfriend."

Welp I guess I walked right into that. "Ah."

"I'm sure Jake already warned you that I can be a bit nosy. But isn't every mother?"

"Alright, Mom. Let's get the interrogation over with," Jake teases. "Hit us with your hardest questions."

I kick him under the table while trying my best to keep my composure. Her hardest questions? Why would he encourage her like that? Maybe I can sneak away to the bathroom or crawl to one of the emergency exits.

"Oh c'mon, stop making me seem so bad. I just want to know how you two met...and maybe a few other details."

"Eliana's tutoring one of the guys on the team. You remember Ollie, right?" The lie comes so naturally out of Jake's mouth I nearly believe him.

"Of course I remember Oliver. He nearly ate an entire pot of pasta when you brought him over for family dinner last semester. So, he introduced you two?"

"Not exactly," Jake continues. "Eliana would come over to Hockey House to help Ollie, and from the moment I saw her, I knew I wanted to get to know her. Find out who she really was behind all the layers and walls she puts up." I try my best not to roll my eyes at his dramatic retelling, especially since I could tell Katherine was eating up every bit of it. "Admittedly my approach to interrupt their sessions was not my smartest move. I was a bit of a nuisance during some of the early sessions."

"Oh you think?" It was very hard to reconcile the cocky asshole hockey player side of Jake Keeley I had first met, with the kind thoughtful guy who got upset that I hadn't eaten breakfast and had showed up with two large bags of groceries for me the next time we met.

"So suffice to say, you did not have a positive impression of him when you first met?" Katherine smirks.

While I know Jake said to be honest, I highly doubt any mom would take it well if they heard their son be called a pompous asshole. So I play it safe. "Oh...um...I wouldn't say that. Jake was fine." *Fine.* Suuuuper convincing, Eliana.

"C'mon, Ellie. You can tell her the truth. She probably already knows what you're going to say ." He moves his hand from my hair up to my neck, drawing soothing circles up and down my skin.

"I may have initially thought he was a bit entitl—"

"She thought I was an asshole." Jake summarizes. "And in her defense, I was acting like one."

"But you still gave him a shot?" Katherine raises her eyebrow at me.

"Nope. I told him off. Let him know that I wanted nothing to do with him." I did crack eventually, but that was only after he looked so down and in need of a friend.

"Which is when I realized I had messed up. Big time. The usual Jake Keeley charms had finally run their course. I apologized and begged for a second chance. A second chance that she granted, and I don't think I'll ever be able to fully articulate how grateful I am that she did." Jake gives me a small smile, and I can see the sincerity in his eyes.

For some reason that's enough to draw a blush from me, my entire face heating up and exposing how much his words affect me.

It takes me a second to realize Jake is waiting for me to respond. Dammit what would his actual girlfriend say in this moment? *Think Eliana, think.* "Looks like not all of your charms have been lost."

Jake takes one of my shaking hands into his and gives it a squeeze. I try to ignore the voice in my head that tells me how nice of a gesture that was. This was all an act. Nothing more.

"You two are cute." She makes a content noise. "Jake's sisters are going to be so jealous that I got to meet you before they did. I let them know that the three of us were going out to dinner."

Jake's eyes widen. Oh shit. So much for keeping this lowkey. "Please tell me you're joking."

Katherine just shrugs as Jake reaches for his phone, and pulls up what I can assume is the family group chat. "Dammit. You've really done it now mom."

"What? I'm just the messenger," Katherine teases.

"I hate to be a buzzkill..." I hesitate, hoping what came next wouldn't come off wrong. "But a part of the reason why Jake and I kept this from you was because he knew I was applying to work for you. I don't want people to think that the only reason I got the internship position is because I'm dating your son. The cat's clearly out of the bag, but maybe we can keep it between us?"

Katherine gives me a sympathetic smile. "Don't worry honey. I know all too well how hard it can be for a woman to make her name in academia. And so do Jake's sisters. I support your decision to keep your private life private. I just hope you know that his sisters won't relent until they get to meet you. You may have to come over to our house for family dinner."

If my heart wasn't already in my stomach, it certainly would've dropped there now. I don't know if my heart could handle a series of dinners pretending to be Jake's girlfriend with his entire family. Hopefully she would forget this invitation, and the fact that I followed up with, "That sounds great. Looking forward to it."

Chapter 22

Jake

I've been dodging my mom's requests to bring Eliana over for dinner for the past two weeks, but knowing my family, they won't stop until they get what they want. Which means I need to fess up about lying soon. My stomach churns just thinking about it. Somehow I had managed to get myself into two majorly shitty situations in the span of a couple of months.

Unfortunately in my attempts to get to know Eliana more she would just divert back to asking me questions either about course material or my life. Stalking her on the internet proved to be basically futile. I did learn she had a substantial One Direction obsession when she was a kid — Zayn was her favorite — but given there I had no way of getting in contact with him I was back on my hunt to find out who she really was. It had become somewhat of an obsession the more time we spent together. The more I revealed parts about myself the more I was desperate to get underneath her rough exterior, beautiful mind, and brown eyes that made my heart jump to my throat every time she beamed at me when I answered a question correctly. I was starting to get the same rush I did scoring goals every time I work a smile or a laugh out of a girl who managed to carry the whole weight of the world on her shoulders.

Somehow Eliana had gone from being someone I tolerated to ensure I wouldn't lose hockey, to one of the first people I wanted to talk to as soon as I woke up, or after I got out of a practice. When I told her we were friends a few weeks ago I meant it. Whether or not she believed me was a different story.

After dinner with my mom I realized that Eliana had saved my ass twice now when she didn't need to. Even though I told her how much it meant to me, I figured it wouldn't hurt to also show it. Plus if that meant spending more time with her and proving to her that I'm more than just some new emotional baggage in her life, then it would be a win-win. I knew asking her to hang out would be a futile effort. Her schedule was filled to the brim and I had a feeling if I suggested a break I would either be fully dismissed or set her off the edge completely. Both were options I wanted to avoid. So instead I got a little creative.

I make it all the way up the stairs of Eliana's apartment when I run into her roommate, Nicole. She looks really confused by my presence.

"Jake?"

"Nicole, good to see you."

Nicole stands in the doorway, not letting me in. "If you're hear for Eliana I need to warn you she's really freaked out about her midterms coming up. I'm not sure if she can help you right now."

Ah that explains the lack of her inviting me. She thinks I'm here to add more to Eliana's plate, not help lessen some of the burden she was carrying.

"I know. She mentioned being stressed about some big term

paper earlier this week. I wrapped up all of my exams and figured I'd come and help out a bit." I lift my arm to reveal a bag filled with groceries. "I was planning on making her some dinner while she writes. I bought enough to feed a small army."

Portion size was never something I could get right, especially as an athlete who could eat mountains of pasta before and after a game with no problem.

My response appears to completely throw Nicole off. "You're being serious."

"Yup." I open the bag wider. "All of this will be made into spinach and ricotta stuffed shell pasta covered in vodka sauce."

Nicole steps aside from the door, eyes still locked on me. "That's her favorite."

Perfect. I had hoped as much given she ordered the same dish at dinner the other night. "Yup."

She looks back at the door, then at me, and shrugs, propping the door open. This time her tone is a bit lighter when she addresses me. "Come on in. Eliana's got tunnel vision so she may not even realize that you're here. Or that you're making her food. I'm heading to the library for a last minute Orgo cram session."

I head straight for the kitchen, leaving the groceries on the counter, and decide to make my presence known so I don't cause a jump scare when Eliana inevitably comes into the kitchen. I stop outside of her room. Her door is propped open, providing me with a full view of her typing feverishly on her laptop.

I find myself frozen in place at the sight of Eliana. Her long wavy hair is thrown up haphazardly on top of her head, strands spilling out of the hair clip in all directions. Her deep brown eyes are slightly hidden behind black-rimmed glasses, while she lounges in long pajamas decorated with a faded "1D" logo —— no doubt a leftover clothing item from her earlier days where she was obsessed with the boy band. I was mesmerized, and debated for a moment how weird it would be to continue to stand in her doorway and soak up the parts of her she kept hidden. *Incredibly weird. Even weirder that you even considered standing here watching her do homework like a stalker. Who even does that?*

Siding with my inner monologue, I knock on her door, which barely does anything to shift her attention away from the screen in front of her. "Hey Nic. I thought you were heading out to the library?"

"It's just us now."

My voice causes her to jump out of her seat. Her hands fly to her desk as she grabs a pencil and points it at me like one would hold a knife towards an intruder. It takes her a second to snap out of her alarmed state. "Jake?"

"Were you really going to stab me with a pencil?"

"I thought you were a burglar. Or a serial killer."

"What serial killer would announce their presence?"

"An overly dramatic one that likes to draw out the process? I don't know." She finally lets go of the sharpened writing utensil.

"Maybe you should lay off the true crime podcasts."

"I prefer murder mystery novels to true crime podcasts, also love an episode of Law & Order SVU. Plus, you chose to announce yourself in one of the most ominous ways possible. Next time try 'Hey Eliana, it's me Jake.' instead of *'It's just us now.'* You have to realize how creepy that sounded."

"Fair enough. I apologize. I just wanted to let you know that I'll be hanging here for a bit."

"Right of course." She nods her head as if this a regular occurrence, turning and typing a few extra words before freezing. "Wait what? I really need to finish this paper tonight, and there's a strong chance I may need to pull an all-nighter, so if you're hoping to get some last-minute tutoring in tonight, I really don't think I'll be able to make it work."

"I finished all my exams for this week."

"Oh. Right. I knew that." She pulls up her calendar, which also includes reminders related to my schedule. My throat tightens at the reminder that she only includes alerts for super important things in her calendar and evidently, I made the cut. "How did your psych exam go?"

I make a show of knocking on her wooden desk, "It felt good. There weren't any questions that I felt totally lost about which is a huge step from how the first exam went. Hopefully we'll get some good news soon."

Her lips form into a proud smile, "That's amazing Jake, I knew you could do it." She gestures back to her computer. "We should celebrate once you get your grade back, but I don't really think I have time to hang out tonight…"

"I figured as much, but you do need to have dinner. Which is why I thought I'd come over and make some food for us while you work."

She looks so uncomfortable at my declaration I almost wonder if she would've preferred I was a serial killer instead of her friend and occasional fake boyfriend. "You really don't need to do that."

"I know, but you tasting my dad's famous vodka sauce is number one on the priority list for me. He's been showing me the ropes in the kitchen for this very moment," I joke, trying to lighten the mood.

The look of discomfort remains on her face.

"What is it?" I ask.

"I appreciate your help, really I do. But I don't want you to feel like you have to swoop in and fix all my problems. I know I'm bad at prioritizing my own needs sometimes, maybe even a lot of the time, but that's something *I* need to work on. Not something you need to feel responsible for."

"It's just one dinner, Eliana. Not a permanent contract for me to be your private chef. You spend most of your time taking care of other people. The thought of someone spending a couple hours taking care of you makes you that uncomfortable?"

Her eyebrows furrow together, and I catch her jaw clench like I struck a nerve. Ah shit. I expect her to yell at me but instead she bites her bottom lip before finally conceding. "Dinner sounds great, thanks Jake. I do really need to finish work though, so I can't help."

"Not a problem. My dad's recipe is a big family secret. Like I'd have to kill you if you found out. And given you made it very clear you have an aversion to being murdered..."

"I'm sure most people would have an aversion to being murdered."

"It's for the best that you stay here while I work my magic," I tease, catching an eye roll from her before I head back into the kitchen.

Chapter 23

Eliana

There was a seventy percent chance I was currently dreaming about Jake spontaneously coming over to cook me dinner while I finished this paper. I probably fell asleep hungry and any moment now, I would wake up. Except the scent of tomato sauce and garlic filling my room was too real to be a dream. Also not a dream, Jake Keeley had discovered one of my biggest insecurities — my tendency to overwork myself because it makes me uncomfortable to ask for help.

Over the years I realized two things. The first was people would never leave you if you had something to offer them. My dad left me and my mom because in his eyes all she did was take, and I was just a kid so I couldn't give much. The second thing I learned was that the only person I could truly rely on was myself.

With these two truths I had lived my life for others and never asked, or expected, much in return. I had learned to do everything on my own. Learned that even though I *wanted* someone to care for me, I didn't necessarily *need* someone to take care of me. And that was okay...But some days, when I could feel every single bit of the weight of all I had to carry on my shoulders, I couldn't help but wonder what it would feel like if someone could burden some of that weight with me.

Jake cooking me dinner on a night when I was going to spoon some ramen and ice cream into my mouth and call it a meal meant more than I could put into words. And I tried not to feel embarrassed about the fact that something so small had such a big impact on me.

"Hey." I look over to see Jake casually leaning against my door frame, a towel thrown over his shoulder. "Dinner should be ready in five. I'm gonna set the table while you wrap up."

Finishing this paper in five minutes was easy, given that I had a home-cooked meal waiting for me and a hockey player who had made it his mission to ensure I wasn't burning myself out as motivation. It felt nice to be cared for.

My mouth waters as I take a seat across from him and lay eyes on the vodka sauce pasta, steaming on top of our plates. "Ya' know Keeley, if this is how you treat your fake girlfriends, I can't even imagine the stops you pull out for your real ones."

"You'll have to keep imagining, given I've never really had one."

"You've never had a girlfriend? How is that even possible?"

"This coming from the girl who snuck in the back entrance of the psychology building just so she wouldn't have to see me?"

"That was under different circumstances. Don't try to change the conversation."

"Why do you care so much?" Jake smiles, though it doesn't quite meet his eyes.

"I just find it surprising given your well-known history..."

"My well-known history....on the hockey team?" He raises an eyebrow.

"Don't be smart. You know what I'm talking about."

"Maybe, but I'd like to hear you say it."

"You're insufferable."

"You say the kindest things to me."

"I'm also starting to believe you have a degradation kink."

"Oh, so we're sharing kinks now?"

"Only my real boyfriends get to know my kinks. Sorry to disappoint."

He rolls his eyes before finally answering my question. "I never really felt like turning any of my hook-ups into something serious. Hockey takes up all my free time and the girls I've been with know the deal. If they're looking for a relationship, they won't get it with me."

"Fair enough." Sub out focusing on hockey with focusing on research, and he basically summed up the reason why I haven't had a serious relationship in...a while.

"And what about you? Any ex-boyfriends I need to track down and give a talking to?"

"Adding protective to the list of fake-boyfriend traits now, are we? You really commit to a bit."

"The more you deflect the more I plan on annoying you about this. And for the record if someone *did* hurt you, you can tell me. I'd make sure they'd never do it again." His tone is light-hearted but there's a sincerity in his eyes that makes me think he would follow through on his words.

"My answers are not that different from yours. I've been so focused on my research and doing what I can to help my family out, that I feel like I don't have much time for anything else. With how busy I am, I'm scared I'd be a bad partner, so I just keep to myself instead..."

My eyebrows draw together as I reveal another one of my

insecurities. Many people have commented on my lack of work-life boundaries. The biggest hurdle I have yet to overcome is acknowledging that I can love my research, nannying, and tutoring while also making time for myself. Helping people genuinely did give me joy, but everyone has their limits. And I have a bad habit of pushing mine too far.

Jake reaches across the table and squeezes my hand, "Well if you treat your real boyfriend as good as you treat me. There's no chance you'd be a bad partner, Ellie."

"I could be a good partner...one day. Once I figure out how to take better care of myself. I don't want to be overly reliant on my partner. Or have them enable my bad habits."

"I think it's possible to work on that, while in a relationship. My mom will be the first to admit she was really bad at giving attention to anything that wasn't research until my dad came along. And even then, I know the start of their relationship had some rockier moments. I think you just need someone who understands how important your work is to you and respects the fact that an academic career is really time-consuming."

My heart clenches. "Your dad sounds great."

"He is. Honestly everyone in my family is. They've always been supportive of my hockey career, and never once pushed me to do something else. But I still can't shake the feeling that I'm the black sheep of the family. I took this psych class with the hopes I'd finally be able to understand what my mom and sisters have dedicated their lives to and instead..." He shakes his head. "Let's just hope I didn't bomb the exam."

"You didn't. I know you didn't." I give him a reassuring smile and we spend the rest of dinner in a comfortable silence and I sigh in contentment as I take bite after bite of pasta. "This might be the best pasta I've ever had. Thanks for taking the time to make this."

He gives me a soft smile. "I'm glad you liked it."

I finish my plate and find Jake staring at me. "What is it?"

"You just have a little..." He gestures to my face, before cupping my face in his hand and using his thumb to wipe what I'm assuming is some leftover sauce from my chin. His hand lingers in my face and he leans closer, our faces only a few inches apart. "You know, if you connect these freckles right here, it'd look like a heart."

I feel my cheeks start to heat up and suddenly all I want to do is close the distance between us and learn what it feels like to have his lips pressed against mine. The feeling of his large hands dipping under my shirt while my own hands explored his body. *Bad idea. Get those thoughts out of your head right now Eliana.* Listening to the voice in my head, I pull back and try to ignore the fact that my heart is racing at what feels like a hundred miles an hour.

"Sorry about that." Jake stares at his hand and clenches it a few times, as if touching me had burned his palm. "Do you want some help cleaning up?" He's standing up and washing dishes in the sink before I can respond.

"Let me help you. You did all the cooking, so it's only fair I help with dishes." My eyes take in all the muscles of his back that I can see through his athletic shirt.

"Sounds good. So you've heard a bit about the Keeley household. What's your family like?" Jake leans against the cabinet next to the sink as I clean.

"My dad's out of the picture, he left me, my mom, and my little sister Josie when she was just a baby—"

Jake's jaw clenches as I give him a quick recap of my childhood.

I give him a small smile, "My dad's definitely a dick, but I honestly don't think of him much anymore. Josie and I are 11 years apart, so our dynamic is less like siblings and more like I'm her second mom. She's so witty and outspoken, and I love her so much. Moving away from her for college was really diffi-cult." My heart squeezes thinking of how hard we both cried when she and my mom dropped me off at my dorm freshman year.

"She sounds amazing." Jake smiles tucking a loose strand of my hair behind my ear so it doesn't get wet. His warm touch grounding me in the moment.

"She is. So is my mom although our relationship is also complicated." I rinse off the final dish, setting it on the drying rack before looking back up at Jake who looks eager for me to continue. "Once my dad left, she had to step in and become the provider. Which meant I was often left alone to parent Josie. There were moments growing up where I resented my mom for that. Not because I didn't love Josie, but because I would watch my friends get to just be kids and I was jealous. But at the same time I saw how much she sacrificed for us. How much she had to give up when she immigrated to the states. So even now, I feel like I must support them. We're all each other has."

Before I can fully process what's happening, Jake's wrap-ping his arms around my waist and pulling me into his embrace. To my surprise, I don't resist the hug. Instead, I just rest my head on his chest, and let out a long sigh. "Sorry I feel like I'm constantly being a downer."

"No. You're not. I appreciate you sharing this with me. You have an incredible heart, and I just wish you gave yourself the same level of kindness you give others." Jake rests his cheek on top of my head as he holds me close.

"Well, you have inspired me to take some baby steps when it comes to self-care. I started a new murder mystery series by one of my favorite author's the other night. I'm about halfway through and I *think* I know who's responsible for shoving the mayor into a woodchipper."

Jake snorts, "Remind me to never get on your bad side."

"Eh you can annoy me sometimes, but never to the point where I contemplate murder." I tease, lifting my head so I can wink at him.

"Glad to hear it. Though I have a feeling my next question may test the limits of your patience." He smirks.

"Oh? Now I'm incredibly curious."

"How long have you had those One Direction pajamas?"

My eyes drop down to my legs. Shit. I had totally forgotten I was wearing them. My mouth hangs wide open as his smirk turns into a shit eating grin "I-um. A while."

Dammit my face is hot. I try to break from the hug, but he holds me in place. Though if I was being honest with myself, I probably could escape if I wanted to...

"Don't be embarrassed. I think it's really cute. Any chance your favorite member is Zayn?" His eyes are filled with mischief.

My eyes narrow, "Yes it is. Was that a lucky guess or should I assume foul play?"

"Didn't realize checking my girlfriend's social media to see what she's interested in was illegal."

"*Fake* girlfriend." I protest, ignoring how my heart twinges when I correct him. "And my last One Direction related post has to be a few years old at this rate."

"Yeah well you don't really post often so it didn't take much snooping." He counters.

"Ya know, usually when you internet stalk someone, you don't admit it. You just drop nuggets here and there so it can feel like coincidence. Or fate."

"I feel like you'd appreciate an honest and direct approach more."

He was right. There's something about Jake's bluntness that I find incredibly attractive.

Jake's expression turns sheepish. "One more question. Any chance you're free this Saturday to join our family night? The longer I delay introducing you to my sisters, the more rabid they'll become. I'm running out of excuses as to why we can't hang out with them."

"I thought we agreed you'd tell them the truth soon?" I worry my lip between my teeth.

"Riiight about that..."

"Jake." I protest.

"I promise I'll tell them before the summer. I just want to get the final confirmation that I didn't bomb the midterm. Can we just keep pretending until then?"

"I don't know. I get it's a hard conversation to have, but I'm already nervous about how this fake relationship is going to be perceived once people learn I'm going to be working with your mom. Getting close to your family is definitely not going to help that perception."

"Don't researchers go out to happy hour all the time with each other? To discuss future collaborations?"

"Sure, but game night is different..."

"No one from school is going to see us there. And you can just default to talking to my family about research, so no personal boundaries are crossed."

I guess that could work. Maybe. I stay silent.

"Just think about it, okay? I promise it won't be anywhere near as bad as you're making it in your head."

"I'm not saying yes. But I do feel the need to state that I'm extremely competitive. Like it can be a little ugly to watch."

"It sounds like you'd fit right in with my family."

How does he always know the right thing to say? Though I loved my family, I can't say I ever felt truly understood by my mom. Over the years, I've learned to accept the fact that I always felt like I was a stray puzzle piece that got thrown in the wrong box. I'd always hoped I'd finally find my place, and would feel like I not only belonged but I also helped complete the set. That I was someone's missing puzzle piece. "I'll think about it and get back to you."

Chapter 24

Jake

"Try not to get too upset when I embarrass you in front of your girlfriend," Sienna teases as we walk into the familiar bowling alley in Fenway. To say my family gets competitive during our game nights would be an understatement. The last game night featured a very intense laser tag session and ended with Sienna refusing to talk to me for two weeks. Maybe I should've just opted for a family dinner instead of feeding Eliana to the wolves. The only thing that would outmatch their competitiveness tonight would be their nosiness. Maybe I could use that to my advantage.

"The only person who's going to be embarrassing themselves tonight is me. I'm really bad at bowling," Eliana chimes in.

"I find that hard to believe. You're way too determined not to master anything you set your mind to." I give her hand a gentle squeeze.

"I once got a ball stuck between the guardrails and the gutter." Eliana blushes.

Normally I'd be stressed about losing my win streak, instead I'm fixated on the nervous look on her face as we stop at the table in front of our lane. My parents and Charlotte are already making their way through a pizza and a pitcher of beer.

Charlotte runs over to us, or really to Eliana, as she gently shoves me away. "I'm so excited you're here. Jake's never brought a girl to a family game night before. A bit of a bold choice if you ask me. Has he mentioned how competitive he gets?"

"How competitive *I* get? Are we forgetting the paintball fiasco of 2012 from which I still have a scar?" I scoff.

"You were in the line of fire. What was I supposed to do?" Charlotte rolls her eyes.

"I don't know, maybe not aim for my neck?"

"Let's not rehash the past. I'm much more interested in learning about how this happened." Charlotte eyes my hand that's entwined with Eliana's. She grabbed it the second we ran into Sienna at the entrance and hasn't let go since.

Eliana tells the lie we both agreed upon. "I'm tutoring his friend Ollie. We ran into each other a few times at Hockey House."

"Each time she made it clear how she wanted nothing to do with me."

"But eventually he won me over."

"With my charm—"

"And the fact that he apologized for being such a dick in the beginning."

That draws a snort from Charlotte. "Keeping him in line I see. I definitely like her, Jake."

"Are we going to spend the whole night yapping or can we get this game started?" Sienna calls out, pointing towards the bowling lane. Charlotte practically marches to stand next to her, and the two start a best-of-three series of rock paper scissors to decide whose team is going first.

"You weren't kidding about being competitive," Eliana whispers.

"Oh trust me. You haven't seen anything yet."

"Should I warn them about what a disaster I am?"

"Nah, I'm sure my mom told them to be on their best behavior around you. Which they'll try to be, especially since they can tell how much I like you." The words are out of my mouth before I can stop them, and I wait for a feeling of regret to follow, but it doesn't.

"Hypothetically speaking?" A flash of something appears in her eyes. Longing?

"HA— Jake, Eliana, you're with me. Charlotte gets Mom and Dad." The smug look on Sienna's face tells me she thinks we already have this in the bag. Charlotte looks down-right pissed and I swear I hear her mumble something about cheating. How one can cheat in rock, paper, scissors is beyond me, but I wasn't about to argue.

"Um, do the bowling pins look weird to anyone...?" Eliana's eyebrows knit together at the sight of the straight pins and bowling balls that can fit entirely in the palm of my hand.

"We're candlepin bowling! Longer pins, smaller balls — no laughs from the audience, please. Same rules apply, except you get three tries each round instead of two." Sienna offers Eliana a soft smile before shooting me a look that screams, "We will *not* lose tonight."

"This is about to be a nightmare," Eliana mutters under her breath.

"Who knows? Maybe candlepin bowling will be your calling."

* * *

A professional bowler, Eliana was not. But she was holding her own and had managed to score two spares. The first time, she froze in place as Sienna screamed and hugged her. The second time Eliana was ready for all the high-fives and cheers coming her way. She even did a little strut back to her seat that I'll never forget.

"Alright team, huddle up." Sienna pulls us over to the corner, checking regularly to ensure Charlotte (who's angrily gesturing at my parents) can't overhear us. "There's one more frame left and we have the lead. Knowing Charlotte, she's going to try for a comeback and bowl next even though it's really Dad's turn."

"She always was a sore loser," I confirm.

"We need a strike to win the whole thing. Eliana you're on fire tonight, so I say we send you out to finish this." Sienna pats her on the shoulder for assurance, before pushing her towards the lane.

Eliana freezes, dragging her heels in place. "I think this is a bad idea. Maybe you or Jake should..."

"No. I have a good feeling about this. My gut is never wrong. You got this." Sienna pushes and I send out a small prayer that she's right. Sienna would never admit it but she's just as sore of a loser as Charlotte is.

I hold my breath as Eliana braces her shoulders, takes a step forward and releases the ball. It's angling just right until it turns and rolls into the gutter. I shoot Charlotte a harsh look as I hear her celebrate.

Eliana walks back to where I'm standing with a defeated look on her face. Without thinking I pull her into my arms and relish the way she fits so perfectly as she leans into me. "Hey, listen to me. It's just a game."

"I know, but I want to impress your family. I know that sounds silly, but..."

"No trust me I get it. Kinda what got me into this situation in the first place." I gesture between us and smile. "You've been on fire tonight, you got this. Just know that I'm here, cheering you on. I'll always be in your corner rooting for you."

She takes a deep breath, shutting her eyes for a few seconds before putting her game face back on. *That's my girl.* The thought pops into my head before I can stop it. Before I can remind myself that this whole thing between us is fake and that she is, indeed, not my girl.

My leg starts bouncing the way it does during a big game as I watch Eliana swing her arm back and let the ball drop. Gutter ball again. Dammit. "Shake it off, babe. You still have one more shot. You can do this."

If she's affected by my words, she doesn't show it. I watch her take another deep breath, shake the nerves out for a few seconds, and then send the ball rolling down the lane. I'm on the edge of my seat as I watch the ball knock down pin after pin until there's nothing left. Holy shit.

"I got a strike..." Eliana mumbles like she can't even believe it before turning around and seeing the massive smile on my face. "I got a strike!" She starts running towards me, and I meet her in the middle, scooping her up into my arms in celebration. Sienna clears her throat behind me, making a comment about how she wants to also get in on the celebration. I let the two talk about Eliana's strike, while I console Charlotte.

Though I can tell she's a bit upset, she also can't stop the smile that forms on her face as she watches Sienna and Eliana interact. "Next time, I'll make sure she's on my team Jake. You can take Dad."

"Sorry Char. Eliana and I are a package deal. You can't separate us." From the corner of my eye I catch my parents shooting each other a knowing look. Though they didn't voice it I had a feeling I already knew what they were thinking. I was absolutely falling for Eliana, if I wasn't fully gone for her already.

Chapter 25

Eliana

The downside of living in a student apartment, specifically one pitched as "rustic" (read: old and broken down), was having no control over the heater. When I woke up this morning covered in sweat, I immediately called our maintenance line and was met with their voicemail. I anxiously checked my schedule, trying to find a time to squeeze in another call to them, of which there was none. Forget finding a time for them to come fix it. I found myself wondering if Jake would be bothered by the heat. Maybe he'd even need to take his shirt off. It was then that I realized it was a random Thursday, and I expected to see him soon. I guess our optional morning hangouts had become so routine that it felt like an event. One I would schedule in my calendar. I was starting to feel a sort of...pull towards him. Like I was a magnet who didn't realize I was missing my other half until I found him, and now all I wanted to do was to be with him.

Our bowling adventure last week had clearly done a number on me. I knew he was just putting on a show so his family wouldn't suspect anything, and yet the entire time everything felt so...real. The way he always held on to a part of me, whether that be my hand, waist, or the small of my back. I usually hated it when people touched me, but something about Jake's gentle yet steady presence made me want more. Add in the moment when I had jumped into his arms like I was reenacting a scene in one of my favorite 2000s rom-coms, and he held onto me like I was his world...Well let's just say my brain had been replaying that moment one too many times in my head.

I was trying my *hardest* to remind myself that everything that happened that night was fake. Not real. All a part of our plan to trick his family into thinking we're together. I repeated that mantra in my head over and over again as I heard a knock on my door, which was either Jake or a serial killer who targeted his victims first thing in the morning. Maybe I should stop watching reruns of Law and Order before bed.

I quickly glance in the peephole to confirm the person behind my door was indeed Jake before throwing the door open. He gives me a quick smile before walking in and handing me a breakfast sandwich — sausage, egg, and cheese on a rosemary bagel. My favorite from the Beanery and now a regular part of my Tuesday and Thursday mornings.

"Sorry, my apartment is a million degrees. The building sets the heat, which means it toggles between the Arctic and Dante's Inferno in here." I roll my eyes, taking a seat at my dining room table.

"No worries. It's kinda nice after being outside in the cold. I'm sure I'll defrost in seconds." He smiles, taking his hoodie off. The shirt underneath lifts up slightly, exposing a hint of his abs and a muscled V before he adjusts the Henley back into place.

My arms start to form goosebumps and I silently curse

myself for being this affected by a little bit of skin. I needed to distract myself before I did something incredibly dumb, or awkward, or both. "Any updates on your exam?"

Jake worries his lip between his teeth. "Should be getting my grade back any day now. Which probably explains why I haven't been sleeping well these past couple of days."

His nervous expression forms a pit in my stomach. "I'm sure you did great. You've been working so hard."

"Yeah, but that doesn't mean it's going to pay off."

I wanted to tell him that it would. Wanted to get rid of that somber expression of his, but he was right. I couldn't say for certain that everything would be okay, but I did know I wanted to be there for him regardless of what happened next.

"We'll figure it out. Whatever happens." I reach out to give his hand a squeeze, which he accepts, entwining our fingers together.

He rubs his thumb in soothing circles on the back of my hand like I'm the one who needs comforting. If you had told me a few months ago that I would not only call Jake Keeley a close friend but also one of the most caring people I know, I would've probably asked if there was another Jake Keeley you were referring to. But now I knew who he really was.

He was the guy who always made sure his friends were okay, going out of his way to drive them to airports or help fix their flat tires. He was the guy who cooked dinner for Hockey House after grueling practices, and would run to help Sienna as soon as she called him. As someone who always takes care of others, I felt small watching Jake do nice things for me. Like his help meant I wasn't capable on my own. But looking at him now, unwrapping our food and laying it out on the table, I just feel incredibly grateful. And hopeful. That he'll continue to want to eat breakfast with me. And make me dinner. And tuck my hair behind my ear. Shit. I really was starting to fall for him. There was no way this was going to end well.

His eyebrows knit together, my hand still in his. "Are you feeling okay?"

Did I accidentally speak my thoughts...I hope not. "Hmm?"

"You just feel a little warm. And I know you mentioned feeling hot in your apartment earlier, but it feels fine to me. Any chance you're getting sick?"

I couldn't get sick. At least not this week. I picked up an extra nannying shift after my mom called and asked if I could help spot the cost of Josie's inhaler for this month. Plus, I promised Violet that I would cover her shift this week at the MRI center. I glance at my schedule on my open laptop. I could get sick next week...or in a couple of weeks when the semester is over, but getting sick now is not an option. *Eliana's immune system, if you can hear me, please don't fail me now. Too much is happening.*

"I'm fine." I had to be. There was no other option.

"You sure?"

I did a quick assessment of my symptoms. Sure, my nose may be a little stuffy, but winters in New England always dried me up. Same goes for my slightly scratchy throat. All I needed was a humidifier and a warm cup of tea with honey and I'd be A-OK.

"I'm positive. As healthy as a horse." For some reason, I opt to give him an incredibly awkward thumbs up. Greeeeat. Now I'm being awkward.

Thankfully he lets it slide. "Well if you are feeling off and need to skip today's hang, it's not a problem. I don't want you to over exert yourself."

"I'm fine. Let's eat." As I look down at my favorite breakfast sandwich, I feel a little queasy. I scarf it down just to prove to my immune system that I am not sick.

* * *

My biggest red flag is the fact that I'm not a water girlie. Tea and flavored seltzers were acceptable, but I found plain water so bland and thus had a bad habit of being dehydrated. Which is why I woke up this morning feeling incredibly dizzy, my throat dryer than the Sahara. It also didn't help that I couldn't fall asleep last night because of how unbearably hot it was in this apartment. I was genuinely surprised Nicole didn't get up in the middle of the night to complain to me about it. Hopefully a shower would wake me up. That and chugging a couple glasses of (gag) water.

To my disappointment, I still felt a bit on edge after my shower. But I opted to go about my day as I normally would. There was nothing like a solid and predictable routine to center me. I know it probably sounded crazy (or perhaps just a bit lame), but nothing made me more excited than checking things off of my to-do list. No matter how tired I was, knowing I was accomplishing the things I had set out to do always gave me a boost of energy that allowed me to push through.

Unfortunately, today, nothing was going my way. By the time I made it to the lab, I had developed a cough that was supplemented by a series of never-ending sneezes. Bethany had taken one look at me and gently ordered me to go home, *"As much as I appreciate your dedication to your job, the health of our participants is most important. Go rest."*

The admin tasks I had to do today could be pushed off for another day or two, but I was still fully determined to cover Violet's shift tonight. I hadn't ever let Violet down before, and I certainly didn't plan on doing it now. So I forced myself to take a power nap that would hopefully leave me feeling rested and less achy by tonight.

As soon as my head hit the pillow, I knocked out— a true

sign of my exhaustion because usually it takes me at least an hour to fall asleep. Mercifully, I set my alarm before I knocked out or else I'm sure I would have slept until tomorrow morning. When I wake, I feel groggier than ever. This is why I don't take naps. You always feel worse after. I resort to my lowest point — the expired energy drinks sitting in my fridge. Given my slight caffeine sensitivity, these notoriously fucked up my sleep for a few days. But a girls gotta do what a girl's gotta do.

I'm about to take a sip of a disgustingly sweet beverage when I hear a knock on my door. To my surprise, I am met with the 6'4 hockey player who has been occupying a bit too much of my headspace lately. He smiles wide, and before I know it, I'm wrapped up in his massive arms and being spun around. The movement doesn't help the dizziness but I don't want him to let me go. I rest my head on his shoulder and close my eyes, relishing the way I fit so perfectly into his embrace and the subtle smell of aftershave that hits my nose.

I bite my lip to hide the smile that threatens to break free. 3 p.m. Jake is much handsier than 6 a.m. Jake. Why the big hug?"

"Because you're my favorite person." He shuts the door behind him after he releases me. I head to the living room, back turned to him so he hopefully misses the redness of my cheeks.

"Oh? And what did I do to receive such honor?" I take a seat on the couch, extending out my legs so he can't sit next to me. I didn't know if I could trust myself not to do something embarrassing around him, especially now that I likely had a high fever and was addicted to being touched by him.

My attempts at putting distance between us are moot as he takes a seat on the floor beneath me, arm resting on my leg, and shows me his phone screen. It takes me a minute to process what I'm looking at when I see the words "exam", "Jake Keeley", and "B+" on his course portal. I feel the grin take over my whole face. "Holy shit. This is amazing. You did it!" When

I look up from his phone, his matching smile makes the butter-flies in my stomach take flight.

"*We* did it," he corrects, giving my knee a small squeeze. His hand lingers, giving me another addictive hit.

"I didn't really do mu—" I'm cut off by the tightening of my throat as I break out into a massive coughing fit, one that feels like I'm choking. Jake's quick to grab me a bottle of water which I immediately chug, though it does little to really soothe me. I try to thank him, but the coughing just worsens, so I just continue to drink until eventually I can breathe...sort of. "Sorry about that. Must be the expired energy drink."

Jake gives me an amused look, then shakes his head. "No need to apologize for being sick."

"I'm not sick," I protest like a petulant child. Jake raises an eyebrow. "I'm serious. I just drank a Red Bull that expired like 2 years ago and—"

"That explains the stuffy nose? And the fever—"

"I do *not* have a fever."

"Eliana. You've been complaining about how blistering hot it's been in your apartment. I just peaked at the thermostat, and it says 75."

"No it doesn't."

"It's okay to be sick, you know. Doesn't mean you're weak or anything."

"I know that." In theory. "Just like I know I'm fine. In fact, I'm so fine, I'm going to help Maya run a participant tonight. I should actually start getting ready now or I'll be late." I stand up a bit too fast, and immediately lose my footing, tripping over Jake before unceremoniously tumbling towards the floor. He breaks most of my fall, but the fact that I couldn't even stand without issue was not helping my case.

"Eliana, you need to call out sick."

"Nope, not happening. I already had to bail on my lab shift

earlier. I can't let Violet down either. It's the first time she's had a break in a while."

"You wouldn't be letting anyone down. You're not feeling well."

"I would be letting Violet down because I'm dependable. That's what I'm known for. You know how you get people to rely on you? By always being there for them." I don't know why I felt the need to lecture him about this. He knew exactly what it meant to have people rely on you.

Jake shifted strategies, realizing there was no way I'd listen to logic. "Either you call out sick now, or I'll email Violet and tell her how you're deathly ill and still working. I'm feeling a little spicy and may even call my coach to make sure Violet gets the message."

What he was doing was sweet. Jake was looking out for me, knowing I wouldn't do it for myself. Unfortunately, my tendency to define my self-worth by how much work I crammed into a day caused me to snap at this nice man rather than respond with gratitude. "You are the bane of my existence."

"Noted. But I doubt any parent would want someone coughing and sneezing all over their child. So if that makes you feel any better, you're really doing them a service by not showing up."

He was completely right. Why was I so upset at the idea that I was a human and humans got sick? I curse my mortal shell.

"Make the call Eliana. I'm serious," he warns before typing on his phone.

I step into my room, dialing Violet. She sounded understanding but I still couldn't stop the barrage of self-deprecating thoughts from flooding into my head. *Great job Eliana. Now Violet's entire night is ruined. All Violet has ever done is support you and the one time she asks for help, you let her down. She's not the first person you've disappointed today, either. What were you thinking, showing up sick to the lab? What if you spread whatever's wrong with you to everyone else? The whole lab is going to have to shut down because you've been so careless. And with the lab shut down, we can say goodbye to continuing to make progress on all the studies going on.*

Breathe. Just breathe. Anxious thoughts are not accurate thoughts. Catastrophizing and trying to think of all the worst-case scenarios isn't helping anyone. You're okay, Violet's okay, the lab is okay. Everything will be okay. Except in moments when I got stuck in my thought spiral like this, nothing felt okay.

My lungs felt useless, my heart felt like it was going to burst out of my chest, and my stomach churned. I sank to my feet and put my head between my knees. I attempt to take deep breaths or think of happier moments, but I swear the world is caving in around me. Before I know it, my body's shaking while my mind spirals over every mistake I made this week.

"Hey, I ordered some soup for— Oh shit! Are you okay?" Jake kneels in front of me, and I can feel his eyes trying to inspect my face.

"I just need a minute," I whisper through my tightening jaw.

He shifts so he's sitting beside me, and places a hand on my shoulder, using his thumb to rub soothing circles.

After a few minutes of silence, I drop my head to my knees. My body feels so heavy after several minutes of holding my muscles string tight. "Do you ever feel like the whole weight of the world is sitting on your chest, crushing you?" I whisper.

"Sometimes, before a big game or tournament. Do you feel that way often?"

"Somedays I feel it less than others. The days where I'm

able to juggle a dozen different things at once. The days where I meet all my deadlines and check everything off on my to-do list. Go to class, go to lab, tutoring, nanny on the weekends, checking in on my mom, calling Josie every night to check in and help her with her homework, finish my own homework... the list goes on."

"That's a pretty extensive list, Eliana."

I hear this a lot. And there is nothing that can be done about it, so I stay quiet. "Have you ever thought of cutting back?" No judgment in Jake's words, just a question.

"I don't know what I would cut out. I can't stop work because I need to pay my bills and help my family. And I won't give up on research because that's the only thing that's just mine."

Jake is silent, so I risk looking up. He's got a sad smile on his face, I his eyes filled with understanding. "Research is the only thing that feels like it's yours. And losing it would feel like losing a piece of yourself," he summarizes.

He's so on the nose it stuns me. "Exactly."

He contemplates for a few minutes. "I wish there was something I could do to help, lessen the pressure you're under."

"This helps. Being here. Listening to me. That helps a lot. Except maybe you should put some distance between us. Don't need you getting sick too." I give him a sheepish smile.

"At this rate, we've been together long enough that whatever you have has already been passed on to me. We can just cross our fingers and hope my immune system is stronger than yours," he teases. "Do you think you'd be up for some dinner?"

"I'm not really hungry."

"Let's try and get some chicken noodle soup in you. Then a cold compress to get that fever down. And sleep, lots of sleep." He lifts me up, an arm wrapped around my waist for support as he guides me to the kitchen.

"You know, if hockey doesn't work out, nursing might be a solid backup."

"As long as you let me take care of you Eliana. I'll be whatever you want me to be."

Surely that's my fever talking.

Jake

"Now that I've gotten a B+, I feel like we can ease up on the practice questions, don't you?" I ask, already knowing her answer.

"You want to change methods now that you've gotten proof that they work?" Eliana snorts.

"Yes?"

"Not a chance Keeley. Not a chance. I have a bunch of old practice tests from old clients I can bust out. Don't tempt me." She challenges me.

"You wouldn't."

"You seem to be running out of things to do the past few times we've hung out. I don't want you to lose your momentum. More assignments would mean more things for us to discuss."

"That's a funny way of saying, 'I get my kicks from torturing you'," I scoff.

"So spending time with me is torture now?" Eliana teases.

She had no fucking idea. It had been about a week since I'd spent the night taking care of her when she was sick. A week since I had realized how gone I was for this girl. Like, I would pass the Beanery on my way to class and think of getting her favorite drink, or hear a song playing on the radio and think about sending it to her because she'd like it. *That* gone for her.

When I got my exam grade back the first person I wanted to share the news with was Eliana, and not just because she was partially responsible. Because I wanted to see her again.

And I'm glad I chose to go over there or else who knows what state she would've been in. Feverish and panicking over the weight of the world. I'm glad I was there so she could see she wasn't alone, and I wasn't scared of her vulnerable state. Say what you want about me, I do have a sensitive side. Years of being forced to play house with my sisters taught me all about how to treat women. Which is why I heated up some soup and then offered to head out, giving her space to decompress. But instead of taking the space, she asked if I wanted to watch a movie. And halfway through 10 *Things I Hate About You* she drifted off on my shoulder.

I don't know much about relationships, but I do know that night was more than friendly. No kissing, no sex, just being real. I think they call that intimacy.

Nicole had come home about an hour later, gave me an appreciative smile, and left me with parting words that have replayed in my head every day since.

"It's nice to see Eliana let someone else take care of her for once."

I knew it was hard for Eliana to lean on other people, and I was determined to show up for her. I wanted her to feel like the world was a place she could enjoy, instead of a burden she had to manage.

"I feel like we're due for a celebration."

"A celebration?" She looks instantly skeptical.

"Yup. I passed my exam, and you were a big reason for that. So a celebration is in order."

I wait for the immediate shut-down. Instead she says, "What are you thinking?"

"We have a big game against Boston College this weekend. Why don't you come out and watch?" *Come watch me in my element.*

"Oh I was already planning on it."

That catches me off guard. "I'm sorry?"

"Jake, I grew up in New England. You can't be surprised that I'm a hockey fan."

"Well you didn't exactly treat me like a fan when we met."

"That's because I was trying to be professional. And you pissed me off by showing up late."

"Fair enough. So you'll be there Saturday?"

"I wouldn't miss it." She gives me a smile like it's no big deal. "I can't promise I won't heckle you if you mess up a play though."

"I'd expect nothing less. This doesn't count as our celebration then, since you already had this planned."

She hesitates for a minute, looking a little shy. "Is there a party planned at Hockey House after the game?"

For once, there actually wasn't. We'd been pretty swamped with practices and exams the past two weeks so no one had time to coordinate. "If there was, would you be interested in attending?"

"Potentially..." She hesitates, likely wondering what she might be getting herself into.

Her openness to the idea gives me newfound energy to plan something. "We can keep it small. It'll be fun, and less chaotic." I would make sure of it. The last thing I wanted was for Eliana to finally let her hair down and regret it.

"Then count me in. But only if you score a goal."

"Make no mistake, Ellie. I'm scoring a goal."

* * *

"Are we playing a game or taking a nap out there!" Mason yells in frustration. He's fallen into the assistant coaching position with ease. There'd been a bit of tension between us after he'd moved me down to the second line and stuck me with two freshmen but that tension was resolved after we beat UCONN, one of the best teams in our division, and I had to admit there was a method to his madness. "If you boys actually want to make it to the Frozen Four this year, we have to try harder. We have to act like every game we play is the last game. Understood?" He locks eyes with each and every one of us before leaving the locker room.

He's right. It didn't matter who we were playing or that this was one game of many we'd have to play before we started tournament season. But I also wasn't going to play it safe knowing Eliana was in the stands. I was never one to let an opportunity to show off go to waste. I wave Craig and Johnny — my new linesmen — over and break down our next few plays before we get called back for the start of the second period.

From the bench, I watch Adam win the face off but struggle to get any pucks past the goalie. Mason waves for a line change and I come barreling onto the ice, ready to knock any Boston College player on their ass if they even try me. As I skate over to center ice, I take a second to scan the student section for Eliana, and I manage to find her in a sea of navy blue, screaming one of the chants the band was leading.

"Looking for your mom, Keeley? Pretty sure she's still sleeping sound in my bed." James Conoway's irritating voice is in my ear.

"Five years on the team and still on the fourth line." I click my tongue. "Not looking too good for you."

The ref yells at us to stop running our mouths, and I lock

back in, eyes fixated on the puck. The second my stick drops to the ice, I make contact with the puck, easily pushing aside James and his feeble attempt to block me from moving into their zone. I pass the puck to Craig when I see one of BC's defensemen come charging behind me, and snicker when he loses his footing and falls in a failed attempt to intercept my pass. We close in on the goal, and I call for Craig to take the shot. The goalie is able to block it with his stick, but he loses control of the puck immediately after, allowing me to scoop it back up.

James comes up on my left and forces me into the boards. We struggle to overpower each other when I decide to send the puck around the boards, hoping either Craig or Johnny is there to get it. I hear the puck hit the goalie post and turn to see Craig with a look of disbelief on his face, wondering how his shot didn't make it in.

"Get the rebound, get the rebound!" I shout, nearly diving in front of the net, extending my stick out to block a BC player from icing it. I skate back a bit from the net, looking for a better angle when I find it. I settle the puck before making contact with my stick and send it flying towards the top right corner of the net. I watch the puck hit the back of my net and the entire student section rises up and screams. During our on-ice celebration my eyes find Eliana in the middle of the student section, screaming her head off and decked out in a blue and white Westchester U t-shirt. I would definitely be upgrading her to a jersey soon.

We're white hot after I score. Adam hits the ice as soon as my line heads back to the benches, and next thing I know, the puck is sliding between the BC goalie's legs and we're up two.

"Look at the two vets leading the charge tonight," I shout, patting my best friend on the back as he comes around to celebrate. I redirect my attention to Mason. "Hey Coach, you still think it was a good idea splitting us up? If we're on fire apart, just imagine how many goals we'd have now if we were together."

"If you were half as good at leading your linesmen as you were running your mouth, Keeley, we'd be up by four right now," he retorts without even giving me a glance.

If he was trying to rile me up, he succeeded.

"Craig, Johnny, watch number 75 out there. He's big, so he gets winded fifteen seconds on the ice. And their captain? He likes to act like he's God's gift to hockey, but he telegraphs nearly every shot he's going to take. Craig, the next time we're on the ice and you see an opening, I want you to watch James's stick and take the puck from him. Pass it over to me whenever you get an opening. Johnny, I want you near the net ready to take a shot as soon as I send the puck towards you."

The freshman looks at me, eyes as wide as saucers. "You want *me* to take the shot?"

"Did I stutter?"

"I-uh-um, no. No sir."

"*Sir?* I'm your captain, not your grandfather." My attempt at a joke does little to settle him. "Listen to me. We've run this drill at least a hundred times in practice. You got this. I wouldn't be telling you to take the shot if I didn't think you could handle it."

He gives me a small nod before taking a big gulp and following along with the action on the ice, tracking the players I pointed out. I can tell he's nervous by the way he barely celebrates Adam scoring another goal. "Don't overthink it Johnny, you got this." Or at least I hope he did. All I could do was hold my breath and get him the puck.

I suddenly felt a pit form in my stomach as I watched Johnny anxiously fiddle with his gloves as he skated onto the ice. Craig sends me a look that screams, "Are you sure about this?" and I give him a shrug. Best case scenario, Johnny scores and builds his confidence. Worst case scenario, I'd settle the rebound and score the goal myself.

"Damn, they have you babysitting the freshman Keeley? How badly did you have to fuck up to get stuck with that gig?" I roll my eyes. James was on a mission tonight.

"Being a captain is more than having a fancy letter on your jersey, Conoway, not that you would know."

"You're one to talk. Everyone knows your boy Adam is the one who holds down the team. You're just a pigeon riding his coattails."

My jaw slams shut so hard if not for my mouthguard, I'm sure I would have chipped a tooth. It was semi-public knowledge that Coach Jameson had needed some convincing to make me alternate captain, despite the fact that the team had voted me into the position. Whereas Adam was an obvious decision, Coach hadn't been sure I could handle the responsibility. I'd like to think I'd more than earned my position over the years, but the topic was still a sore spot for me.

Conoway was one word away from being rammed into the boards so hard he wouldn't know which way was up. I feel the blood pumping in my veins — a sign of how much he's managed to piss me off. *Keep your head on straight, Jake. Win this game and wipe that smug ass grin off his face.* A strong part of me wants to tell Craig and Johnny to step back and let me handle this. With how riled up I am, I have no doubt I would send the puck straight into the net if I got possession. It felt like I was going against every single one of my instincts by not jumping in and taking the lead, but I could feel Mason's eyes burning into the back of my head.

Where Johnny is shaking like a leaf, Craig is cool and composed as he sets up for the face-off against Mark Remmington, one of BC's top players. Though I can't hear it, Craig says something to Mark that manages to throw him long enough for Craig to toggle the puck over to our side and send it towards me. Johnny takes a second too long to get into position, and I let out a string of curses as James sneaks up behind me and steals the puck.

I dash like a madman across the ice, legs on fire, as I manage to regain control over the puck. With Johnny clearly too in his head, I look for Craig hoping he's nearby and ready to take the shot. I see him wide open to my right and we lock eyes as I motion for him to get ready. Like a parasite, James is immediately on top of me, relentless. He slashes me in the leg followed by a hard cross-check to my lower back. I listen for the ref to call a penalty that never comes, so I decide to give James a taste of his own medicine. If the refs had blinders on, I may as well use it to my advantage. As I send the puck towards Craig, who's finally right where I need him, I angle my elbow to jab James right between the ribs.

With him officially off my back, I refocus my attention on adding another point to the scoreboard. I close in on the goalie who has his eyes trained on Craig and I. He's one of the best in the league, and most days, if you're lucky enough to get one past him, it's because he's distracted by the chaos down in front. I skate back to the center line looking for another angle to attack when I hear Johnny. "The goalie's locked in on you guys and he'll never even see me coming. Get me the puck and I'll go in for the kill."

"You sure?"

He gives me a firm nod and I notice his nervous look is now replaced by one of sheer determination.

I skate back to my original spot, close to the goal, and make a show of passing the puck back to Craig. We go back and forth, ensuring the goalie's attention is on us like a cat tracking a laser pointer. When I'm sure we have him right where we want him,

I shout, "Now!" my eyes locked on Craig, while my stick is aimed at Johnny. The goalie's too preoccupied with Craig that he has no idea Johnny's goal has landed until the buzzer goes off. 4-0 Westchester. I skate over to Johnny, giving him a big bear hug as he stands there, eyes wide in shock. "Atta boy Johnny! First goal of many for you."

I scoop Johnny's puck out from the net and bring it back to the bench where I settle in and watch our third line head out. Mason throws me my water bottle and I would've nearly missed the faint small on his lips if not for the words he uttered after. "Alright, Keeley. I see you."

I give him a small shrug like it's no big deal, while my heart tightens. It's about time he sees that Jake Keeley could handle his own.

Chapter 27

Jake

The last time I was this uncertain about a party I was 15, had an awful mullet I thought looked amazing and really solidified me as a hockey player, and had never gotten drunk before. Not even the athletics and greek life crossover rager I coordinated last year, which resulted in over a thousand drunken college students flooding in and out of Hockey House, caused me as much anticipation as I feel tonight.

"'Sup, man ." Oliver calls out as he and Adam bring a keg down to the basement. "Tonight should be relatively chill. We didn't invite that many people tonight. It should be like sixty people max."

Sixty people was nothing given that ten of us already lived here. I honestly can't remember the last party we had that was less than a hundred people, but I wasn't sure what Eliana was expecting. Given the girl had never even been to a college party, I knew that whatever was tame to us would seem like an absolute rager to her. "Are the boys all showing up?"

"Yeah most of them are coming by and some girls from Tri

Delt and Gamma Phi. A solid chunk of the men's lacrosse team, and some other people I can't remember now. Should be a good time."

"That sounds like a lot of people, Ollie..."

"Relax man it'll be like no more than like a hundred people."

"You just said sixty."

"Well I never claimed I was good at math. Does your girl know any math tutors? Maybe she could set me up with one." Ollie winks.

I don't correct Ollie, even though Eliana and I are just friends. No matter how many times I caught myself counting the freckles on her cheeks or wondering how her soft lips would feel against mine, she'd never indicated she wanted to turn our fake dating situation into something real. So I just stayed in my lane, and tried to fight the urge to touch her every time we were together.

"So are we all good on booze?" I ask hoping the question deflects his attention.

"We should be. Though it would've been nice if you also got salt and vinegar chips for the rest of the party and not just Eliana." He smirks

"I want her to have something here if she gets the drunchies. It does me no good if she leaves halfway through in search of Taco Bell."

"No one likes salt and vinegar chips, Jake."

"You have no taste." I scoff, hiding away the family-sized bag in the cabinet. Drunk college kids are heathens, and this bag would be gone in seconds if I left it out.

* * *

In the hour since people started flocking in, the place is already packed to the brim and more people will continue to pour in. We've already gone through a whole keg of beer, busted out the emergency keg, and had to send the freshmen out with fake IDs to get more alcohol. I didn't know if it was a good or bad thing that Eliana wasn't here yet. It was certainly a plus that she missed my total meltdown over the fact that the lacrosse team had tried to sneak in a wild turkey. It never made sense to me how Boston got infested with turkeys every year, and all it took was a couple of college athletes getting drunk enough to capture one and keep it as a pet.

I was a few beers in and loosened up enough after the turkey incident that I didn't even notice her arrival until I felt a small hand squeeze my shoulder. "If this is your definition of a small party, I'd hate to see what happens when you guys throw a rager."

"You should've seen the wild animal I—" I turn my head to finally look at her, and immediately feel like I'd been punched in the throat.

In place of her usually cozy cardigan and leggings combo is a short black ribbed dress that hugs her body like a second layer of skin. Her legs are nearly covered with her thigh-high boots, and she looks lethal as sin. I can't even help it. I fully gawk at her.

The best part is I can tell she knows how good she looks from the way she cocks her eyebrow at me and flashes me a smile that makes me want to fall to my knees and worship her ten times over. Who was I? I hadn't been this nervous about a girl in....well, ever. And I've definitely never been left speechless by one either. But Eliana had a way of throwing me completely off my axis, in a way that made me question whether I even really knew what it meant to feel alive until I met her.

I pull us further away from the living room into the hallway so we can hear each other. "You look…" Beautiful? Incredible? Neither of those words seemed to do her justice. "Breathtaking."

She dips her head slightly to hide the blush on her cheeks. Standing on her tiptoes she raises her voice so I can hear her over the chaos surrounding us. "You can sweet talk me all you want Keeley. I plan on still seeing you studying your ass off at 6 a.m. We can't let this B+ on your exam be a one-time thing."

"I wouldn't dream of skipping out on my unofficial tutoring session." I wink, nudging my hip against hers. "Thanks again by the way. For not giving up on me."

Her eyes soften as they lock with mine. "You're welcome. Thanks for pushing me to be a normal college student for once." She does a once over, taking in the living room, "So, where's the bartender?"

I can't help my laugh. "I'm sorry?"

Her eyes widen as they lock with mine, and I see a slight hint of embarrassment. "Given your reaction, I take it most people don't hire bartenders for their house parties?"

"That would be a negative."

"Also going to assume DJs aren't really a thing?" She blushes.

Damn, this was pretty adorable. It was becoming very obvious her only knowledge of house parties came from the movies. "Nah. We have Spotify, an aux cord, and speakers. Gets the job done."

"Makes sense. I guess that serves me right for thinking Mean Girls and 10 Things I Hate About You were accurate portrayals of party culture. Although I do have to admit I thought they only did *that* in the movies." Eliana nods her head toward Oliver, who's doing a keg stand in the middle of the living room. "That's pretty impressive."

"We can get you up there next if you want. Get the full college experience."

"Mmm, I'd rather not flash anyone tonight, given my outfit choice. Probably best to sit this one out."

"Fair enough. While there's no bartender, I'm happy to serve you up a drink." I wink. Without thinking, I grab her hand, locking our fingers together as I walk us over to the kitchen. Eliana has yet to pull away from my touches the past few weeks. She follows my lead and lets me hold on to her as I pull two cherry Jello shots out of the freezer and hand one to her.

Her face turns serious. "Is now a bad time to tell you I'm allergic to cherries?"

I feel my heart hit my stomach and immediately snatch the container out of her hands. "Shit. You might've just touched cherry juice! How allergic are you?! She smirks at me, then licks her fingers. "...You're not really allergic, are you?"

"No." She shakes her head. "But it was really sweet to see how fast your life, and mine, flashed before your eyes."

"I would say it's nice to see you making jokes and letting loose, but that was a sick joke."

"That was barely a joke," she laughs. Then she seems to consider something. "Do I really come off as that up tight?"

"You're the tightest," I respond, getting an eye roll from her. "I'm just messing with you. Did you know you get this cute little crease between your eyebrows every time I say something obnoxious and you don't want to laugh?"

"You think you know me so well, huh?"

"Not nearly as much as I'd like to." The confession leaves my lips and hangs in the air for a moment. I don't want to put her on the spot, so I pivot. "So, are we doing this or not?" I hand her back the cherry Jello shot.

She brings her container up to cheers mine before

squeezing the Jello into her mouth. "That's actually not half bad. I can see how those get dangerous real quick."

"One day, I'll tell you about the time Ollie double-poured the Jello shots and then ate most of them."

"Yikes, that sounds like a rough night."

"And a rough morning," Ollie interrupts. "So what's next on your 'college party' bucket list Eliana?"

She looks around casually. "Where's the beer pong table?"

Chapter 28

Jake

Eliana handles beer pong the way she tackles any to-do item in her calendar— with tact, a game plan, and a determination that could rival an Olympian's. She does a few practice throws before the game starts. She manages to sink her first shot and the next one touches the rim before bouncing off the table. She decides to up the ante in her next attempt, bouncing the ball off the table and sending me a wide smile when it sinks into the cup a few feet across from her.

"You're a pro already, Ellie." I had been using the nickname for weeks now, and if she minded, she hadn't told me.

She walks around the table to where I'm standing and taps her hip against mine. "Well you gave me some pretty solid pointers earlier."

She takes a ping pong ball from my hand and sends it flying across the table and into the leftmost cup with ease, and I know immediately we're going to sweep any team that comes against us. I liked that idea a lot. The thought of us as a team.

We play a couple of rounds just the two of us. Eventually, I swap out the beer in the cups for water after Eliana confesses that she can't have more than a few sips without wanting to gag over the taste. We had set up a few beer pong tables outside and closer to the kitchen to keep the party controlled to the front part of the house. I set up this table specifically for us, far away from all the alcohol, the debauchery, and decently hidden from the rest of the party. For a moment, I forget that anyone else exists except for her and I. That is until Ollie rolls in with Adam and a mix of guys from the hockey and lacrosse teams.

"Well well, what do we have here?"

"Jake's showing me how to play beer pong." Eliana's expression shifts from calm and confident to sheepish. She turns her head to shoot me a quick wink before going back to looking despondent. I'm very intrigued by the game she's trying to play right now.

"Oh *is* he now?"

"Yeah...it's not going super well though." She sighs and tosses a ball so far back it doesn't come close to any of the cups. Her second "attempt" isn't any better, and if I didn't know any better, I'd say she was very bad at beer pong.

"Don't beat yourself up over it. You just need some practice. And maybe some better competition." Ollie smirks playfully at me. "Jake why don't you and her pair up against Adam and I? Hockey House rules."

And by that he means loser has to clean the winner's bathroom and do their laundry for the next two months.

"I mean, it'll probably be a shutout but I'm down." Eliana shrugs. Her nonchalant tone matches the look on her face.

"I'll rack the cups."

"Excellent." Ollie smirks. "Jake why don't you and I start so Eliana has time to adjust?"

"You sure you wanna play House Rules again? My track record speaks for itself."

"Oh yeah. I think it's about time for me to get a win. I'm

feeling pretty good about tonight. Letting your heart control your head is a rookie mistake, Keeley. I thought you knew better," he tsks.

Eliana was going to burst his bubble eventually, but for now, I'd let him have his moment. No harm in letting my best friend get excited over finally beating me in beer pong.

"Ready?" He gives me a small nod as we lock eyes and send the ping-pong balls flying. Each round we face off, he lands a ball into one of my cups. Eliana is keeping the team alive, scoring against Adam with ease. Ollie's eyes narrow in on me as if he's starting to piece together what's unfolding in front of him.

"It's probably beginner's luck." Eliana comforts him. She sinks the next cup and we are now tied with 5 cups left.

Ollie seems to be taking the tough competition in stride, and shoots me a smirk when he notices my arms wrapped around Eliana's waist.

Somewhere between my 5th or 6th cup, I went from giving Ellie small hugs in celebration to holding on to her. She doesn't seem to mind, as she leans into my chest and places one of her hands on top of mine. With her so close to me, the scent of her shampoo— a mix of apples and honey— hits my nose and all I want to do is hold on to her for as long as she'll let me.

Towards the end of the game, Ollie takes the lead, leaving us with two cups to his three. On her next toss, Eliana bounces the ball on the table and we watch, holding our breath, as the ball circles the rim of the cup before finally falling in. She lets out the cutest little squeal before turning her head to look at me, pride beaming on her face. "I can't believe that actually worked."

"You're absolutely incredible." I press a small kiss on her shoulder. "That counts as two by the way. Which puts us in the lead."

"Really?" Eliana beams, and it takes everything in me not to kiss her. Everything about being with her felt right. Even in the moments when we butt heads, there's no one else I would want to be with than her. And that realization was centering.

"Yes, really. You played me Ellie, didn't you? What a shark." Ollie groans as he pulls two of the cups off the table. His shoulders hunch in mock defeat, but by the smile on his face and his use of Ellie's nickname I can tell he isn't really upset.

"Mmm maybe a little bit," she admits. "Are you mad?"

"Mad? No. Annoyed that I'm going to have to wash Jake's laundry again? Yes. Next time I'm going to be smarter when I pick my team." He winks at her.

"Hey man, don't act like I'm dead weight over here," Adam scoffs.

"I would never." Ollie claps a hand on his shoulder, which Adam shrugs off.

I grab the final ball and slide it into Eliana's hand, which draws a look of confusion from her. "But it's your turn."

I shake my head. "It's all you." *It's always been you.* "Unless Ollie wants to protest."

Ollie is unbothered, "Honestly, I kinda want to see if she's able to make it shooting from behind her back. Consider this an audition for being my partner next round."

My eyes stay trained on Eliana as she wraps an arm around her back, angles her wrist up, and lets the ball fall from her fingers. I can't look away from her, but I hear the beautiful "plop" of the ball making contact with the beer in the cup. She gives me a a smile that could stop tides and make the earth fall off its axis.

"Holy shit. We won! We won!" She wraps her arms around my neck. My hands fall to her hips and I pick her up in celebration, spinning us around in a circle before setting her back down. "That was so much fun."

I tuck a stray piece of hair behind her ear and relish in the way she slightly leans into my hand. "You crushed it."

"Maybe you should give Ollie a break. For being a good sport?"

I tap a finger on my chin. "Hmm I'll take it under consideration."

"C'mon. You knew we were hustling him."

"Alright fine. I'll forget this game ever happened Ollie. Consider this your lucky day."

Ollie pumps a fist in mock celebration. "I knew I liked you, Ellie. Should we go for round two?"

She looks to me for confirmation before saying, "Eh, why don't you and Adam play and we'll cycle back. I want to see what other trouble Jake can get me into tonight."

Well damn. I take her hand in mine as I weave through the bodies. I have no doubts Adam would demand we scrub the place clean tomorrow but that was a problem for future Jake. Current Jake had much more important things on his mind. Like how it felt all too natural having my arms around Ellie or feeling a sense of pride when she absolutely destroyed Ollie at beer pong. All I wanted to do was figure out how to bottle up this moment and make it last forever.

We head into the kitchen to grab some snacks as I plot my next move. Throwing the cabinet open I groan at the sight of a missing bag of chips.

"Dammit. Freaking animals. Hang on, I stored some in the closet upstairs." I leave Eliana tucked in the corner of the kitchen as I run upstairs and grab the bag of chips. As I head back down the stairs, I see Eliana, still in the kitchen, looking incredibly uncomfortable as some random drunk guy is talking to her. Fuck that.

My blood starts to boil as I get close enough to hear her.

"Listen, I told you I'm not interested, so if you could please give me some space—"

"Aw c'mon baby. There's no need to play hard to get." He lifts a hand to touch her hair, but I smack it away before he can make contact. The jackass lets out an irritated noise before looking up, his eyes widening when he notices me.

"She told you to leave her alone man. I recommend you listen to her and fuck off. Because if you don't, I can promise you I won't be as nice about removing your hands as she was."

"Whatever. Fuck this." He grabs his cup and stalks out of the kitchen. Wise choice.

I pull Eliana closer to me. "I shouldn't have left you. I'm so sorry—"

She cuts me off. "It's not your fault, Jake. Nor is it your responsibility to stop every asshole guy that can't respect my boundaries. But I do appreciate you jumping in and helping me out." She reaches out and takes my hand into hers, and I can't help but notice how good we fit together.

I don't want to make a big deal of it and risk freaking her out, so I just lift the massive bag of chips I brought down. "Here you go."

She pops a few chips in her mouth. "Excellent choice. Salt and vinegar chips are my favorite."

"They're definitely superior. And I would even argue underrated."

"*Right?* Like not only are they salty but they're also perfectly tangy. What more could you want from a chip?"

I watch as her tongue dips out and traces over her bottom lip, and it takes me a few seconds to realize she asked me a question. "Maybe if they were kettle cooked?"

"Ooo or even a waffle cut." She stops before she can finish her sentence and I watch as someone's beer sprays all over her dress — drenching it.

"Damn my night really peaked with winning beer pong." Eliana laughs as she shakes the beer off her arms.

My head snaps to the stranger standing across from us in the kitchen. He throws his hands up in defense. "I was just trying to shotgun it..."

Eliana's hand wrap around by bicep, "Jake, it's fine. It was an accident." I look down and see her arms covered in goosebumps.

"Well he can at least say sorry." I roll my eyes.

She presses her lips together, clearly enjoying my uncharacteristic irritation. Her eyes soften and my arm feels like it's on fire as she trails her hand down my bicep. "Thank you. For defending me."

"No need to thank me. Now let's get you cleaned up."

Chapter 29

Eliana

Jake keeps a firm hand around my waist as he leads me upstairs. I send out a quiet "thank you" to the universe that my skin was already covered in goosebumps from being drenched in beer, so he wouldn't notice the additional ones that formed from his touch. I had a problem. A massive one in fact. And it was all tied to how I wanted more. More of his touches, more of his jokes, more of him coming to my defense. *More of Jake Keeley.* That's all my brain could think right now which was incredibly dangerous given he was leading me up to his room.

The first time he wrapped his arms around me during beer pong, I thought my heart was going to explode. I was never a super touchy person and cringed whenever my exes tried to engage in PDA, but with Jake everything just felt right. I wanted to have him draped all over me in public, and in private, the same way I wanted to see him defend me again because damn, that was hot. I would gladly sacrifice a dozen dresses if it meant I got to see him all riled up like that.

He leads me down the hall and unlocks the door, holding it

open for me. Jake's room is mostly what I would expect from a college athlete, with hockey memorabilia and video game posters covering a majority of the walls. A thought about whether he had recently shared the bed with someone pops in my head and my stomach immediately drops. Ugh. I had no reason to feel insecure. It's not like we were *really* dating, and we never talked about being fake-exclusive. He had every right to do whatever the hell he wanted.

He walks over to his closet and pulls out a basket of what I presume to be unfolded clean clothes. "What are we feeling? T-shirt? Flannel?"

"What about your hockey jersey?" I tease. *Not every intrusive thought needs to be spoken Eliana. In fact, all should probably remain inside.*

"I, uh. What?"

Fantastic. My awkwardness left him speechless. "I was just joking. Any chance I can borrow a sweater? I'm hoping I can pull it off as a dress."

"Oh sure. Let me see what I have here." Jake ducks into his closest. "Here you go." He hands me a large cotton sweater and points to the private bathroom inside his room.

I quickly change into his sweater and am covered in his scent. Forget feeling hot, I was on fire. I splash some water on my face in an attempt to cool myself down. Looking in the mirror, love that I'm currently drowning in Jake's sweater, and I contemplate how I can keep this long after this night is over. Keep *him*. Shit. There's no way this is going to end well. We had agreed that once he got his midterm grade back, he would tell his mom the truth. Which meant there would be no need for us to keep this dating façade up. That should make me feel better but instead it bummed me out. The more time I spent with him, the more I wanted our dating situation to be real, even if it made my work life more complicated. *But maybe it would be worth it.*

"You alright in there?" I jump at Jake's voice from the other side of the door.

"Yup sorry. Coming out now." I take a few deep breaths to settle my heart before I open the door and lean against the frame. "What do you think?"

My throat goes dry as I watch him peruse my body and lick his lips. His fists are clenched at his sides like he has to hold himself back.

"I think you should wear my clothes more often."

"Practicing your fake-boyfriend lines again?" I laugh awkwardly.

"I'm serious." He sounds like he means it as he steps closer. Eventually he is right in front of me, and I can feel the heat radiating off of his body.

I crane my neck a bit so I can look into his eyes. "Jake."

"Eliana."

"What are we doing?"

"What do you want us to be doing?" He braces himself against the doorframe, his arms caging me in.

"I don't know." It's a lie. We both know it is.

"I think you do. I think you're just too scared to say it. Too scared to let yourself take what you want."

I lift my chin higher in defiance. "I'm not scared."

"Then prove it," he challenges, his eyes fixated on my lips. "Tell me what you want. Tell me all the things going on in that brilliant head of yours."

"I don't want to pretend to be your girlfriend anymore," I confess.

He takes a minute to compose himself. "And why's that?"

"Because it's messing with my head."

"Well, that makes two of us." He tucks a strand of hair

behind my ear as I stand there frozen in place. I try not to show my disappointment as he pulls his hand away.

"What are *you* thinking?" I ask, needing to shift the attention off me.

"I'm thinking of how I can convince you to let me keep you."

A flutter of hope fills my heart, but I can't bring myself to believe him, "What game are you playing Keeley?"

"No games. Just truths. I want you, Ellie. More than I've ever wanted anyone. And I don't mean I want you just for tonight. I want *us*. I want you to be mine. Really and truly *mine*."

My eyes search his face, looking for a hint of that classic Jake teasing. But all I see is sincerity. "Yes."

"Yes?"

I give him a small nod before tugging on the collar of his shirt, bringing his head down, and locking our lips together.

Chapter 30

Jake

I wrap my hands around Eliana's waist and deepen the kiss, relishing the way she melts into me. I feel my cock twitch in my jeans as she parts her lips, allowing me to taste her. Her grip on my collar tightens as I hoist her up, wrapping her legs around my waist. I break our kiss to trail kisses up and down her neck as I walk us back toward my bed.

Eliana settles onto my lap. I trace idle circles on her exposed thighs as she slowly strips my sweater off her body. With the fabric tossed aside she moves her arms so they're covering her stomach, a sheepish look on her face. I'd chalk the look up to first time jitters but something about the way she kept biting her lip and avoiding my gaze told me there was more going on. *Maybe she didn't want to do this?* My cock protests at that idea, but if that was the case I'd stop things right here. I move my hands off of her body, and instead take her hand into mine, giving it a gentle squeeze. "What's wrong?"

She shakes her head, schooling the expression on her face. " I'm just having a little insecurity moment. I'll get over it." She leans down to kiss me, but I pull back. If we were going to do this, I wanted her to feel comfortable and be present. Not worrying about a dozen different things in her head.

"Can I do something to help?"

"No. It's just..." Her gaze travels down to her arms which are still partially hiding her soft stomach. "I don't exactly have a six-pack going on so..." She relents, moving her arms to her sides so I can finally take her all in.

Damn she's stunning. She has no reason to be insecure but given her shyness and her lack of knowledge about the "typical college experience", I don't think it was a stretch to say she was probably inexperienced in this department as well. Which, as far as I was concerned, was a major turn on. We could take things nice and slow.

"You're beautiful, babe. You're fucking breath taking." I reassure her.

I knew all too well that sometimes the biggest critic is the one inside your own head. I cup her face in my hand and press my lips to hers. Once softly and then a little harder, showing her how hungry I was to have her. The sound of her moans fill my room and I swear I've never heard anything sweeter.

When I pull back, she lets out a soft whimper and I smirk as I bring my lips to the shell of her ear. "It's taking everything in me not to lose all my self-control right now Ellie. If you keep making noises like that, I won't be able to restrain myself anymore."

Eliana places a hand on my lips, her cheeks flushed red. "Such a dirty mouth on you."

That was tame compared to the other things I wanted to say to her, but we'd get there eventually. I adjust myself so I can slide my jeans and shirt off, loving the way her eyes track me the entire time. When I bring her back on top of me, I trail my hand down her spine until I brush against the clasp of her bra. She gives me a nod before I unhook it. My mouth waters as I watch her pink nipples harden from being exposed.

"You still feeling okay?" I check in.

"Yes... I have a practical question for you right now."

I snicker. "Let me hear it."

"I'm feeling a bit sticky and gross from the beer, so I was wondering if we could move this into the show—Jake!" She squeals as I lift her into my arms with ease. I walk us over to my bathroom and turn on the water.

We both strip off our remaining clothes as the steam starts to fill the room, and we step inside my shower. Her eyes are trained on me as I lift the shower head off its hook and trail it over her long hair and slowly down her body. I do the same to myself before placing the shower head back.

Eliana reaches for a fresh washcloth, lathering it with soap before rubbing it in between her breasts and *fuck me* if it isn't the hottest thing I've ever seen. I've had a lot of women in my bed, but showering with one was a first for me. She closes her eyes and takes a step back, leaning into the water so it can wash away the suds. As she moves into the water her wet body slides against mine, and I feel my self-control weakening with every passing second.

"Jake?" She whispers, reaching her hand out with her eyes still closed.

"Reporting for duty," I tease, entwining our fingers together.

"Can you kiss me, please?"

I wrap my arm around the curve of her waist and place my mouth on her soft, pouty lips. I moan as she uses her free hand to play with my hair and deepen the kiss. I adjust us so our chests are pressed against each other, and it feels like absolute heaven. We pull apart for a second to catch our breath, and I shift to press a trail of soft kisses down her sternum. Her nipples are practically begging to be played with. I move my hand to cup one of her breasts.

"*Oh* Jake," she moans, her grip on my head tightening.

"That feel good, baby?" I ask, already knowing the answer.

"Really, really good—" She gasps as I take her nipple into my mouth and trace it with my tongue. I take my time toying with her breasts ensuring her nipples always have either my fingers or tongue on them, when I notice her squeezing her legs together. Desperate to release some pressure.

"Ellie baby, can I touch you?" I groan.

Gripping my shoulders, her eyes widen as she watches me trail my hand down her stomach, pausing right above her bare pussy. "God yes," she pants, snapping my patience into pieces.

Slow. Jake. Slow. I drag a finger up her slit before sinking a finger inside of her. Holy shit she's soaked. Pausing, I wait for her to take charge of the situation and start telling me what to do next. She looks up at me and pouts her lips. So the bedroom was the one place where she was okay not having full control. "Fuck, Ellie. What did I ever do to deserve you?"

"More Jake, I need more." She groans in frustration, resting her forehead on my chest. I place a kiss to the crown of her head as I plot out my next move. I don't think I'd ever given this much thought into hooking up before, but Eliana deserved more than just a quick round of sex. Though I could tell that while she was enjoying herself, she was still building her confidence when it came to being with someone. Hopefully after tonight she would have no doubts how special she was, and how special I felt to call her mine.

I wrap her into my arms and bring her into my chest, just wanting to hold her for a second before I turned her into a mess underneath me. The thought makes my cock stir and I place a kiss on her neck, knowing exactly what I wanted to do next. I move us back slowly toward the bench in the shower. I take a seat before gently gripping Eliana's waist, moving her down until her bare pussy was settled on my thigh. I bring our mouths together, nipping at her bottom lip before taking her hips and guiding her to grind on my leg.

Her hands immediately come up to my shoulders, nails digging in, as I remove one of my hands from her waist and use it to part her lips so her clit can rub up against me. She throws her head back in ecstasy as she fails to put together a coherent sentence. "J—Jake ...*Oh god*. That feels so good. Please, *please*."

"You're making such a mess Ellie, riding my thigh like a good girl." I move my hand that's toying with her clit up to her face to tuck away the stray strands of hair covering her eyes. I search them for any sign that my dirty words are unwanted, but all I can see is the opposite as her pupils dilate. So my girl likes being praised? Noted.

"You like that don't you? Getting commended for all the hard work you're doing. God you're amazing," I groan, bringing my leg up higher to add more pressure to her clit. The only response I get from her is a whimper followed by her leaning her head back and biting down on her lip. How she managed to look so damn innocent and sexy at the same time I had no idea. All I knew was that I needed her to come more than I needed my next breath.

"You getting close, Ellie?" I get a small nod in response as she reaches for my hand and brings it back down to her clit. "Use your words, Ellie. Tell me what I need to do to make you come."

Her cheeks turn red at my request, and for a second I think she's about to retreat back into herself before she widens her legs a bit more and whispers, "I'm so close, Jake. I just need you to play with my clit."

I'm drawing circles on her swollen bud a second later, adding a bit more pressure than I did before to tip her over. I can't stop the smirk on my face as a stream of moans fall from her lips, her body shaking as her orgasm takes over. "That's my girl. Let go, baby. Let go."

I hold her tight in my arms as she continues to come down, placing soft kisses on the crown of her head almost instinctively. I have never been the type to want to cuddle after sex, and often dreaded it when a girl would come up with an excuse to sleep over that night, but with Eliana everything felt different. I wanted her to feel cherished and know how much I cared about her. Wanted her to know that I would be there for her, and that she could rely on me. Always.

She releases a content sigh as she traces the muscles of my bicep with her fingers. The completely innocent touch manages to light my body on fire again, and I groan, feeling the precum leak from my cock. Dammit I was acting like a teenager who'd just hit puberty.

"What's wrong?" Eliana asks, as I let out a small self-deprecating laugh.

I tuck her head under my chin, loving the way she fit with me. She's like a missing puzzle piece I didn't even realize I needed. "Nothing, beyond the fact that you touching my arm feels like foreplay and my dick is screaming at me. Take it as additional proof for how gone I am for you."

My words cause her to perk up and before I know it, she's sliding down on her knees in front of me. She grips me in her hands tentatively. "Can you tell me how you like it?"

This fucking girl. A question that innocent shouldn't have such an effect on me. "Grip me hard. More. More, sweet girl, I can take it. Mmmm, perfect." My hips buck instinctively as she applies the perfect amount of pressure to my cock and starts moving it. The determination on her face, paired with the way she's squeezing me, is more than enough to get me off, and then I feel her soft lips around my head. "Holy shit, Ellie," I groan.

She stops immediately. "Sorry. Was that bad? I can stop."

"No. No, babe. It was good. So good. Do you think you can take more of me in your mouth? It's okay if you don't feel up to it." At this rate I'd take anything she'd be willing to give me.

She gives me a soft smile and nods, lowering her mouth back on me and moaning as she takes me further and further into her mouth. She reaches her limit, so I thread my fingers in her hair to stop her from taking on more than she can handle. She uses one hand to wrap around what's left of me and the other she places on top of mine, holding my grip on her hair firm. Eliana trails her tongue down my length, and my hips buck. She moans in response and squeezes my hand, encouraging me to continue.

"Jesus, you feel so good wrapped around me. You're such a good girl." She moans at my praising words, which only adds more pressure to my cock. Shit. Shit. "Ellie baby I'm coming, I'm—"

Her grip on my cock tightens and the next thing I know I see stars. It takes everything in me not to shut my eyes but I need to see her. Need to watch her as she swallows every last bit of me. As I come down, she pulls away with a satisfied smirk on her mouth. "Huh I think I might actually like giving blow jobs. Who knew."

I snort, not able to form words following what might be the best orgasm I've ever had.

"I guess that's what happens when you actually want to give one." she says softly.

The muscles in my arms tighten. "Did someone try to pressure you into..." I can't even finish my sentence. The thought makes me sick.

Eliana's eyes widen. "Sorry I didn't mean to kill the mood. Don't worry about."

I reach down, bringing her back into my lap and cupping

her face with my palms. "You didn't kill the mood. And you don't have to tell me anything if you don't want to. But I'm all ears if you need."

"One of my exes was pretty big on trying to guilt me into doing stuff with him when I wasn't feeling it. I wrote it off in the beginning, but then it happened a few more times. I would usually find an excuse to get out of the situation, but the last time he was a bit more aggressive. He said that if I didn't get him off then I must not love him. I stormed out of the room, but he tried to follow me. I kneed him in the balls, got away and never looked back. I knew no one who truly loved me would ever try to force me to do something I didn't want to do." She shrugs as if what happened to her was no big deal. As if I wasn't now determined to track down her shithead ex and break his nose (or worse) for treating Eliana like shit.

"I'm glad you didn't take his shit. If you ever see him in public again just give me a call and get ready to bail me out of jail."

She snorts, leaning her forehead against mine.

We sit there in a comfortable silence long enough for her eyes to drift close. "Alright I think it's time for bed." I shut off the shower and we take turns drying each other before heading to bed. The last thing I remember is bringing her into my arms before we both fell asleep, exhausted and incredibly sated.

Chapter 31

Eliana

Jake Keeley was a cuddler. The kind that wrapped their limbs around you like a koala bear to a branch and clung on all night. His weight on me gave the same effect as my weighted blanket, and it was the best sleep I'd had in a long time. Currently he was using my chest as a pillow while I played with his hair. In the middle of the night he brought us some water and snacks—namely salt and vinegar chips— before he crawled back into bed and buried his head into my neck. He pressed soft kisses along the curve of my throat until he fell back asleep. The whole thing felt so intimate I thought I'd freak out at some point but instead it all felt so... normal. Like we had been doing this all along.

At some point I would freak out like I normally do when I realize I've taken on a task I have no idea how to accomplish. But freaking out would be a waste of time—time I really wasn't going to have now that I had a...boyfriend?— so I planned to do what I did best: prepare. A common misconception about psychology majors is that we knew everything about human behavior, but the reality was we found our niche and stuck to it.

180

Mine was babies, not adult human relationships. Tonight, I would research articles on communication and long-term relationships, and maybe even listen to a podcast or two from Jane and Mark Ellis, my favorite podcasters, researchers, and husband and wife. They frequently discuss the hurdles faced in modern dating on college campuses on their podcast, The Dating Method, and now that I had a relationship to nurture, I needed them more than ever.

Normally I would prepare *before* I actually started something, but Jake and I were officially, well, official. Lots of googling would be needed because what the hell did I know about being in a serious relationship? Especially given my only past relationship experience was incredibly toxic and I didn't really have good models to reference either. But this was Jake. Someone who went from being one of the biggest annoyances in my life to one of my closest friends— and now boyfriend— in the span of a couple of months. And I would do my best to be a good partner for him.

I've never opened up to someone so quickly. But here I was in his bed, after three months of knowing him, post shower hook-up, thinking about how to make him happy. He practically forced himself on me, this soft, caring, and protective man who was hiding behind deep blue eyes and a cocky smile.

I press a small kiss to the crown of Jake's head and try to slide myself out from under him. Every small movement I make results in him tightening his arms around me like a boa constrictor. "So clingy," I hum with approval, leaning my chin on his head.

"I don't remember hearing any complaints last night." Jake yawns, his voice deep and scratchy from having just woken up.

"Admittedly I was a big fan earlier, but now I have to pee and there's a 6'3—"

"6'4," he corrects.

"Hockey player on top of me who refuses to let me go."

"How dare he. Who is this guy? Tell me his name and I'll go talk to him."

I roll my eyes and gently push him off, freshening myself up in the bathroom before returning to bed.

"I could get used to this." Jake smiles, cupping my face in his hand and kissing my forehead before wrapping his arms around me again.

"So could I." I let out a content sigh. "But I do have to go soon."

His arms tighten around me. "Mmm I don't think so."

"Jake."

"Ellie."

"I need you to let me go."

"No can do." He shakes his head, burrowing his head in my neck.

"But I have work to do."

"You can just do it here."

"I could, but I need my laptop and books..."

"Well why don't I drive you over to your apartment, grab everything you need, and then I'll bring us back?" He yawns, making no move to get out of bed.

"Wow. Who would've thought you'd be so clingy," I tease.

He clicks his tongue. "I am *not* clingy."

"You using me as a pillow last night isn't really helping your case, Keeley."

"I wouldn't call that clingy. I just wanted to be closer to you. I like being close to you." His eyes lock with mine, filled with such vulnerability and adoration I would've melted to the floor if not for the fact that I was already lying in bed.

"Hmm...I suppose it doesn't matter where I work as long as I get it done," I concede. "Head out in 20?"

"That's more than enough time." A wild smile forms on his

face as he brings our lips together and I lose myself underneath him.

* * *

"I'm going to share my Google calendar with you," I announce on the drive over to my apartment. "I basically live and die by the Gcal so you'll know which weeks are particularly rough for me."

"Sounds good. Do I also get editing privileges?" Jake asks. I freeze in response. "Yup that checks." He laughs.

"It's just, if something gets accidentally shifted or deleted it could throw off my whole day, really my whole week." The thought puts me on edge, and my leg starts to bounce. "I promise I trust you, I just get a lot of anxiety when I feel like I'm losing control, which is why—"

"Hey, it's okay I was just joking around." He reaches over and gives my hand a squeeze. "Didn't mean to rile you up."

"Sorry. My anxiety decided to act up for a moment there."

"Nothing you need to apologize for," he reassures me.

"Maybe it is something we should talk about, since experiencing anxiety is unavoidable, especially for me. I honestly can't remember a period of time when I wasn't constantly swimming in worries and thinking of thousands of 'what if' scenarios in my head. Once I got to college and was put on student insurance, I was finally able to get a therapist. She's been great in helping me realize how my attempts at controlling my anxiety are not very effective. We're working on thinking more flexibly now, but I still slip back into my old ways of trying too hard to control things. I used to think that because I was so anxious I couldn't do anything I really enjoyed, which I realize isn't true. The therapy and medication have helped a lot, but it was definitely a journey getting here. When I was

183

younger, it would mainly manifest in physical symptoms like stomachaches. My pediatrician gave me some meds for nausea but when that didn't help either, my mom just thought I'd get over it eventually."

Jake draws his eyebrows together. "What do you mean?"

"It's a bit complicated. I can't fully blame her because Middle Eastern culture has a stigma surrounding mental health. She definitely experienced depression when my dad left us, but she would never admit it. It's too taboo. When I was younger, it bothered me that she thought I would just outgrow my anxiety, as if that's how it works. I can't say that I'm not still upset with her when she makes insensitive comments, but being in my field has taught me that the stigma for mental health was prevalent not just in my culture, but lots of other cultures. It's definitely getting better, but we still have work to do. And the older I got the more I forgave my mom, seeing that there was only so much she could have done for me." I shrug. "It did take me a while to address my own internalized stigma, though, and finally reach out for help. Nicole helped a lot with that."

"I'm really happy that she was there for you."

"Yeah, so am I."

"Anything else I should know, or do, that could be helpful?" Jake pulls up to the curb outside of my place.

"Just be patient with me. Even on my good days I still have my moments. Anxiety never goes away, and to some extent, that's a good thing. Normal levels of anxiety are evolutionarily adaptive, which is why everyone experiences it at some point in their life. It's just at the heightened levels where I feel consumed by it, like you saw that one night, when I lose control of my coping strategies. You being there helped. And doing things I enjoy. Anxious feelings can exist, and I can still engage in behaviors that make me feel fulfilled. Or at least that's what my therapist keeps telling me."

Jake smiles and then hesitates.

"What is it?" I ask.

"Well it's just that you mentioned doing things you enjoy, and in the entire time I've known you all you've done is work."

I freeze. I couldn't exactly deny that, but the truth is, "Well I really enjoy my work. Especially research. It makes me happy."

"Sure. I totally get that. It's how I feel about hockey. But research and hockey are also careers for us. We can enjoy them, but they're more than just hobbies or things we do to decompress. You don't really do things that are just for you." His tone is very matter-of-fact.

"Guilty as charged." I attempt to joke, but it doesn't really land.

"Maybe I can help you brainstorm things to do for fun. Any thoughts on video games?"

"Um I'm really bad at Mario Kart, and that's the only game I've played so..."

"Got it, okay. Are you into crafting? Charlotte really likes knitting. I call her a grandma all the time, but she has made me some pretty nice beanies."

"Mm I tried it once and made a sweater with no arm holes."

"Alright well let's scrap that idea then. Let me think..."

"I have always wanted to write a murder mystery novel. I actually wrote a few chapters like two years ago and I think about adding more at least once a week. Just never have the time." I shrug.

"Well maybe you should make the time. I would love to read what your twisted little mind comes up with." He winks.

"Maybe I will." I smile as Jake pulls up to my apartment and follows me inside, where we run into Nicole.

"Wow so you *are* alive? I was about to call campus police and report you missing." She raises an eyebrow at my outfit (Jake's sweater, as my dress still needed to be washed).

"Hey, I promised I'd get her back home safe." Jake gasps in mock offense.

"Which is why I was also going to report you as the prime suspect," Nicole deadpans.

"Just when I thought we were becoming close, you lose faith in me again."

"In my defense, you set the bar in literal Hell. You can't be surprised by how much more work you have to put in before being in my good graces."

"Well you should know I never back down from a challenge," Jake warns. "Especially when it comes to ensuring my girl's best friend likes me."

Nicole shoots me a look that screams, "Is this guy for real?", followed by a small smile when Jake isn't looking. To an outsider, it would appear like my best friend hated my boyfriend, but I knew better. Phase 1 of Nicole starting to warm up to a person and enjoy their company always included her giving them a ton of shit. Like an unofficial hazing or testing of limits and buttons she could push. Jake's ability to let whatever's thrown at him roll off his shoulders was definitely winning him some points in her book.

"We'll be out of your hair soon. I'm just grabbing a few things and then heading back to Jake's," I announced nonchalantly, knowing a barrage of questions was about to follow.

As I head into my room. I hear the door shut and turn around to see Nicole with her arms crossed. "You really didn't think you'd be able to just walk away from me without giving some answers, did you?"

"I had hoped you'd be a bit distracted with... whoever is

here." I reference to the heels and fancy coat strewn across our living room that don't belong to me or Nicole.

"Oh, don't you worry. I always have time for my best friend. Especially when I catch her in the middle of a walk of shame."

"I wouldn't call it a walk of shame," I protest.

"AND she announces that she's now dating Jake Keeley. The same guy she's been "tutoring" and a few months ago wanted to push in front of a Green Line train—"

"That's not true! First-degree murder comes with a 25-year sentence, and I wouldn't last a day in prison," I protest, schooling the smile on my face as I watch Nicole's fill with irritation. "Alright fine. I admit things may have come together a bit unexpectedly but...it just felt right. Like something clicked into place, and I knew I wanted us to be more."

Nicole's apprehension fades. "He did win major points taking care of you when you were sick."

"So you approve?" There were very few people's opinions I cared about, and Nicole's was one of them. While my people-pleasing tendencies had a history of misleading me, Nicole was always there to steer me straight when someone was taking advantage of me.

"I do. I can tell he really cares about you and wants you to be happy. That's all that matters to me." She gives my shoulder a squeeze. "I did have a feeling you two would get together ever since you told me Jake bought you groceries."

"Right?! Who could resist that?"

Returning back to the living room, night bag in tow, I see Jake scrolling through my calendar on his phone. "Ellie has two participant visits next Friday, and I have a game on Saturday. Maybe the three of us could do something on Sunday?"

"Have you had Dim Sum before? I know the perfect spot in Chinatown. We could aim for 11?" Nicole offers.

"That works great. Do you want me to drive?"

Nicole shakes her head. "Probably best to take the T. Parking is going to be a nightmare."

"Works for me."

"Great. See Ellie, I told you I would use my shared access to your calendar for good." Jake winks at me, Nicole snorts, and I roll my eyes. I could get used to this.

Chapter 32

Jake

For a building that housed ten members of Westchester's Hockey team, Hockey House was oddly quiet today. With the exception of Ollie, most of my roommates were out, taking a rare day off of practice as an opportunity to explore the city.

"Are you our new Mommy?" Ollie extends his arms out to Eliana for a hug, eyes wide like a golden retriever. I tap the back of his head, but he reacts as if I'd smacked him hard. "Ow! Dammit, what the hell was that for?"

"Don't be so dramatic. I barely touched you. Plus, her being your mommy implies that I'm your daddy, and that's something I wouldn't even wish on my worst enemy," I tease.

"What's that supposed to mean?" Ollie huffs in mock offense.

"Just the fact that you're super weird. Which, like, you do you man. Let that freak flag fly. But not everyone appreciates your...charms."

Ollie rolls his eyes. "I'm a goalie. We're naturally wired to be weird and often inappropriate. It comes with the territory.

Plus, with how attached at the hip you two are, Ellie's on her way to becoming an unofficial member of the team. So she needs to get used to it. I was just trying to break the ice."

"It's fine Jake. I adapt quickly." I watch as Eliana walks over to Ollie and places her hands on his shoulders. "I'm not here to be your mom, but I am more than happy to connect you with my therapist if you want to work through some of your unresolved issues," she snickers.

"You just met me and you already want to fix me? I can't tell if I'm offended or attracted," Ollie teases, flirtatiously moving his eyebrows. "You already fixed up Keeley, you wanna take a stab at me too, Ellie?"

"There was nothing about Jake that needed fixing." Eliana corrected him immediately, and in doing so, I let out a breath I didn't know I was holding. "He just needed some help with one of his classes. And there's nothing wrong with asking for some help. That's what he's taught me." She takes my hand into hers and gives it a squeeze.

"You two are so sweet it actually makes me nauseous." Ollie gags, rolling his eyes.

"Don't be jealous Oliver. You'll find someone to match your own energy one day...probably."

"Wow, such a huge vote of confidence from one of my captains. You really know how to build a guy up."

"Well if half of your goalie skills translate into relationship skills, I'm sure you have nothing to worry about. Better?" I offer.

"Much. My bruised ego is now healed. So what are you two up to today?" Ollie heads towards the kitchen, likely digging through the fridge for whatever leftover meal prep I made earlier this week.

"I'll probably watch some of Bolton's game tape while Ellie gets some work done. I don't want any surprises when we face them in a couple of weeks." Over a century's worth of rivalry between our two schools meant there was no love lost between us. Every game against Bolton felt like a championship faceoff, with how rabid the crowd was. They'd beaten us both times last year when we faced off, but now that their star seniors, Chase Matthews and Shepard Carlson, graduated, I liked our odds.

"Have you talked to Coach yet about whether you'll be playing that night?" Ollie lowers his voice in case any of the other boys are around. Adam and Ollie were the only two teammates who knew how close I'd gotten to being cut because of my grades.

"We're meeting with Mason and my TA next week to talk about it. Eliana said I shouldn't have anything to worry about given the grade I just got on my exam." She crunched the numbers three times to ensure her estimates were correct. I was in the green — we just needed to update Mason and Coach Jameson.

"Good because we need you on the ice against Bolton. That game falls on family night, right? I should make sure my parents are set." Ollie pulls out his phone to send a quick text.

"Shit, good call. Ellie, I'll make sure you have a spot in one of the suites." I wrap an arm around her waist, tucking her head under my chin. "That way I'll be able to find you from the ice. Plus, the fam is already dying to see you again." I should also look into getting her a jersey by then. Couple of weeks should give me enough time.

A faint blush reddens her cheeks. "Any chance you could add Nicole too? We've been planning on going for a while now."

"Done. I'm sure Nicole will be dying to hear all the embarrassing stories about me from my sisters."

"Sienna's gonna be there?" Ollie interrupts, freezing in place.

"Yeah, why wouldn't she be?"

All I get is a shrug. "Just asking." Followed by him grabbing a bag of chips and running upstairs.

"That was weird, right?" I turn to Eliana who looks equally as confused as I feel.

"A little bit, but we established all goalies are a little weird so that was probably normal for him."

"Fair enough." I let it go, leading us upstairs. In the back of my head I couldn't help but wonder why Ollie got so spooked at the mention of my little sister.

* * *

"What are we doing for lunch?" I rest my chin on Eliana's shoulder as she feverishly types away on her laptop. She's fully locked in, which is why I'm not surprised when she doesn't respond. I place a kiss on her neck, hoping that works. She just shuffles back into my chest as dozens of words fly across the screen.

While I was watching game tape, Eliana plopped herself in between my legs and continued making her way through her never-ending to-do list. I can't say I minded. Something about Eliana made me want to hold her whenever I could. Like she was my own personal safety blanket.

When I think she's finally about to respond to my lunch question, she turns to me and says, "We should probably discuss how you want to handle our meeting with your assistant coach and Violet."

I look down and see her Google calendar open to an event titled, "Talk to Jake about tutoring meeting" scheduled for now. "Wow you really do put everything in your calendar."

"If it's not on the calendar it's not getting done. I wasn't joking when I said I live and die by it." She laughs.

"Just so we're on the same page. As far as Violet knows you're still my official tutor?" I check.

"Yup. She is aware we had a rough patch in the beginning, but I didn't tell her I quit on you. I wanted to avoid you getting in trouble with the tutoring center. It all worked out in the end." She shrugs, though there's a tension to her.

"What's wrong?"

Eliana worries her lip between her teeth. "Would you be upset if we kept our relationship a secret? At least in front of your assistant coach and Violet."

Of all the things she could've asked me, I wasn't expecting that. "Why?"

"I just don't want to come off as unprofessional. Dating the guy I was tutoring could be seen as crossing a boundary I shouldn't. I'm already nervous about what the people in your mom's lab this summer will think of me when they realize I'm dating you, and I just don't want Violet to be upset with me."

I struggle to silence the insecurity that's building in my chest. Why did she want to hide our relationship? "Are you worried about what Violet will think?" I bite.

Eliana's eyes widen as she shakes her head and turns her body around to face me. "No, that's not it at all. I promise."

She looked and sounded sincere but the twinge in my chest wouldn't let up. "Are you sure? Because I really don't think Mason and Violet would care. It feels like you're hiding me."

Eliana settles her hands on her knees, clearly nervous. "It's not that at all. It's more so related to my own anxieties about what people will say about me working with your mom this summer."

"I don't really understand what Violet has to do with that. You might just have to accept that people are going to say whatever they want."

"I know, I know. It just hits deeper for me. I always feel like

I need to be overly cautious about the things that I do or say." She takes a deep breath, letting it out before continuing. "As a woman of color in academia there have been many moments where someone has not so subtly alluded to the fact that I've been given the scholarships or opportunities that I have because I'm a diversity hire, or that I have ties to someone who gave me a handout. Over time the more you start to hear those things the more you assume everyone must be thinking that about you. Which is why I want to keep my personal life separate from my professional life. Especially in instances that might add fuel to the fire and give people another excuse to say I didn't deserve the opportunities I've earned. That's why I was so against fake dating in the beginning. And why, even now, I can't stop thinking about what other people are going to think of me."

Out of all the things that could've come out of her mouth, I never expected it to be that. "Anyone who thinks that is a piece of shit that isn't worth a second of your time."

"Thanks. And I *know* that deep down...but I still feel like I need to protect myself. That's why I want to keep our relationship from Violet and Mason. At least until the semester is over. I know Violet wouldn't judge me, but if word got around somehow to the tutoring center I know eventually someone would have an issue with it." Her sentences speed up with each word, matching the anxious energy she was omitting.

I place my hand on her shaking knee and smile as I watch her relax with my touch. "It's okay, I can wait a few months to share the news with everyone. If you haven't guessed, I don't plan on going anywhere soon. You're stuck with me," I tease to lighten the mood.

Eliana brings herself closer to me, wrapping her arms around my neck as she leans in for a hug. My hands move to play with her curly hair, drawing a content sigh from her lips.

"I appreciate you hearing me out and understanding where I'm coming from. It means a lot to me. You mean a lot to me," she whispers into my chest, sending goosebumps up and down my arms.

"Always Ellie. You're my girl now. I'll always be there for you," I promise.

"I like the sound of that." She hums against my chest.

"Good, because it's a promise I plan on keeping."

Chapter 33

Jake

My racing heart had nothing to do with the brutal practice Coach just led us through. It's from the feeling of uncertainty heading into this meeting where Violet is going to confirm whether or not I'd be benched for the rest of the season. Eliana's assurances had kept me calm up until this point. Approaching Mason's office now is bringing up feelings of anxiety I didn't even know I had. I'm hyper-aware of every movement as I enter. Like the way Mason and Violet pull apart abruptly from each other as if I'd just caught them in action. The way the seats are laid out in his office like an intervention. The tense look on Mason's face as he glances at the whiteboard on his desk with drawn game plays. Plays that may or may not factor me in.

Before I can start, Eliana flounces in behind me, a large mocha frap with extra whipped cream in hand. While she immediately sits down in a chair across the desk from Mason and Violet, I remain frozen, leaning against the door frame. I can tell I'm pissing off Mason, but that was what Eliana and I had planned. For me to play the role of the cocky hockey captain who was still acting like a brat to his tutor. *If only they knew.*

If my acting is convincing, then Eliana should win an Oscar for the way she turns around to nod her head towards the empty seat next to her, all while sending me a menacing glare that makes my cock twitch. Fuck, forget having her beg for me. I wanted her to boss me around and tell me exactly how to own her body. I move to sit down and look down at my hands entwined on my lap, knowing if I made eye contact with Eliana now, I would blow our whole cover.

"Alright, so why don't we get started," Violet offers. "I'd like to first hear from you two about how tutoring has been going. What's been working and what hasn't been? Can we make any changes to help you both out during this process? And then we can end with discussing where to go next and Jake's eligibility for the rest of the semester."

Violet hands Mason my class report, where he will clearly see how hard I've been working.

Eliana is the first to respond. "We had a bit of a rocky start—" I snort, "But over time, we came up with a plan to stay on track. And things have been better since then."

"'Mutual agreement' is a very nice way of saying she threatened to let me flunk several times if I didn't do all of these assignments on her hellish timeline," I say not-so-subtly under my breath.

"Part of my responsibility as your tutor is to make sure that you complete all your assignments in a timely manner. It's not my fault you have issues with planning and prioritizing your responsibilities."

"And it's not *my* fault they gave me a drill sergeant instead of a tutor." I watch her eyes turn dark in a way that lets me know she's enjoying our game. "Seriously, could you *be* any more uptight? I don't respond well to authoritarianism."

"You can get snippy with me all you want Jake, but that doesn't change the fact that my methods have been working." Damn right they were. I was one sultry look away from getting on my knees and begging her to do whatever she wanted with me. From the smug look on Eliana's face, she knows just how wrapped around her finger I am. Eliana continues, "You're welcome, by the way."

"You are so full of yourself," I press, hoping it comes off as seething.

"Just giving my student a dose of his own medicine."

"You know what?" I lean over my chair to bring myself closer to Eliana, who doesn't cower away. If anything, she leans closer and looks just as ready to go head-to-head with me. I needed one of the adults in the room to interject or else I was about to drag Eliana to the closest trainer's room and lock us in until we got all of this "tension" out of our systems.

"Okay," Violet interjects. "I hear that some things have been really effective. Jake, from looking at your assignment grades before you started tutoring to now, you've really turned things around, which is great." A sense of pride fills my chest. "But maybe we can work on being a bit more flexible when it comes to scheduling and check-ins?" Violets offer. A compromise. Now is the time for me to perk up in response.

"So, he can keep playing?" Mason speaks for the first time, asking the real question we'd all been waiting to ask. Eliana looks offended, as if he's questioning her capabilities as a tutor. If only she realized he wasn't skeptical about her performance, he was skeptical of mine.

Violet looks at her laptop for a few seconds before turning her attention back to Mason. "He can keep playing—"

"Thank *fuck*." I exhale.

"But I do recommend he keeps up with his tutoring. At least until the end of the semester. And maybe next semester too if he plans on taking more psych classes." *Fat chance that would be happening.* "Pending Eliana is available. She's our best psychology tutor and tends to be high in demand." The latter comment is not-so-subtly aimed at me and my snarky attitude.

Violet didn't need to remind me of how incredible Eliana was, but I hoped hearing it out loud would ease any doubts Eliana had in her head about how she was perceived. I turn my attention to Eliana and shoot her a sincere look, "You are a really good tutor, even though you may act like a drill sergeant."

"Thanks." She rolls her eyes and turns her attention to Violet. "I have to head over to the lab, if that's okay? I'm helping Maya run a scan soon."

"Yes, definitely. We'll talk more soon." Violet gives her a wave as she heads out of my office.

She's working another shift? I must have missed that in her calendar. She was already pushing nearly 40 hours of work this week on top of being a full-time student. I knew she could handle herself, but I hated seeing how exhausted she was at the end of every day. Once Eliana's out of the office I turn to Violet. "Have you considered giving her a day off or something? She practically lives in that lab."

Violet looks caught off guard. "I'm sorry?"

"It wouldn't kill her to have some fun. All she does is school, tutoring, and research."

"Research can be fun," Violet challenges.

"God, no wonder you hired her. You're like, the same person." Does every academic have this incurable desire to burn themselves to the ground? I've seen it with my mom, my sisters, and now my girlfriend. "So, am I good to go?"

"Yeah, you're all set," Mason responds. "I do want to finalize some things with Violet though so just shut the door on your way out."

Eliana texts me as I leave Mason's office, telling me she wants to make dinner for us tonight to celebrate my being back in the team's good graces. I smile to myself, realizing that a few months ago my definition of celebration would probably look like hitting up a couple of bars or throwing a party at Hockey House. Now the thought of a night in with my girl sounded perfect.

Chapter 34

Eliana

Walking through Westchester's Hockey arena, I'm surprised by how quiet the building is. There's no game today but I expected some level of chaos. "Where is everyone?"

"Practice ended over two hours ago, and we have a rare weekend free of games. That usually means going home for the weekend or spending it at frat row. You know hockey players, we can never sit still. Jake smirks as he guides me towards the back of the arena.

"Oh I know. My boyfriend was once the team's prime playboy up until a few weeks ago." I tease.

Jake throws a hand up in defense. "Actually, Ollie had me beat, but I am willing to admit I was in a steady second place."

"Wow. I never thought I'd hear you be okay with coming in second."

"There are some moments in life when coming second is a privilege." Jake winks at the double meaning behind his joke.

My cheeks start to redden. "You're such a child."

"Hey, if you got the joke then your head is just as in the

gutter as mine." He places a kiss on my cheek to stop himself from laughing.

We reach the end of the hall and Jake swings open a massive door that leads to the locker room. ESPN had ranked Westchester's Men's Ice Hockey locker room as one of the top three in the nation. I'm a big hockey fan, and yet I struggled to understand why 1) ESPN would even bother reporting about it or 2) why that was something to boast about, but I now understood it.

The room was covered in navy blue and white — our school's colors. Posters of former players that went on to play for the NHL covered the leftmost wall, along with their autographed jerseys. The individual cubbies that served as lockers were massive enough that any large player could comfortably sit down in it. I walked around the room until I found Jake's locker.

The photos of his sisters and parents taped to his locker don't surprise me, neither do the ones of him, Adam and Ollie celebrating a big win. What does surprise me is the photo of us together at Cornwall's sharing a milkshake after Westchester beat UMass Amherst a few days ago.

"Had to make sure all my good luck charms were represented." Jake speaks from behind me, wrapping his arms around my waist. "That and I couldn't get the pure look of bliss on your face after you took a sip from that milkshake out of my head."

"Best Oreo shake in town. Don't think I ever tasted anything that good in my life." My eyes are locked on his lips, mere inches away from mine, and yet they didn't feel close enough.

"I'm inclined to agree, but there's one thing I can think of that tops it." Jake moves a hand to rest on my stomach, his fingers so long the tips of them brush against the hem of my knit sweater.

All it took was a simple touch to leave me a fluttering mess. "I—Impossible."

"Is that a challenge, Ellie? You may not know this about me, but I love a challenge." His small smirk turns into a wicked smile as he turns me around to sit on the bench and then sinks to his knees. Jake moves his hands to the waistband of my leggings, waiting for me to give him a nod before tugging them off. I swallow hard as he places his hands on my thighs and spreads them apart, inching his face closer to my core as he does.

I feel the heat creep up to my face and neck at the sight of him in front of me, eyes filled with such hunger and adoration, as if he were under a spell. While his intentions were clear he waited patiently for me to confirm whether or not I wanted him to continue. "Jake," I pant.

"Eliana." He takes my hand into his gently.

I use my free hand to run it through his hair. "What are you going to do?"

"Whatever you'll let me do, whatever you want me to do."

"I think I want whatever you want," I confess, tightening the grip I have on his hair.

"You think?" Jake's eyebrows furrow together.

"No one's ever...done that to me before. I've wanted them to, but the guys I've hooked up with in the past thought it was gross so—" I stop myself, realizing I'm over-explaining and rambling like I always do when I'm nervous. To Jake's credit, he just listens and holds onto me, keeping me grounded. Secure.

"I probably don't need to tell you this, but they sound like fucking idiots. You should know I'm not above begging you to let me taste you."

My nipples harden at the desperation in his voice. "Beg, huh?"

"I'm already on my knees for you, so I'd say I have a head start." He winks, then groans as I tug at his hair.

"Watching you beg could be fun," I tease. I knew what Jake was doing. He was letting me take full control of the situation, even with my lack of experience, to make sure I felt comfortable. His hands move from my thighs to the waistband of my underwear, then he stops. My eyebrows furrow together when I realize he's waiting for me to stop him, as part of our game. Well, if he wanted me to make him beg...I click my tongue. "You haven't earned that yet."

Jake's entire body shudders in response. He pulls back, placing a trail of kisses down my thighs to the top of my knees on both legs before looking up at me. "Please Ellie."

I trace his lips with my index finger. "Please what?"

"Let me taste you. I've been starving for you for days, no, weeks now. I need to taste you more than I need my next breath." His shaking hands confirmed his declaration.

I struggle to ignore the voice inside my head that's screaming at me to cave in now and let him have his way with me. I remind myself that the more I drag this out, the more ravenous Jake will be. And that's exactly how I wanted him. I loved how sweet and careful he was around me, especially when it came to being intimate, but I was also really enjoying this game we were playing.

Using my hand that's wrapped in his hair, I lift his head up, entwining our lips together and teasing my tongue into his mouth before abruptly pulling back. "There. You've tasted me."

He drops his head to rest on my knees, grunting in frustration. "You *know* that's not what I meant, Eliana."

"What did you mean?"

His mouth parts and his hands twitch as if he's moments away from snapping. Worrying his lip between his teeth, Jake closes his eyes and takes a deep breath to compose himself.

My confidence and comfort when it came to having sex was a work in progress, but I felt it growing more and more with Jake. "Don't be shy, Keeley. I promise I won't break."

My words are his undoing. "I want to bury my tongue in that sweet little pussy of yours until your screams fill this whole damn arena as I make you come over and over again." The heat in his eyes along with the huskiness of his voice cause me to spread my legs even wider.

I ignore the voice in my head that says I should be embarrassed for wanting him so much. Still, I decide to drag this out, see how much I could push him. "And why should I let you?"

"Because I'm on my knees on the verge of absolutely losing it if you don't let me. I promise I'll make you feel so damn good, Ellie." He presses another kiss to my knee then looks up at me, waiting for my permission.

I run my hands down my thighs, taking his hands into mine and placing them on the top hem of my panties. "Well don't keep me waiting then."

Jake immediately slides off my underwear and shoves them in his pocket before throwing one of my legs over his shoulder. "God how did I get so lucky," he moans as he uses his tongue to trace from the side of my knee all the way to the top of my thighs. "Look at you spread so wide for me. Dripping on my locker and I haven't even touched you yet. You're such a good girl. My girl."

Fuck. Is it possible to orgasm just from listening to someone speak? I was very close to losing all control I had over the situation. "If I didn't know any better, I'd say you were stalling—oh... god..." I moan as Jake traces my swollen clit with his tongue. The pressure feels so damn good I can't help but tighten my grip on the back of his head and bring him closer to me. He adjusts his movements ever so slightly, and before I know it, I'm grinding my hips into his face.

A sexy chuckle forms in his throat as he dips his tongue lower into my slit, lapping me up. Jake lets out a moan that shakes his whole body as he continues to bury his tongue in me with such insatiable hunger. The noises that are coming from the both of us are so obscene that goosebumps form on my arms. That with the added knowledge that he was eating me out in the locker room where anyone could walk in on us, had me dangerously close to coming. When Jake brings his thumb up to my clit, drawing torturous circles that bring me closer and closer to the edge, I can barely breathe. Jake must feel the same as he replaces his tongue with a finger, sitting back for a moment to lick his lips and take me in. "You look so beautiful Ellie, and you taste even better."

"Then why'd you stop?" I whine.

"It's a bit embarrassing." His cheeks redden as he looks down at the wet spot on his pants. Oh. *Oh.* Jake had come, without me even touching him, just from— "I promise I'm not usually like this. But something about seeing you move on my tongue...I lost control." Before I can tell him that's the hottest thing someone has ever said to me, Jake slides another finger inside of me, curving them both to hit a spot that has me seeing stars. Whatever we were talking about completely leaves my mind as he keeps stroking me.

"Jake, fuck. Right there. I'm so, so close. Please."

"Let go baby, let go," he encourages, placing a soft kiss on my knee. It's a stark juxtaposition to the way he's edging me with his finger.

"I—I can't."

"Yes, you can. Just tell me what you need."

"Your tongue. I need your—" I gasp as he takes my clit in between his lips and sucks hard, following it with the sensation of fingers continuing to move in and out of me. I can't even warn him as my thighs close around his face and I ride his tongue until I explode. Jake showers my legs with soft kisses as I lean my head against the side of his locker, catching my breath. "I fear you just created a new obsession for me."

"Trust me, that makes two of us." He looks up at me with a sly grin before helping me stand up, bearing most of the weight as my legs feel like mush. "Let's get you cleaned up."

He walks me back to the trainer's room and lifts me up so I'm sitting on one of the made beds. I snake my legs around his waist, burying my head into the crook of his neck to stop him from walking away. "What if I don't want you to clean me up?"

Jake brings his lips to my temple. "Hmm then what should I do?"

Leaning down onto the bed, I dig my fingers into his t-shirt and tug him on top of me. With my legs wrapped around him, I gently rock my hips until I can feel his cock start to harden. I bring my lips to the shell of his ear, while tugging on his hair. "I need you inside of me, Jake."

"Is that so?" With his free hand, Jake slowly removes his belt and unbuttons his jeans. I whimper as he traces a hand down his abs and dips it into his boxers. He hums in approval and takes his cock into his hand, teasing it. "Tell me more."

"I want you buried so deep I'll feel you for the rest of the week," I pant.

Jake's eyes widen. "Fuck Ellie, and you said I had a mouth on me." He shakes his head while he removes my sweater and tosses it across the room. My sports bra earns similar treatment shortly after. I wait for the wave of insecurity to hit me the way it always does when I was naked in front of a guy, but it never comes. Instead, I feel...confident.

I had no doubt this was Jake's influence on me. He palms me with his calloused hands and I moan at how good it feels. "My sweet girl is so perfect." He hums in appreciation, pinching one of my hardened nipples between his fingers and traces the other with his tongue.

Attempting a verbal response is futile, so instead I grind my hips against him. Wetness pools down my thighs. "You have too many clothes on," I observe, my ankles digging into the back of his t-shirt. "That's not fair."

"If you wanted me naked, all you had to do was ask." Jake winks, placing a rough kiss on both of my nipples before leaning back and slowly teasing his shirt off his body. My hands claw at his shirt, desperate for him to move faster. In a blink, Jake locks both of my wrists with one of his hands and pins them above my head. "Not so fast, babe. You made me beg earlier. Now I think it's only fair that I return the favor."

Jake groans as he strokes himself. "You wish this was your hand, don't you?".

"Yes. *Yes.*" I struggle against his grip, which he immediately releases. I would've been more than fine if he hadn't, thoroughly enjoying the game we were playing, but I loved how even when he was being rough, he was still gentle with me.

"I also wish it was your hand on me now. Stroking me. Feeling how hard I am for you."

"Jake, please. That's all I want." All my self-control is gone as I grab his boxers and tug them down so he's fully exposed to me. Jake quickens his strokes and my mouth falls open at the sight of him.

"I'm all yours, Eliana." He leans down to place a kiss on my forehead and threads his fingers through my hair. "Every part of me is yours."

"Do you have a condom?" I ask, impressed with myself that I'm able to even think straight right now.

Jake reaches over me, throwing a cabinet open and pulling out a handful of protection.

"They have condoms in the trainer's room?"

"There was an STD outbreak a decade ago. I'm negative, but they've practically thrown them at us since." He puts on the condom.

"Got it. Also negative." I bite my lip. "Hope I didn't kill the moment."

"Eliana."

"Jake."

"I've been dreaming about this moment every night for the past few months, and none of my dreams compare to what I feel right now. There's no way you could kill this moment, but you might kill me if we drag this out any longer."

His eyes are locked on mine as I take his cock into my hands and guide the tip in between my thighs until it hits my clit. We both moan at the contact, and I motion for him to take control. He grabs my legs and places them over his shoulders. He teases my clit with his thumb, all while slowly edging his cock inside of me. "Fuck baby, your pussy is so damn tight." He groans, halting to give me a moment to adjust.

I'd never felt this full in my life. I probably shouldn't be surprised, given Jake was 6'4 and well over 200 pounds, but I wasn't sure how much more I'd be able to take. My concerns must have been written all over my face because he immediately comforts me. "It'll fit baby. You're already taking me so good, we just have to give this little clit a bit more attention." His thumb quickens in pace, and a jolt of pleasure rocks my body. As if on command, my hips start to move against him until he's fully buried inside of me.

Jake peppers kisses on my forehead and cheek before locking our lips together. He pulls out slowly, adjusting himself so he rubs against my clit with each thrust. The sensation is so good it's almost overwhelming. I dig my nails into his biceps as tears form in my eyes from the pleasure.

Jake freezes. "Shit, am I hurting you?"

"No, no. It feels good, so good. Please don't stop, please." I beg, moving my hands to his hips and urging him to go faster, deeper. If that was even possible.

"You're the best thing that's ever happened to me." Jake moans as he continues to move in and out of me, hitting my clit with every movement.

"More, Jake, more. You're making me feel so good. I'm so close—" I gasp as he plays with one of my nipples while he hits my g-spot. The combination sends me toppling over.

"That's it, Ellie. That's it. Come all over my cock as it's buried inside of you, like a good girl." Jake lets out a final moan before he finishes with me, holding onto me tight as he comes down. He pulls out of me gently and then cradles my face in his hands. "You alright, baby?"

"I'm more than alright," I assure him. "Although I can't say this is what I expected when you asked me to come to the arena because you had a surprise for me."

His eyes widened. "Oh shit. I forgot to give you your actual surprise." He rolls off me and the table, and runs naked back into the locker room, returning with a jersey in hand. "I promise 'surprise' wasn't a euphemism for sex. I wanted to give you my jersey, for you to wear at our game against Bolton."

I clutch the fabric to my chest. "I'll wear this if you promise to embarrass them."

A smile lights up his face. "Oh Ellie, you have my word."

Chapter 35

Eliana

Being abruptly woken up at 6 a.m. on a day when I didn't have to be up this early was my definition of cruel and unusual punishment. Someone was currently pounding on my door like they were determined to break it at the hinges. When I opened the door and saw my mother standing on the other side, a remorseful look on her face, my heart dropped to my stomach. *What was going on?*

"I'm sorry to have to wake you up this early. Can we come in?" In my state of shock, I had completely missed my sister hidden behind her, gripping onto our mom's arm in a feeble attempt to stay warm. My heart breaks as Josie gives me an apologetic look, like she felt like a burden in this situation. I never wanted her to feel that way.

"Of course. Sorry, I'm still half asleep. C'mon in." I step aside for them to enter, Josie giving my hand a squeeze as she walks in. Our universal sign for *'Life is really tough right now, but at least we have each other.'* "Why don't we go into my room since Nicole's sleeping?"

My mom switches to speaking Farsi, a sign of how tired she

must also be. Speaking her native language probably requires less brain power this early in the morning. Tears form in her eyes.

"Your grandma is sick. Your aunt called me, and I don't think she has much time left. I need to fly back to Iran so I can say goodbye."

"Oh Mom. I'm so sorry." I take her hand into mine, giving it a big squeeze. I didn't know much about my grandma other than that she was the one who arranged my mom and dad getting married. From what I could tell the two never saw eye to eye, but that didn't make it any easier to lose a parent.

"I need you to watch Josie for me. I know it's unfair to ask, but I can't leave her alone, and I'm really desperate."

"Of course. Don't even worry about it. I can show Josie campus and Nicole and I can keep her busy."

"Thank you. I packed a small bag for her, but there may have been things I forgotten. I am not in the best headspace." She looks at me sheepishly.

"Don't worry about it. We'll figure this out. When do you leave?"

"In a few hours. I'll be back in a few days. I wanted to stay longer but I couldn't afford to take that much work off." She shrugs as if it's no big deal, but from the expression on her face, I can tell she's stressed. International plane tickets weren't cheap, especially last minute. That paired with taking off work, she was going to be in the red for a few months. *"I should probably head out now. I don't want to miss my flight."*

"Call us when you get to Auntie's house if you can." Josie and I give Mom a big bear hug, and walk her out the door.

I don't even have to ask Josie what she wants to do next as she follows me back into my room and plops down on the bed, falling asleep almost instantly.

* * *

"Does take-your-ten-year-old-sister-to-work day exist?" I groan at the endless barrage of to-do items on my calendar. "That's the only way I can keep an eye on her while not falling behind."

"If it's not a thing, I'm sure you can make it one. I doubt anyone would mind. You could just say it was a family emergency."

"Ugh I feel so bad for my Mom I wish there was something I could do to help." I take a sip of tea from my mug.

"You're watching Josie, that's a big help." Nicole gives me a hug as I let out the sigh I was holding in.

"Yeah, I just feel like I could be doing more." My mom's bills come to mind...

"You're doing all that you can. And that's what matters. Maybe we could do something fun this weekend as a little pick-me-up? I can look into what's happening in the city."

"Have I ever told you that you're the best person ever?" I give an appreciative smile.

"At least a handful of times, but I wouldn't mind hearing it again."

"You're the best. I should probably grab Josie and get going. Long day ahead." I groan before heading back to my room, throwing my backpack over my shoulder, and taking Josie's hand as we made our way out of my apartment and to the bus stop.

Chapter 36

Jake

"What are the odds I can convince you to drive me to Foxborough this Saturday?" Sienna gives her best puppy dog face as we FaceTime.

"What's going on in Foxborough?"

"Mel and I have tickets to go see ITZY at Gillette Stadium."

"What's an ITZY?"

"Hello, only like one of my favorite K-POP groups."

Shit, I had definitely gotten her a birthday present from the wrong group then...Maybe I still had time to return it. "What happened to BLACKPINK?"

"Oh I love them too, but I've already seen them live like twice." Crisis averted. "This is my first time seeing ITZY, so I'm really excited. We tried to get tickets for the commuter line, but they sold out immediately, and I'd really like to not pay for a hundred-dollar Uber."

"So naturally you want your big brother to play chauffeur?"

"We have a couple of spare tickets from some friends who bailed. We were going to sell them, but you can have one?" she offers, her puppy dog face intensifying enough to make me cave.

"It's fine. I'll drive you."

I pull the phone further away as she starts screaming. "THANK YOU, thank you. You're the best big brother ever."

"Yeah, yeah. Let me know what time I should pick you up."

* * *

"You wanna hit up Cornwall's this Saturday?" Ollie asks, stretched out on the couch while I prepare dinner for the house.

"Can't. I have to drive Sienna to Foxborough." I throw the pasta into the sauce that's been simmering on the stove for the past hour, adding extra salt, pepper, and garlic powder.

"Sienna? I can drive her if you want."

"Then how would we both go to Cornwall's?" I loved Oliver but sometimes I had no idea how his brain worked.

"...Right. My bad. How's the food going?"

"It's ready. Feel free to dig in. I'm going to take some over to Eliana." I nod to the giant pot on the stove and the Tupperware filled with food.

I hadn't heard from Eliana all day, and at the risk of sounding like an extra clingy boyfriend, I missed her. A lot. Her Google calendar informed me that she was swamped this week and I had no intention of adding additional stress to her life. But I was hoping that I could hang out in her room while she worked.

When Nicole opens the door, I assume Eliana's out. Likely at the library to increase her efficiency. "The library holds a certain aura of anxiety that makes me go into hyper-productive mode" she'd once confessed to me. I made her take an extra long break that day. Nicole gives me a slightly concerned look before stepping aside and gesturing to the dining room.

A sense of joy fills my chest when I hear the sound of Eliana's contagious laughter fill the apartment. She didn't do that enough. Another thing I would have to change.

"Now I need to figure out how to make you laugh like that after one of my jokes." I freeze when I notice a kid sitting next to Eliana.

Their similar features clue me in to who she might be. Josie. Eliana likely would have informed me about this, which probably meant this wasn't a planned trip. I try to gauge how she's feeling, but her eyes are locked on her sister.

"Hi. I'm Jake." I smile at the child, who holds her chin up at me.

"So you're the boyfriend." She eyes me down like she's not sure what to think of me yet. Evidently my first impressions with both Jasper women would be rough.

"That would be me. And you must be the incredibly smart and funny little sister?"

"Flattery will win you some points, but I have more questions for you." She cracks her knuckles like a mob boss, then points to the seat across from her. "Sit down. We have a lot of things to discuss."

"Josie! Stop harassing him." Eliana exclaims, pressing her lips together to suppress a smile.

"No, it's fine. I imagined this day would come." Eliana spoke about her little sister the way a proud mom would. She also emphasized how she admired Josie's ability to speak her mind and stick up for herself. "Please continue."

Josie stares me down. "State your name, age, and occupation."

"Jake Keeley, 22, Westchester U Hockey Player and alternate captain. You watch a lot of crime shows, don't you? Probably with your older sister, right?"

"I'll be asking the questions today," Josie states. "Your intentions with my sister?"

"To make her happy." Josie gives me a look that screams, "Well duh." My palms started to feel clammy. Damn, she was really sweating me out. "And to support her. In any way that I can."

Josie's expression softens for a moment. That seemed to win her over. "I want to make it clear that Eliana and I already have plans to live together when I turn 18. You can take the guest room if you want." A compromise.

"That works for me."

"You do have to promise to be clean. I refuse to live in a boy-house." She locks eyes with me to say she means business.

"Noted. No messes and no boy-house vibes." I nod.

"So, what brings you here, Jake?" Eliana smiles, entwining our hands together.

"I made dinner for Hockey House and wanted to bring over some leftovers." I take the large Tupperware out of my bag and place it on the table.

Josie turns to Eliana. "I like him. He can stay."

"You heard her. She said I could stay." I beam like I just won the lottery.

"Let me grab some plates. Nicole, will you be joining us?" Eliana calls.

"That depends. Did Jake make his homemade tomato sauce?" Nicole asks from her room.

"And fresh pasta," I confirm.

"I'll be there in a second." Nicole's enthusiasm draws a small chuckle from my lips. One way or another I knew I'd win over every resident of this apartment.

I head to the kitchen to help Eliana set up.

"Josie really busted my balls back there." I could handle someone harassing me just fine; I was a hockey player, after all. But I was starting to notice a pattern. "So did Nicole when we first met."

Eliana takes a second to process then gives me a regretful smile. "That's on me. I definitely had some preconceived notions about hockey players, and paired with how our first tutoring session went...Let's just say when I vented to them, I didn't paint you in the best light. Which is unfair to you. I'm really sorry."

"Ah I see." I can't say I was surprised she had bad mouthed me to her little sister and best friend. I managed to win Nicole over so hopefully I could do the same with Josie.

"I promise I've told Josie nothing but good things about you since we started getting closer. She's just a little protective of me. Or really, we're protective of each other."

"I'm the same with my sisters. So, any big plans for the rest of the week, now that Josie's here?"

"That's what we were going to figure out tonight. I feel like there's not much going on in the city." Eliana gives me a soft smile.

"Yeah, I suppose you can't exactly take her bar hopping," I tease.

"Definitely not. And she goes ice skating with her friends all the time, so taking her to the Frog Pond probably won't be exciting." She sighs as we walk back to the table where Nicole has joined us. "Did you end up finding anything fun for us to do?"

"Still looking into it but you know how the city starts to go into hibernation around November. Which is funny given how all the New Englanders will still have their iced coffee even when it's cold enough to cause hypothermia if you're outside long enough."

"What about the little market at Seaport? There's hot chocolate and fun games," I offer.

"Doesn't open until next week after Josie leaves."

Damn. I hated the disappointed look on Eliana's face, especially knowing how much she cared about Josie and no doubt wanted to make her week.

"It's fine Ellie. You know I don't care. I'm just glad I get to hang out with you." Josie stands up to give Eliana a small hug before we all dive into dinner.

The rest of the night is spent in high spirits, and I can't think of a time when I'd seen Eliana crack so many jokes. On the surface, she could easily convince you that she wasn't stressed or overthinking a million things in her head. But I knew better. Something I've realized about Eliana the closer we've become is how she's a master in hiding her true emotions. Her tells were subtle, a slight tension to her jaw, an eye twitch here and there, the way she would worry her lip between her teeth for minutes before realizing. I wasn't sure what was causing her so much anxiety, but I had a feeling it was related to her sister's surprise visit.

Once Josie and Nicole left to get ready for bed, I decided to broach the topic. "I didn't realize Josie was coming to visit this week."

Eliana's shoulders tense. I come behind her, slowly massaging her shoulders while placing a soft kiss on her temple. We stand in silence while I wait for her to speak. Eventually she turns around to bury her head into my chest, and I take that as an opening. "What happened?"

"My mom dropped by this morning." She lets out a deep breath. "My grandma is sick. She had to fly back to Iran to say goodbye. They don't have the best relationship, but I think this is still really going to hurt my mom. Goodbyes are hard for most people, but especially for her, ever since my dad left."

I tighten my arms around her. "Jesus, Ellie. I'm so sorry. So, Josie's going to be staying with you until she comes back?"

"It's fine. Or at least it will be. "

Knowing there's not much I can say, or do, I simply squeeze her tighter into my chest and tell her all the things I love about her. Her caring heart, her strength, her willingness to always help people, her ability to have a snarky response to anything stupid I ever say, and most of all, her. "I love you, Eliana. I love you so much, and I want you to know how much I see you and everything that you do."

She places a kiss on my chest and finally looks up at me, eyes still shiny. "I love you too, Jake. Thanks for being here today. It really means a lot."

"Always. Whenever you need me, I'll be here."

We stay in each other's embrace until we hear the sound of footsteps.

"Don't let me break up your love fest." Josie announces with slight disgust in her voice. Glad to know preteens still spoke in sarcasm.

I open my mouth for a snarky older brother response when I notice Josie's sleep shirt. "Do you listen to ITZY?"

"*You* listen to IZTY?" Josie asks in a state of disbelief and horror. Like a teenager who found out they have something in common with their parents.

"I don't, but my sister does. She has tickets to their concert this Saturday."

"Wait what? Those sold out immediately!" Josie's jaw falls open.

"My sister had some friends who bailed last minute so maybe—"

"OH MY GOD. THIS IS FATE. MEANT TO BE. WE HAVE TO GO," Josie screams, jumping up and down before she contains herself. "Ellie can we go, pleaaaase."

"Maybe...How much are the tickets?" Eliana looks at me, concerned.

"Don't worry about it. Sienna was just going to give them away anyway. Also I'm driving, so you don't have to worry about getting there."

"Can we Eliana? Please, please, please, please, pleeeease?" Josie begs, throwing her arms around Eliana.

"You're sure Sienna won't mind?".

"Nope. In fact, I'm sure she's dying to talk to someone who's as big of a fan as she is."

"Alright, then let's do it."

Josie lets out a scream that rivals the one prior and will probably get a few noise complaints from the neighbors.

"This is so exciting. I can't wait to tell all my friends. Thank you, Ellie!" Josie runs back to Eliana's room before stopping and turning around for a second. "And thanks Jake. You made my day."

"You hear that? I made her day." I beam at Eliana.

"From interrogation subject to best friends in a couple of hours. That's impressive Keeley."

"What can I say? I'm just irresistible."

"I think you mean incorrigible," Eliana teases.

"Same difference."

"Thank you, Jake. For the tickets. For everything."

"You're welcome, but you don't need to thank me. I meant what I said to you earlier. I'll always be here for you, whenever you need me."

Chapter 37

Eliana

My mom arrived on Tuesday to pick Josie up after putting her mom to rest two days before. Unsurprisingly, my mom didn't speak much. She just held onto me tight, and when Josie went inside my room to pack her things, my mom finally let a few tears fall. I offered to let them stay the night, but my mom had to get back to work the next day for a double shift. She said her boss had been relatively understanding about her missing work. She got a coworker to cover her shift, and in exchange, my mom was taking her Christmas shift. A bit of a bummer, but I'd try to find a way to make it up to Josie.

"Why do you look like you're in the middle of getting a root canal?" Jake's voice snaps me back to reality. We were curled up on his bed, a Bruins game playing on the TV.

"Just thinking about my mom and Josie."

"That kid has an impressive set of lungs on her." A smirk comes over his face. Josie had been in full fangirl mode the night of the concert, dressed head to toe in merch courtesy of Sienna, who had deeply undersold the tickets she had gotten.

These tickets included backstage passes where we got to see IZTY practice for dress rehearsal and even take selfies with them. After that, we got personally escorted to our front row seats where she spent the entire opener teaching Jake different dance moves. The lock screen of my phone was now an image of the two of them dancing along to one of Josie's favorite songs.

"I can't thank you enough for all you did for her, for us, that night."

"The only thanks I require is seeing you happy." He presses a kiss to my temple.

"Wow, looks like the romcoms we've been watching have been rubbing off on you. That was a solid line."

"One day, my sweet Ellie, you'll learn how to accept a compliment or term of endearment without following it up with a sarcastic quip."

"I've already been talking to my therapist about that. It's a work in progress."

"Aren't we all?" Jake winks, likely remembering our first few encounters.

"Some more than others." I laugh as he rolls his eyes and gives my hip a gentle squeeze. "Any updates from the Bruins on your contract?"

"They're sending me and my lawyers a draft of my standard player contract, which is like an entry-level NHL contract, in the next week or so." The excitement in his eyes makes my heart squeeze.

"That's so amazing. I'm so freaking proud of you." I give him a soft kiss. "So, what are the next steps?"

"My lawyers will look it over and consult with me. Sometimes, people decide to go into negotiations, but I'm hoping I won't need to. My plan is to sign it at the end of our season, and this time next year, I'll officially be in the NHL."

"So you won't get to finish your senior year at Westchester?"

"No. At least not on the hockey team, per NCAA rules. I can remain a student, but I'm going to try to take some extra courses next semester and in the summer, so I can graduate early."

"Is that why you're putting so much pressure on yourself this season?"

Jake lets out a long sigh. "I just want to leave on top. Want to be able to say I won the Final Four in my last year of college hockey before I went professional. That probably sounds dramatic given I have a contract lined up and have nothing left to prove really—"

I shake my head. "It doesn't sound dramatic. It makes sense to me. You're one of the best and you want your last season to reflect that."

He places a soft kiss on my forehead, and we turn our attention back to the TV.

"Fair warning. Emotional Christmas commercials always hit me in the feels, so if any of those pop on, you may see me shed a tear or two," I joke.

"Speaking of Christmas, what do you and the fam usually do?" Jake asks.

"Nothing too special. Usually we get takeout, put on a Christmas movie, and have some hot cocoa. I want to do something more this Christmas since my mom has to work, and I know that's really gonna bum Josie out."

"Damn, are you serious? Working on Christmas blows." Jake groans in frustration.

"Agreed. Josie and I will figure something out." I assure him.

Jake shakes his head, not having it. "Isn't Christmas your favorite holiday?"

"Technically I said I *wanted* it to be my favorite holiday," I correct. "I love everything about it, the snow, the gingerbread houses, the lights and decorations. But I've never gotten to experience any of those things myself."

"Well I think it's time we fix that." Jake pulls his phone from his pocket, shoots off a quick text, and then takes my hand in his. "Pack your bags. You and Josie are spending Christmas at my family's cabin. Your mom can also come if she can make it. We'll be there for a whole week starting on the 23rd."

"What? No. I can't. I don't want to impose on your trip—"

"First, you could never impose, and second, I already texted the family group chat, which means I'll have to deal with the wrath of my mom and sisters if you don't come. And we wouldn't want that, now would we?"

"Jake, this is your family trip."

"Well I love you, so I think that means you've more than earned your right to crash," he teases.

"I don't know..." The last thing I wanted to be was a clingy girlfriend who dumped all her problems onto her partner.

"Would it make you feel better if I told you Ollie was also going to be there, so you're not the only non-Keeley present?"

"Ollie's coming?"

"Yeah, his Christmas plans fell through, so I invited him to tag along."

In that case..."Okay count me and Josie in then."

"Done. Now I have a homework assignment for you."

"Oh?"

"Make a bucket list of all the Christmas things you want to do. I plan on checking them all off."

* * *

Josie was over the moon when I updated her on our Christmas cabin trip. I also extended the offer to my mom, but she couldn't get any of the days off. A large part of me felt guilty for going out and having fun while my mom was so tied up with work, but she insisted that I go and enjoy myself for once.

The alarm on my phone goes off, letting me know that I have an hour until I need to head out. I groan at the half-finished report on my screen, let out a deep breath, and start typing away. It's definitely not my best work, but I repeat, "It's just a draft; you can always edit it later" in my head a dozen times. My brain feels like absolute mush by the time I finish typing the final sentence, and I nearly jump out of my seat when Nicole knocks on my door, signaling me to get dressed. Tonight was our big rivalry game against Bolton University, and nothing would keep me from attending this game.

With the semester coming to an end, I no longer felt like I had to keep my relationship with Jake hidden. I threw on my Westchester U Wolves jersey that Jake surprised me with last week that had his last name on my back. The jersey and the sweet glass seats he scored for Nicole and I had me dying to announce to the world that I was his girlfriend. Being shown off was another thing I'd never experienced before but could get used to.

"Ellie, we gotta head out or we'll be late. It's going to be crazy getting insi—" Nicole pauses, a smirk on her face as she notices my outfit. "That's new."

"It's from Jake."

"Yeah, I figured. It looks good on you."

"Thanks. It's a little big, but honestly it makes it easier to layer on top of my sweater."

"I meant the happiness looks good on you, but I guess the jersey's nice too." Her smirk turns into a genuine smile.

Her words warm my heart, especially given all the highs

and many, many lows she's seen me through. I return her smile and grab my bag as we head out.

We follow the sea of blue jerseys heading towards the hockey arena. I make a mental note to thank Jake again for getting us tickets because the student section was already filling up.

"Damn, it's freezing down here." Nicole wraps an arm around herself as we take our seats right next to Westchester's bench.

"Yeah, I guess we've never sat this close to the ice before."

On the other side of the rink, Bolton students decked out in maroon start filing in and the tension starts building in the arena. The aggressive nature of hockey definitely rubbed off on its fans. While a century-long rivalry between the two oldest universities in the city would normally increase the odds of a fight breaking out, I hoped Jake would stay out of it.

The NCAA had a very strict anti-fighting policy that would be met with an immediate game ejection and likely suspension to follow. Normally seeing a fight would excite me (two men on ice skates throwing punches itched a part of my brain I didn't want to admit I had), but now that I imagined Jake getting hurt, I couldn't get it out of my head. All I could do was picture the hundreds of ways in which something could go wrong tonight, and I hated how my anxious mind always found a way to taint even the happiest of moments.

A knock on the plexiglass in front of us brings me back to the moment.

Jake licks his lips as he notices me wearing his jersey. "Looking good, Ellie."

"Make sure to score some goals tonight or else. We can't have these Bolton players thinking they run this place."

"One hat trick just for you coming u—" Jake's shoulders tense and he snaps his head back. Following his gaze, I notice a

Bolton player standing behind him, running his mouth with mocking laughter. Though I can't hear what's being said, I don't miss the Bolton player pointing at me and then back at Jake.

"Jake, don't—" He skates away before I can talk some sense into him. Mercifully Adam intercepts Jake before he can reach the Bolton player and convinces him to warm up. While I'm grateful for the distraction, I know once Jake gets started, he won't stop. And it's only a matter of time before he explodes.

Chapter 38

Jake

There was a part of me that wanted to feel the nose of Bolton's star rookie shatter under my fist, but I'd managed to talk myself out of that idea. Freshman-year Jake would've called me a pussy for not challenging the Bolton player who had made it his mission to harass my linemates. If it wasn't for the NCAA's incredibly strict no-fighting policy I probably would have snapped ten minutes ago. But with my contract signing coming up, the last thing I wanted to do was jeopardize it by getting suspended. While I kept my fists to myself, I was putting a little more force into my body checks whenever a Bolton player got in my way. It was a rivalry game after all.

I'd seen red from the moment he opened his mouth in front of Eliana. But once the rookie saw that I wasn't taking the bait, he turned his attention to one of our freshmen — Tristan. I could see that every chirp the Bolton player threw at Tristan was getting to him. By the look on his face, it wouldn't be long before Tristan snapped. I pulled him aside and tried to tell him it wasn't worth it. Tristan was undeterred. Whatever the Bolton player had told him struck a nerve, and there was no going back. The second my puck hit the back of the net, with only two minutes left to play in the period, Tristan threw off his gloves and skated right up to the Bolton freshman.

Before I can pull Tristan away, he lets a fist fly for the center of the Bolton player's face. He keeps wailing away on the guy, and I know if I don't break this up now he'll regret this.

Skating behind Tristan, I wrap my arms around his torso and yank him back.

"Let go of me man!" he protests.

I shake my head. "You already won, and he's not worth any more of your time. Trust me."

"You need your captain to fight your battles for you, Tristan? Pathetic. And what happened to the Jake Keeley who used to knock guys out before he asked any questions? You're getting soft Keeley. Guess that's what happens when you're pussy whipped." Christ, this Bolton player was annoying.

A ref comes over and gently shoves the Bolton player back to his bench while I lead Tristan to ours. He heads straight to the locker room, knowing his game was over for tonight, and all he could do was hope that he wouldn't get suspended since this was his first fight of the season.

Tristan's fight causes a massive shift of energy to all the guys on the bench. Now not only did we want to embarrass our biggest rival, but also had a member of the team to avenge. Mason calls out a play and sends me back onto the ice with Adam. I win the face off, managing to send the puck over to Adam who only makes it to center ice before he takes a brutal body check that sends him flying. I have no doubt that hurt like crazy, but Adam refuses to show it, shrugging off the hit like it's nothing.

He takes the next face off but clearly he's a bit shaken up, resulting in a Bolton player being able to gain control of the puck. I chase after him, but it's futile. The Bolton forward fakes left, managing to confuse Ollie, and sends the puck to the back of our net. 0-1, Bolton.

"Fuck." Ollie screams slamming his stick against the net.

I skate over to him, "Don't let 'em rattle you. We'll get them back."

My words of motivation prove easier said than done. Bolton's defense is relentless, and laser focused on taking me out anytime I hit the ice. In the span of the second period, I get railed into the boards three times, all in an attempt to steal the puck from me. I relented each time, but I know for a fact I'm going to be sore as shit tomorrow. The end of the second period is a much-needed reprieve.

In the locker room, I immediately move to ice my shoulders. The rest of the team follows suit taking whatever ice packs our trainers provide. Adam refuses to leave any ground untouched and dunks his entire body into an ice bath. Mason and Coach Jameson take turns giving us a pep talk. Focusing on what they're saying is challenging as my entire body throbs in pain. I'm sure I can fill in the blanks of what I miss though. Likely how we need to keep our heads in the game and push through.

The third period starts off with the same of level of aggression as the first two, except this time I have all of Bolton's dirty moves spotted. Adam and I pass the puck back and fourth across the neutral zone until we finally cross into their territory. He attempts a shot, that rebounds off the goal post. I'm on it in a flash, sliding the puck between their goalie's legs before he has time to process. Tie game.

Normally goals would garner a much bigger celebration from the bench but the entire team is battered and bruised. Probably best we conserve our energy for what's left of this game. Whether I'm on the ice or catching my breath, one thing is clear — Bolton is not going down without a fight. With only two minutes left of the period and both teams primed and ready to rip each other's throats out, the hope of us ending this game early fades away with the time clicking on the clock. Or so I think.

One of the Bolton freshmen loses it after he has the puck stolen from him and trips our defensemen right in front of the goalie. The crowd goes insane as he gets sent into the sin bin, and we enter a powerplay.

I wave the boys over to huddle up, "Alright boys we're not going to rush this. Two minutes is more than enough time to get one goal and end this game without going into OT. We're going to force them to the inside. Closer and closer toward their goalie, until they're blocking most of his view. Then, whoever has the puck goes in for the kill. Sound good?"

Adam, and the rest of my linesmen, nod in response.

My initial game plan proves harder than I thought, with a Bolton senior managing to get control of the puck and ices it. I rush down the length of the arena and bring the puck back into their zone. The next minute is agonizing. Step by step, pass by pass, we inch closer and closer to the goal. Everytime I think we have an opening their goalie shifts, primed to stop our attempt. With 10 seconds left the crowd starts to get rowdy, yelling at us to shoot. I feel the puck hit my stick and in an hail mary attempt I send it flying toward the net. The Bolton goalie dives, closing his glove. Except when he opens it there's no puck inside — its buried in the side of their net.

The game ends and the arena goes crazy over beating our biggest rival. I lock eyes with Eliana as I skate back to the locker room and from the mix of pride in her eyes, all I want to do is rush over to her and start our post-game celebration early. First I had to get through our post game meeting.

Coach Jameson stands in front of all of us looking like he

went a few rounds himself on the ice. This was an important game for all of us, and the win couldn't feel sweeter. "I won't speak for too long because I know how exhausted you all must be. That was a hard-hitting game, with a lot more good moments than ugly. A win against your rival is nice. But not as nice as being champions. You remember that when I continue to push you all during practice next week. Shower and get some rest." Coach was never the type to let a win get to his head.

As the rest of my teammates file into the shower, Mason pulls me aside. "Can I talk to you for a second?"

That catches me by surprise. "What's up Coach?"

"That Bolton player was coming after you hot in the beginning. You okay?"

I blink. "Uh yeah. He was just a freshman with a mouth that didn't know when to quit."

"I'm surprised you weren't the one to shut him up."

"Trust me, I wanted to, but I realized it wasn't worth jeopardizing my future."

His eyes soften as he gives me a genuine smile. "You've come a long way since we first met Jake. I'm really proud of you."

Damn. "That means a lot coming from you Coach."

"Any chance you can rub off some of your maturity to Tristan? I'm going to talk to him after this but, I don't know if I've ever seen a kid go that hard before. Usually once you know you've won the fight you back off. Tonight you had to pull Tristan off."

"I tried to talk him down. I couldn't hear what the Bolton player was saying to him, but when he was chirping at me earlier, he spoke about someone I love. Someone who's off limits. I nearly snapped too. It's always hard when they come for someone you care about."

"It is. But it's also not worth getting hurt over. You never know which injury will become *the* injury."

I give him a nod. He would know better than anyone.

Mason smiles. "Well I should track down Tristan and see how he's doing. I know Coach Jameson has already pulled him into his office so—"

I wince. Poor kid.

"Yeah, my sentiments exactly. Keep up the good work Jake. I'm really proud of you" He pats me on the shoulder before heading out the locker room.

The pride I feel from his words are one of the things that keeps me going, after my entire body is screaming in pain. The other thing is the reality that soon, so soon, I'd be able to bury myself in Eliana's warm embrace, and pass out for the rest of the night.

Chapter 39

Jake

"Just to be clear, I'm still sitting shotgun, right?" Ollie asks me for the third time this morning.

"Yes, Oliver you can sit shotgun instead of my girlfriend. I promise she's not replacing you." I pat him on the shoulder in mock comfort as I continue to load our bags into my trunk.

"Excellent, because if you decided to switch up on me, I would've had to call you out for breaking bro code. Actually, I would've called you out for breaking up our *brotherhood* and ratted you out to the rest of the team."

"Not sure including the team would work out in your favor. The guys know how annoying it is to sit next to you on car rides."

"I am not annoying. I have the *best* road trip snacks," he protests.

"Yeah, and the worst-smelling road trip farts. Seriously man, you should get that checked out."

"Ha ha, very funny."

"I know. I'm a regular comedian. It's why Ellie loves me so much."

As if on cue, Eliana walks out of Hockey House with Josie in tow. I jog up the porch steps to help Josie, who's struggling to juggle all her bags.

"What do you have in there Jos'?" Eliana laughs as she hands me a bright pink backpack.

"Well I had to bring all my CDs and photocards since Sienna is going to be there. She told me the next time she sees me we can trade merch and have karaoke sessions. We'll be gone for five days, so I had to be prepared for anything."

"Wow you crammed all of that in one bag? That's pretty impressive—" I start.

"SIENNA!" Josie squeals as she runs towards my younger sister, who's coming out of my parent's car. When Sienna was younger she would always complain about not having a younger sister. Now that Josie is around, she finally gets her wish. And it's a role I know she's taken very seriously.

"Josie-Posie, I'm so happy to see you! I have all of ITZY's songs queued up for our road trip playlist!" Sienna leads Josie down the stairs and over to my parents and Charlotte so she can meet the whole family.

I take Eliana's bags off her shoulder and set them down before wrapping an arm around her waist and bringing her into my chest. "Sienna has been talking to me about karaoke nights all week, babe. My whole family's over the moon that you're both joining us." I place a small kiss on her forehead, relishing the way she tightens our hug.

"That makes me feel better about crashing your trip. I think I just have lingering anxiety from the semester that I need to expel." She gives me a sheepish smile.

"Well it's a good thing I have tons of rest and relaxation planned for us on this trip."

I managed to make it through the end of the semester as painlessly as possible, largely thanks to Eliana's help. While final grades for PSYCH101 hadn't been released yet, I felt fairly confident that I didn't fuck up the exam. Between helping me prepare for my exam, studying for her own, and still working in the lab, I knew Eliana was exhausted and ready to relax. Despite the chaos that happens on any family trip, I'm determined to make this the best Christmas for her and Josie.

"Do you need my help with planning anything?"

"Nope, I'm all set. I don't want you to have to worry about anything on this trip. Including bringing your wish list to life." In true form, Eliana emailed me a bulleted, color-coded, Christmas-themed to-do list earlier this week. She'd be thrilled to know I've been plotting away ever since.

"Music to my ears."

We stand there long enough for my whole family to come over and tease us. My mom and sisters get all their annoying but endearing comments in before we decide to hit the road.

"Is it alright if I drive up with you guys?" Sienna asks.

"Yup. You can sit in the back with Josie and Eliana." I respond, unlocking my car.

Ollie shakes his head and playfully smacks my shoulder. "C'mon man. I think your girlfriend should sit in the front, don't you?"

My eyebrows scrunch together. "I thought you wanted to sit next to me?"

"Jake, I love you and all, but we live together. I think I can manage not sitting *right* next to you." He grabs the door of the back seat and holds it open. "Josie, Sienna, after you."

My mouth hangs open as Ollie sits next to them, then shuts the door in my face. Wow. So much for bro code.

"You okay?" Eliana asks.

"Yeah, I just...Goalies are weird." We both get settled in the car before getting on the I-89 towards Vermont.

Sienna and Josie are quick to que up their favorite songs and require Ollie to learn the different dance moves.

I reach over and thread my fingers with Eliana's as she chews on her lip, likely overthinking about coming on this trip. "Hey, look at me."

She gives me a sheepish smile, realizing I caught her in an anxious spiral.

"I'm happy you're here, and I'm happy Josie is here. So is my entire family. The only thing you need to be worried about is whether we're building a snowman or star gazing first."

I get an eye roll in response, but I can see the tension slowly leaving her shoulders. She takes a quick glance at the back seat, finding Sienna and Josie deep in conversation, before she fully relaxes, leaning her head against the window as she falls asleep.

Chapter 40

Eliana

"Babe, we're here." Jake presses a kiss to my temple, and I wake up to him holding the car door open for me.

"Where's Josie?" I yawn, noticing the empty car.

"In the lobby with my family, they're checking us in."

"Lobby?" I freeze in place, finally taking in my surroundings. To my left was a ski lift, currently carrying dozens of people up the mountain. On my right was not one but *three* massive skating rinks, and in front of me was a massive building that made the Four Seasons look like a budget motel. "I thought you said your family rented a small cabin."

"We do have a cabin...Sort of...It's just a cabin-styled suite. And small is in the eyes of the beholder." He winks, dragging me inside before I can protest.

Josie comes barreling towards me and catches me up to speed. Or really screams in excitement about the fact that she was called "Madame" and handed a hot chocolate with whipped cream as soon as she walked through the doors. Sienna's the one to inform me that our luggage has been taken to our cabin suite and that, if I need to, I can borrow one of her dresses for dinner tonight at the upscale restaurant inside the lodge.

I squeeze Jake's hand so hard he winces.

"Why don't you all head over to the cabin and Eliana and I will join you in a little bit?" Jake calls out to our families before pulling me aside to a remote corner of the lobby. He lets me start.

"Jacob Keeley."

"Actually my legal first name is Jake. Not Jacob. I'll let you call me Jacob any day of the week though." He winks.

"Stop trying to be funny."

"Aww you think I'm funny?" he teases.

I shake my head. "No."

"Then why did your lip just twitch?"

"It does that when I'm angry."

"Are you sure?"

"Positive," I deadpan.

"Well now my feelings are hurt. You really don't think I'm funny? How will I ever recover?"

"Well I'm sure we can find a famous comedian in one of the *thousands* of rooms in this place to help you. If we start looking now, maybe we'll be able to finish checking all the rooms by the end of this week."

"Ah so we've circled back to the root of the problem. You don't like this resort?"

Guilt fills my chest as I take in his solemn expression. "The resort is beautiful Jake. It's seriously the nicest place I've ever seen."

"Then what's the problem?" He cocks his head.

The problem is I have never been in a place this expensive, and I have no idea how I can ever pay your parents back— breathe, Eliana. Jake has put in so much effort to make this trip special and to create some time to relax. The least I can do is just try to have fun.

I shake my head. "There's no problem. I'm sorry. I just made some assumptions about what this trip was going to look like, which is my fault. This is amazing, Jake. More than amazing. Truly."

He gives me a soft smile. "I brought you here because you deserve something special. My family always treats this trip as prime time to relax and decompress. I just thought after spending the past twenty-one years taking care of yourself and Josie, you've more than earned a week of relaxation. You deserve a week where you get to experience what it's like to prioritize yourself."

"I love your heart and your kindness, Jake. But I don't want you to put all this extra pressure on yourself to make me happy. Life is filled with stress, and that's okay. As long as I have you by my side."

He presses a soft kiss to my forehead. "Fair enough. Would you at least like to know what I have planned for the rest of the week?"

There's a part of me that screams "YES", but I remind myself that I want to be more spontaneous and go with the flow. And that started with letting go of to-do lists and calendar events. "Nope. You can just surprise me. I know whatever you have planned will be great."

"Just you wait and see what I have in store. I've taken the homework assignment of making this the best Christmas ever very seriously."

"Glad you hear it. Because if you hadn't, I would have to have a word with your tutor." I laugh as he wraps an arm around my shoulder and leads me to our suite.

Chapter 41

Eliana

"So did I do a good job?" Jake's soothing voice echoes off the thin glass walls of the star-gazing room. Because of course this hotel had everything I could ever want all in one place. When Jake opened the door and pulled me inside, I nearly burst into tears at the sheer magnitude of beauty in front of me.

"I can't even remember the last time I was able to see this many stars. I could lay here forever." I give his hand a squeeze while I rest my head on his chest, the two of us spread out on the padded floor.

He extends his other arm to point out more constellations. "That right there is Orion's Belt."

"It's stunning." I let out a content breath. Pointing to the three stars to the left, I ask, "What's that one?"

"Umm...his helmet?" Jake's uncertainty draws a laugh from me.

"Mmm, something tells me that's not quite right."

"Well, I never claimed to be an astrologer."

"Astronomer," I correct

"Same difference."

"You're right, they're practically interchangeable careers," I laugh.

Jake winks, "I'm an Aries and you're a Gemini."

"Interesting. Do you know what that means? I barely know what my big three are."

Jake purses his lips. "When we first started dating, or technically fake-dating, Sienna mentioned to me that Aries and Gemini are historically very compatible."

"Oh. Well, that's good to know." Heat rises to my cheeks. "So Sienna's really into astrology?"

"Yeah, she went through a whole phase last summer. Made star charts for all of us and even spent hours on the phone haggling with some poor admin hospital staff trying to get my exact birth time because it wasn't printed on my birth certificate."

"Damn. Now that's some dedication."

"She was determined to get mine right because she was quote, 'Tired of my whoreish ways and wanted me to find a match that would get me in line and also love me.'"

I struggle to hold back my laugh. "Sienna never holds back, does she?"

"Not for a second. She may be the youngest, but she is the loudest. And maybe the biggest hot head."

"That's funny. I would've guessed that position belonged to you, but you managed to keep your temper in check during the Bolton game."

Jake tenses slightly under me while he clenching his hand into a fist. He refused to tell me what was said, which does little to appease my suspicions that it was about me.

"Can you tell me what the Bolton player said to you?"

"Just a bunch of bullshit. Nothing you need to be concerned with."

"I think if it was about me, which I suspect it was, then it *is* my concern."

He lets out a long sigh before bringing us into a seated position and pulling me onto his lap. Jake takes a loose strand of my hair in between his fingers to toy with, avoiding my eyes. "Any chirps I get on the ice that are about me go in one ear and out the other. Comments about my loved ones however... get under my skin. If the Bolton player had come at me a few years ago, I definitely would have gotten to him before Tristan did."

"I'm glad you didn't go after him. He's not worth risking your health over."

Jake takes a deep breath and gives me a tight smile before whispering, "The Bolton player who fought with Tristan, was basically running his mouth about us. He insinuated the only reason you would be into me is because of my money, and said he would pay you later to sleep with him."

My heart drops to my stomach. Though I knew Jake's family was better off financially than mine was, I never actually thought about how much more money they had. I knew once I agreed to fake date, and then real date, Jake, it would be an uphill battle of handling other people's perceptions of me, especially once I officially started working for Katherine this summer. No doubt I'll run into people who think the only reason I was hired was because I was dating her son. It was going to be a struggle not to let those comments get to me, but I'd been slowly preparing myself (largely due to my therapist pushing me to do so). Looks like Stephanie and I should add "How to not care what other people think when they know nothing about you" to our list of things I need to work on.

"Ellie?" Jake's apprehensive voice brings me back.

"Sorry. Just had a little moment. That guy's a dick, who cares what he says."

Jake doesn't seem too convinced by my attempt to come off

as unbothered. "I love you, Eliana. And I would do anything for you."

"I know you would Jake..." While his words are meant to comfort me, the frown on my face only deepens. I didn't want him to feel like he had to fix all of my problems in order to show his love for me. Not only is that an impossible ask, but I can handle myself. I can admit I have a bad habit of neglecting my own needs, and I may have sent him some mixed messages when I accepted his groceries or let him cook dinner for me when I was feeling lazy. But I wanted him to know he didn't have to do any of those things for me to love him.

"What is it?"

"I don't want this to come off as ungrateful or unappreciative because I love how thoughtful and caring you are, but there's been a few times now where you've mentioned wanting to remove all of the stress in my life and that's just not realistic. There's going to be things you can't protect me from, and that's okay. And just because I had some rough moments growing up, doesn't mean it's on you to fix them. That would be incredibly unfair to you."

"But I like doing those things for you."

I lift my hand and place it on his heart. "I know you do. Trust me, you're preaching to the choir here. Which is why I want to have this conversation. From one person who loves taking care of people, to another, I don't want you to burn yourself out taking care of me."

He places a hand ontop of mine. "I hear you Ellie, I do."

I give him a soft kiss, and shift back to stargazing. We sit content in each other's arms, laughing at our failed attempts at pointing out constellations in the night sky, until Jake's phone vibrates and brings us back to reality. "It's Sienna. She said we should probably head back and start getting ready for dinner."

"I thought we were just grabbing dinner in the hotel's restaurant?"

"We are, but they have a dress code that's a bit strict."

"Strict?" Shit. I had a feeling strict was code for "really formal" and the nicest thing I brought on this trip were my extra thermal LL Bean boots.

"Don't worry Sienna and Charlotte brought a bunch of extra clothes you can borrow. And a surprise for Josie."

I try my hardest to let Jake's words comfort me and silence the voice in my head that's screaming and wondering, what the hell did I get myself into coming on this trip?

"Eliana, you have to see this. It's the cutest thing ever." Sienna drags me inside her and Charlotte's room inside the massive suite. Josie is posing in front of a full-length mirror, decked out in a sparkly plaid pink jacket and skirt combo.

When she notices me, she breaks out into a massive smile and gives me a spin. "Ellie! Look at the outfit Sienna got me. I feel like I'm ready to rock a red carpet." She poses in front of the mirror as I try to stifle my laugh.

"Sienna, you really didn't have to—"

"It's a Christmas gift! Santa just came a few days early. Now, let's get big sis sorted. Josie and I thought long and hard about this, and we landed on evergreen being your color. Not that you don't look incredible in other colors, but we really think this one is absolutely meant for you."

Sienna slides open the closet door and pulls out the most stunning velvet dress I've seen in my life. The soft material goes on for days, and from the shape of the dress, I can tell it would hug me in all the right places. I can't even stop myself from taking the hanger from Sienna's hands and holding it in front of me as I face the mirror. "It's stunning."

"And it'll go perfectly with these shoes." Josie peaks her head in and lays down a pair of black heels with red bottoms in front of me.

My heart squeezes as I take in her excitement. We didn't have a lot of moments where we could do simple things like dress up and just be sisters. So much of our relationship was me stepping up to serve as the responsible mom, and sometimes it was hard to step back and enjoy the moments where I could be a normal older sister.

"It's perfect. This is all perfect." I beam while turning around to bring Josie and Sienna into a massive hug.

"Then go get dressed so I can do your makeup. Time is money!"

I lay the outfit on the bed and walk into the bathroom so Sienna can apply my makeup. If I spent this long on my makeup, I know I'd look like a clown. Before I can say as much to Sienna, she's hitting me with the setting spray. She refuses to let me look in the mirror until I have the dress on. Jake stumbles in a moment later with a wicked smile on his face, as his eyes wander down the length of my body.

"Sienna drew a mustache on my face didn't she?"

"You're so beautiful," he whispers, cradling my face in his hands. His words and besotted expression make me feel like the most special person in the whole world. Even with my heels on, I still need to stretch a bit as I lean in to kiss him.

I'm yanked away by Sienna before our lips can connect. "Oh no, you're not ruining all my hard work. Plus, we're already running late."

Jake lets out an annoyed noise and sends me a wink as we all shuffle out the room and to the restaurant.

Chapter 42

Eliana

"Why is the center pink?" Josie leans over as she attempts to whisper.

"It's a filet mignon. What did you think it was going to look like?"

"I don't know! It sounded fancy and everyone else got it, so I figured it would be yummy."

"It's just medium rare. Totally safe to eat." I try to console her.

"Rare? Like uncooked?!" She crinkles her nose, and I swear she starts to turn green.

Worrying my lip in between my teeth, I search desperately for a waiter and hope that Jake's parents don't notice. The last thing I wanted was to make a scene or have them think we didn't appreciate their hospitality.

"Hey Josie, wanna trade?" Jake reaches over to swap Josie's plate for another piled with chicken tenders, fries, and ranch. Her favorite.

"You see Jake, I knew I always liked you." Josie beams.

I stifle a snort, remembering their first interaction. Jake reaches underneath the table and gives my hand a squeeze.

"I didn't even know that was an option. When did you order chicken tenders?"

"When the waiter announced that the main course was a filet mignon and you looked like you were about to have an aneurysm. I asked the waiter if there was something else the kitchen could whip up for picky eaters. Now, eat your dinner before *I* have an aneurysm about you not eating enough." He nods his chin to my untouched dinner.

Thankfully the rest of meal, including an absolutely delightful Baked Alaska, goes off without a hitch. Jake's mom and Charlotte kept the interrogations to a minimum and instead spend most of the night talking to me about my research interests and goals. To some, that may have felt equally as stressful, but for me, I just felt excited. And understood. My mom never once asked me what my career goals were. All she needed to know was that I was getting a degree that would support me and the rest of us. It felt so comforting talking to other people who understood what I was going through and all the politics of our field.

Beyond the moments when I felt understood, it also warmed my heart to see how close Jake's entire family is. I was struck by the adoring glances his father gave to his wife and children, the genuine interest Sienna and Charlotte had in Jake's season, and the way they made an effort to ensure Josie and I felt included the entire time.

As the hours of conversation continue, I look over my shoulder and notice Josie passed out on the table, leftover chocolate syrup from dessert on her chin. "Josie-Posie, should we head upstairs?" My attempt to shake her awake fails. She was always able to sleep through anything and everything.

"I can take her if you want," Sienna offers.

"Oh, it's fine—"

"Stay. I can tell you want to. I was just about to head up, so it's no problem."

"Are you sure?"

"Yup not a problem." Sienna shakes Josie until she's awake.

"I think I'm also going to call it a night. I'll see you all tomorrow." Ollie smiles. My eyes flicker to Jake, assessing whether he was seeing what I did. From the clueless look on his face, that would be a negative. Seems like he missed the fact that his best friend clearly has had a crush on his younger sister. Maybe for the best. As much as Jake calls me a momma bear when it comes to Josie, he's equally as protective of Sienna.

Ollie stands from his seat, lifting Josie with ease, and following Sienna's lead as she guides them back to my room.

"First soldier of the night down," Charlotte teases. "I know we can be a lot, so I can't say I'm surprised we tired her out. You still hanging in there, Ellie?"

"You can't get rid of me yet, though I do feel a little stiff after all this sitting."

"Why don't you kids head to the bar and bring us all back something fun? A good excuse to stretch the legs." Katherine offers.

"Don't act like I haven't seen the looks Dad's been giving you all night. You two just want an excuse to make out without us around." Jake rolls his eyes, while Charlotte makes a gagging noise.

We head to the back and stand behind a crowd of middle-aged men waiting for their drinks. Admittedly, I loved people watching, especially when I hear the group in front of us talking about plot devices, how tricky it could be to write in the third person, and having to Google instructions on how to decompose a body. My eyes fixate on the older woman in front of me who looks incredibly familiar for some reason...*Holy shit.*

"Excuse me, so sorry to bother you...Are you Margaret Haywood?" I ask, internally pinching myself.

The woman's eyes crinkle as she gives me a soft smile. "I sure am."

Oh.My.God. It's really her. "I'm such a big fan of your writing. *A Murder in Briarwood Manor* literally changed my life. I started plotting my own book after reading it. It's a romantic suspense where she's forced to marry the guy that she believes killed her father all while having to prove he did it," I gush.

"That's sounds super interesting. I'm assuming you're joining us for this writing retreat? I know my assistant mentioned a few people would be arriving later tonight."

"Oh! No. I didn't realize there was a retreat going on. That sounds amazing." I sigh dreamily.

"Well, we did also have some people drop out last minute so there are a few spots open if you're interested. Only requirement is to have a draft of a book ready which sounds like you have. We're meeting in the conference room by the lobby tomorrow at 9 a.m. sharp."

"I...wow. That's an amazing offer. I would love to I just don't know what my schedule for tomorrow—"

"She'll be there. Don't you worry," Jake cuts in, giving me a smile.

"Excellent. Well I look forward to talking more then..."

"Eliana." I put out my hand.

Margaret laughs softly as she puts out hers to shake. "Eliana. Happy to have you join us." She takes her drink from the bartender and gives me a small wave goodbye.

I'm frozen in place as Jake places his hands on my shoulder. "Ellie this is amazing. Look at you putting yourself out there."

"I—I can't believe that just happened. I just saw her and started babbling and next thing I know I'm attending a retreat with Margaret Haywood. *The* Margaret Haywood, I just... I can't go." I shake my head.

Jake's eyebrows knit together. "Umm, why not?"

"Jake, you had this whole list of things planned for us! I can't just abandon you."

"You wouldn't be. All the things I had planned for tomorrow were centered around you doing things for yourself, and I can't think of anything more Eliana that finally getting to write the book she's been thinking of with her favorite author. I'll just hit the slopes with Ollie."

"Are you sure?"

"Positive. So long as you promise that I'll get to be the first person to read your book when it's done."

"Deal."

"Deal." He smiles, lacing our fingers together as he orders drinks for us. I lean my head against his shoulder, and for the first time in long time instead of worrying about all the things in my life, I find myself hopeful for what's to come.

Chapter 43

Jake

"**A**re you sure we're allowed to be in here?" Eliana's eyes are wide as saucers as she takes in the commercial kitchen.

"Positive. This is their spare kitchen they have in case of big events. My dad used to bake cookies down here all the time when we were kids. He had a special understanding with the chef and hotel owner. I would say we helped with the baking, but really the one time we tried I ended up covered head to toe in flour. Sienna slipped and dropped all the eggs and Charlotte nearly had a panic attack over the mess we made."

"And your mom?"

"Laughing in the background the whole time and taking pictures of the chaos. One of them became our Christmas card the following year." I roll my eyes thinking back fondly to the countless number of holidays we spent here.

"Cute. Josie and I make those Pillsbury sugar cookies that have festive designs on them." Eliana smiles.

"Oof sounds like I'm up against tough competition. Hopefully I can pull off this recipe with some of the finesse my dad had."

"As long as I don't end up covered in batter or with food poisoning, I'll consider it a win."

I pull out the tattered recipe card from my pocket and set it on the countertop in front of me. "Four generations of Keeley's used this this little thing. Hasn't steered me wrong yet."

"Well put me to work." Eliana smiles, tying her hair up.

I grab one of the loose curls between my fingers and tuck it behind her ear before handing her an apron.

"Spices are on that shelf right there." I point to her left. "Can you hand me cinnamon, nutmeg, clove, and salt? I'll get the flour, sugar, and bowls."

"Yes, chef." She winks.

"Ellie, only you can make a simple word sound so dirty."

"It's not my fault you have such a perverted mind." She laughs as I reach over and smack her ass. "See. *I'm* not the problem here."

"We'll agree to disagree." I start to lay out the various ingredients and cookware. We breeze through the rest of the preparation. Eliana helps me by making the gingerbread cookie dough with the precision and determination of a surgeon. I reach out and rub my thumb on the crease between her eyebrows that always forms when she's deep in concentration.

She relaxes into my touch before taking the tray of cookie dough and placing it inside the freezer to firm up. "I can't believe we're actually making a gingerbread house."

"We still have to shape the dough, cook it, and stick it all together, so maybe hold off on the celebration." I'd try my best to pull this off, but I didn't want to over-promise either. Frankly, I wouldn't be surprised if our house ended up being more of a lopsided tent situation.

"Well, still. I appreciate you helping me cross something off my bucket list."

"Of course. So no regrets doing this over skiing?" I check, already knowing the answer. Eliana had immediately turned green when I told her what my family had planned for today.

"Definitely not. I manage to hurt myself walking on flat surfaces. The last thing I need is to get on a mountain with gear I have no idea how to use. Recipe for disaster."

"I guess I don't have to ask who the daredevil is between you and your sister."

"Definitely Josie. Wouldn't be surprised if she's out there crushing the adults on some super scary slopes. I was also the more anxious and practical one. Such is the burden of the eldest daughter."

Her tone is light, but I know the truth behind her words. I've seen it first-hand with how she's had to step in as a second parent for Josie, and also pick up as many odd jobs as she can to help support her family. I hoped this week could show her that it's okay to take time for herself. That doing things that made her happy didn't make her selfish.

The writing retreat yesterday was a good start. She had come back to the hotel suite that evening with such excitement and light in her eyes. We'd spent our time at dinner discussing the chapters she had written, the advice she got from Margaret, and how she hoped to keep writing when we got back. I loved hearing her talk like that. About a future where she finally makes time for herself.

DING! The sound of the timer brings me back to the current moment. "Alright looks like it's time to put our artistic skills to the test."

We do a pretty solid job of carving out the pieces of the house, baking the cookies, and putting it together without it crumbling. Eliana and I take turns decorating the gingerbread house with icing, covering the roof with a layer of white to resemble snow, and she's kind enough to let me spoon the remaining icing into my mouth while she adds some multicolored gumdrops to the roof as a final touch.

"Perfect." Eliana beams up at me.

"We should send this in as our audition for the *Great British Baking Show*," I tease, wrapping my arms around her waist and tucking her into my side, resting my chin on top of her head.

"Mmm not sure if making one dessert means we're ready. Plus, we're not British. Maybe we can aim for the American spin-off? After we practice some more?" She winks.

"Fine. Fine. I suppose learning some other recipes wouldn't be the worst idea." I pause before gently broaching the real reason we were in this kitchen. "So how do we feel finally taking a few days for yourself?"

Eliana shuts her eyes and lets out a deep breath. "Like I really, *really* needed it." Her eyebrows scrunch together like she's fighting with herself over the admission.

"What's going on in that head of yours?"

"Just how amazing this trip has been, and how I wish I could continue taking time for myself when we get back."

"Wish? Why can't you just do it?" I try my best to keep my tone curious and nonjudgmental.

"I'm just not sure if it makes sense with how my life is now. I'd love to have more time for myself, but I have to help my family. Not just for Josie's sake, but also for my mom."

"So you take care of everyone else except for yourself? That's not fair to you Ellie." I try not to let my frustration come out. Eliana's heart was one of my favorite things about her, but her selflessness usually came at the price of her own happiness.

"It's always been the three of us. And my mom works hard but it's not enough on her own, so I have to step up." She takes in my frustrated expression. "Don't worry, one day I'll be an established professor, with a salary to match, and will be able to better balance supporting my family and doing things for myself. We'll plan an annual trip to the Bahamas during your off-season."

I notice her deflection and instead of letting it slide, I call it out. "Can I be real with you for a second?"

"Oh boy. Why do I feel like I'm in trouble?" She lets out an uncomfortable laugh. "Go for it."

"You always talk about how right now is a bad time for you to live your life, but is there ever going to be a good time? You've said it yourself, life always finds a way to throw you curve balls and it's impossible to get rid of things that stress you out. Which means there's never going to be a perfect moment when you can do things for yourself. No one is going to force you to take a break or tell you to take time for yourself. You have to be the one to set those boundaries for yourself and stick to them." I can't say I exactly enjoyed giving Eliana some tough love, but deep down, I know she needs to hear it.

She places her hands on the table in front of her, eyes cast down. She lets out a long, deep breath before nodding her head and looking up at me. "You're right. I keep putting off things I want to do, hoping I'll get to them someday but knowing that day may never come. I need to stop doing that...I will stop doing that. Or at least I'll try really hard to."

"You can do it. You can do anything you set your mind to. That much I'm sure of." I wrap my arms around her waist and bring her into my arms, tucking her head under my chin.

She gives me a tight squeeze in response. "Who knows, maybe this time next year I'll have my book finished, and we can celebrate by going to the Bahamas or something tropical. Pending that works with your game schedule."

"Already prepping for my time in the NHL now are we?"

"Of course. I'm not the only one who's working like crazy to pull off my dreams. I hope you know I see how much effort you put into hockey, and that I'll always support you."

I feel my heart swell at her words. "I know. Your heart, and how you have my back, are two of many things I love so much about you."

Pressing my lips to her cheek, I relish in the heat and faint shade of red on her cheeks.

"You just really know how to make a girl feel special, don't you?" She steps up on her toes to place a kiss on my lips.

"I try my best, but it's not that hard given how incredible you are," I whisper into her shoulder.

A shudder runs through her body, and I don't miss her attempts at trying to hide the tears forming in her eyes. "You're turning me into a ball of mush."

"I always knew there was something under your tough exterior."

"Even when you thought I was a drill sergeant?"

My lips turn to a smirk, remembering our first few encounters. "Even then."

Chapter 44

Eliana

My trip with Jake allowed me to reset from the chaos of the past semester. The entire trip felt straight out of a Hallmark holiday movie – magical, heartwarming, and filled with feel-good moments, including roasting s'mores by the campfire and laughing about our favorite Christmas memories. It also made me realize that it was okay for me do things for myself now instead of putting them off. Granted that was much easier said than done. Which is why when we made it back home I planned on adding some reoccurring self-care and book-writing events in my calendar. Nothing held me more accountable than my gcal.

My mom was waiting for us when we got back, eyes tired. She still greeted us at the door with a smile on her face.

"C'mon in. Jake it's so good to finally meet you." She places a kiss on each cheek, a traditional way that moms greet visitors in our culture, which I totally forgot to warn him about.

To Jake's credit, he just rolls with it, adding a hug at the end. "Ms. Jasper, it's really nice to finally meet you. I've heard so much about you."

"Likewise. I really appreciate you taking care of my girls, and for extending an invitation to me. I wish I could've been there, but I got caught up with work. Please take a seat, I know you had a long drive. Let me get you some tea. Eliana can you help me in the kitchen?" She turns her back to me before I can respond.

Josie and Jake get settled as I walk down the hall. By the time I make it to the kitchen, my mom is already spooning black tea into the pot, filling it with water, and placing it on the stove. She finally turns around and gives me a smile, though it doesn't meet her eyes.

Uh oh. I doubt this was going to end well.

"*So did you have a good time?*" she asks in Farsi. Because she didn't want Jake to be able to listen in? Or was I reading into things too much?

Regardless, I respond in her native tongue. "*It was great. His family really took care of us.*"

"That's great, honey. I'm glad you got to relax." She purses her lips like she's holding back, but she doesn't say more, so I continue giving her a recap.

"I even ran into one of my favorite authors and got to spend some time with her, while writing my book. I'm hoping to keep working on it now that I'm back."

"*Wow. How cool. Just be sure not to neglect your responsibilities. The book is a fun hobby, but you need to focus on your schoolwork and building a stable career for yourself,*" she cautions.

Ouch. Not quite the words of support I was looking for. "*Don't worry. I promise I still have my priorities straight.*"

"*Good. That's all that matters.*" She nods.

Okay, what gives? My mom was never one to stop at a few-word responses. "*Why does it feel like you're holding back? What are you not saying?*"

She worries her bottom lip between her teeth before she starts. *"I just want to make sure you keep your head on straight. When I first met your dad, I was enamored by him. His looks, his charm, his finances. I was easily wowed by all the expensive gifts and jewelry he would get me. But over time, that charm faded, and by the time I realized I had given up some of my best years for a man who never truly loved me...it was too late. I missed out on going to college and building my career. I gained you and Josie, which are the biggest accomplishments of my life, but I lost myself. And I don't want the same thing to happen to you."*

"Jake is nothing like Dad. He loves that I have my own dreams and aspirations. He's one of my biggest cheerleaders. You don't have to worry about him. Or me losing myself in him. I promise."

"I'm always going to be worried about you. You're my child. A mother's fear about all the awful things that can happen to her children never goes away. I know you might think I'm being dramatic, but I just wanted to be honest with you. Treat me like a cautionary tale on what not to do in a relationship."

I appreciate where she's coming from, but our circumstances were entirely different. The only similarity between my dad and Jake is that they both came from wealthy families. There aren't a ton of things my mom and I have in common, but one thing we did share was how touchy we became when discussions about money were involved. I couldn't blame her for being a bit sensitive about Jake coming from a different financial situation than us. Being around money was also something that made me uncomfy.

"Once you get to know Jake, you'll see what I see Mom."

"I look forward to it." She places her hand on my cheek and strokes it. "You make me so proud you know. Being the first woman in our family to go to college. Doing your fancy and complicated research that I can never understand. My smart

girl. You are proof that I was able to do something right in the world. Do something good."

A high-pitched noise from the tea pot draws my mom's attention. Turning off the stove, she pours the boiling tea into traditional glasses and sets them on a tray. "*Can you grab the Nabat please?*" She references the saffron rock candy commonly served with tea. "*I'll see you out there.*"

Her serious tone shifts to cheery, and I really see her inability to let strangers see how much she was hurting. I have no doubt our Middle Eastern culture, and the emphasis on keeping our emotions to ourselves, was the largest contributing factor to this personality trait which only made it harder to shake. Fighting against all you know, even when it hurts you, is never an easy feat.

"*Sure.*" I nod, taking my time as I sift through the shelves. Unlike my mother, I needed some extra time to stitch myself back together. By the time I finally enter the living room, everyone has finished their drinks with my tea, now room temperature, being the only one left on the tray.

Unsurprisingly, Jake and my mom seem to be hitting it off exceptionally well. I can't remember the last time I heard a genuine laugh come from my mom's mouth.

Josie shoots me a reassuring smile and thumbs up that he's managed to win our mom over. The news releases some of the tension from my shoulders. Long car rides always did a number on me, and having an emotional conversation with my mom didn't make things any easier. Jake must have noticed the tiredness in my eyes because a few minutes after I sat down, he came up with an excuse for why we had to head back to campus. He gets a big hug from Josie and a kiss on both cheeks from my mom as we walk out the door and get in his car.

"Your mom seems amazing. It was really great getting to meet her." He grabs my hand and brings it to his lips.

"Seems like you've managed to win over all three Jasper women." I smile. Or at least two and a half. My mom would get fully on board eventually.

"You excited to get back home and start writing about burying bodies or whatever it is you're planning for the plot twist?"

His excitement makes my heart skip, and I try to shut out my mom's voice, reminding me not to lose focus. "Yeah it'll be fun. Though I think I'm too tired to write tonight. Maybe tomorrow."

He looks at me from the side of his eye. "That makes sense. Well, I can't wait to get my hands on your first full draft. I know it's going to be great."

"Soon. You'll get it soon." I wanted to believe the words that came from my mouth, but the conversation I had with my mom played in my head over and over again. I couldn't lose sight of what was really important, not just for me but for my family. I give Jake a small smile and lay my head on his shoulder as he drives us through winding roads and pine trees covered in snow, until my heavy eyes shut and I fall asleep.

Chapter 45

Eliana

Something must have happened. That's the only possible explanation. I stare at my phone, re-reading the text exchange with my mom and waiting for the words on the screen to magically change. I pinch myself to make sure this isn't some weird dream.

Me: Might be a day or two late in sending money this week. There's been a delay with student employment, sorry.

Mom: Don't worry about it. No need to send any more. We're all set.

Did she win the lottery and not tell me? Decide to finally take her chances at a casino and win big? Or is she having one of her fleeting moments of shame about relying on her daughter for support? The first two options were incredibly unlikely, and the last one was also unrealistic. I had entirely too many questions and not enough answers. Taking a deep and centering breath, I talk myself out of calling my mom now and demanding an explanation. There was no way I would be able to keep my tone calm and not ask questions that would result in her getting mad, or at the very least annoyed, at me.

While a part of me wanted to relish in the fact that my bank account was now looking a lot less sad since I could use the remaining money for myself, the rational part of my brain told me not to put the cart before the horse. So instead of balling out at the Beanery, I made some overly bitter drip coffee, and poured it into two to-go cups. Then I headed towards the hockey arena.

Jake was wrapping up his pregame practice as I walked across campus, and by the time I made it to the arena, he was waiting in the lobby for me. I feel my chest squeeze as his eyes light up when I walk in. A moment later, I'm engulfed in his warm embrace, and a chill runs down my neck as he presses a soft kiss to my neck, feeling his damp hair brush against my chin.

He gleefully grabs one of the travel coffee mugs from my hand, takes a large sip and clearly tries not to gag. His attempt to spare my feelings was appreciated, despite the expression of disgust he was currently rocking.

"That bad, huh?".

"What? No. Not at all." He takes another large gulp as if to prove his point. It did the opposite as he started to turn a little green.

"Alright. Alright. I think that's enough for you. I promise I won't be offended if you don't finish my coffee. And I'd rather not be responsible for you puking on the ice."

"I've had my fair share of showing up hungover to practice, so wouldn't be the first time."

My nose crinkles. "Gross."

"Admittedly the aftermath wasn't pretty. Not to mention how pissed Coach Jameson was."

He pulls me into the now-empty locker room. My face warms at the memory of the last time we were alone here. Jake's mind must immediately go to the same place because he leans down and whispers into my ear, "Don't get any crazy ideas now. Most of the staff is across the hall and there's no way I'll be able to stay quiet with you wrapped around me."

I trip over my own feet and elbow Jake in the ribs as he laughs at my expense. I'd get him back for that.

Jake sits me down on the bench next to his locker as he finishes packing up his bag. "How's your day been so far?

"Mostly normal except for this text I got from my mom." For a moment I think I see his back stiffen.

"Is she okay?" he asks. Hmm, nothing weird in his voice. Must have imagined the tension then.

"Um, I think so? I told her I'd be late in sending her money this week, and she said she didn't need it." Which still wasn't adding up to me.

"Huh. Did she say why?" Jake places a kiss on my cheek as he takes a seat next to me.

"Nope. I debated asking her, but money is always a touchy subject and I know if I pry, I could upset her, and I don't want to do that."

"That makes sense." He taps his knee against mine.

"I don't know how much longer I can hold out on asking her about it though. None of this makes sense. I just really hope that she's not taking on even more work so she won't have to ask me for money. She already does so much..." Burying my head into my hands, I let out the breath I was holding in.

Jake places his hand on the back of my neck, then moves it down lower to massage my shoulders, squeezing the tension out of them. "What are the odds she found a hidden treasure chest in the backyard?"

My lips twitch, appreciating his effort in trying to lighten the mood. "Given the fact it's the dead of winter and there's no way she'd be able to shovel through solid ground, I'd say none."

"Hmm maybe your mom's a secret assassin who received an

offer she couldn't refuse and decided to come out of retirement for one night."

"Jake, be serious."

"I am! Don't underestimate her. When we first met, she had her eyes locked on me with laser precision. If she wanted to kill me. she totally could."

"You can be so annoying sometimes, did you know that?"

"Is that why you're holding back a smile right now?"

"I am not." My stoic face lasts all of a second before I let out a laugh. "Don't mistake my laughter for joy. I am still very stressed and anxious right now."

"That might just be your permanent state, my love." He presses a kiss to my forehead. "What would your therapist say in a moment like this?"

"That short of having a crystal ball, I can't know for sure what has happened with my mom, and that most of the times I've predicted something bad happening, it ended up being fine or at least nowhere near as catastrophic as I thought it would be."

"Well there you go. Let's ride this wave of joy for a moment."

"Yeah I guess you're right." I wanted nothing more than to believe my own words, but I couldn't stop the nagging feeling in my gut that my world was about to be turned upside down. And all I could do was brace myself for the storm that was to come.

Chapter 46

Eliana

"Your heart's beating a million miles a minute," I state, my ear pressed to Jake's chest as he wraps my loose curls around his finger.

"That's because I have a pretty girl curled up next to me. Whenever she's around, my mind and body go crazy." Jake smirks, pressing a kiss to the crown of my head.

"Good deflection. You sure it has nothing to do with the Hockey East championships tonight?"

His eyes wander around his bedroom, never meeting mine. "Nope, I'm as cool as a cucumber."

Knowing better than to push someone when they were about to go through one of the biggest moments of their lives, I let it be. "Well, I know you're going to kill it tonight, but if you want to talk, I'm here."

We lay in silence long enough for me to slowly fade into sleep, when his voice brings me back. "What if I cost us the game?"

Of all the things he could've said about tonight, this was the last thing I would've expected. It had taken a while, but Jake had slowly let me in on all his insecurities over the past few months. How he felt like the black sheep of his family, how he didn't want to be known as just another athlete who had nothing else going for him. In all the moments he had opened up, he had never once doubted his skills as a hockey player. He was one of the few members of Westchester's team that was already drafted to the NHL and would be signing his contract at the end of this season. He had no reason to doubt his abilities and yet here he was.

"Why would you say that?"

"I don't know. It just feels like so much is riding on this game. More than usual. We haven't made it this close to qualifying for the Frozen Four or even making it to the Hockey East Championship in years. Everyone's hungry for it. We've been going hard practice after practice, game after game. But nothing's guaranteed. One stupid decision is all it takes to cost us this game. This could be my last game with the boys. And I don't know how to process that. And I don't always find it easy to keep my head composed when we play against Bolton."

As if a championship game wasn't enough pressure, this one happened to be against our biggest rivals. Not only that but the last time the two teams had played against each other, Jake had mentioned how hard it was for him to hold back his temper. I'd be lying if I said I wasn't also scared of what would happen again when Jake faced off with the same players. "I believe in you. You're one of the best, if not the best, players on the team. And beyond that, you're one of the most incredible human beings I know. I've never felt so supported, cared for, and loved until I met you." I pause for a moment to let my words sink in. "You've been able to keep your temper in check multiple times on the ice. Even when someone was running their mouth about me. Don't underestimate yourself."

"I appreciate that. I'll be sure to score two goals tonight just for you." He kisses my cheek.

"Only two?" I tease.

"Fine. How about a whole hat trick? Is that better?"

"Yeah I think that will do." I take his face into my hands. "You're going to do amazing, Jake. I know it."

His eyes soften, and he turns his head so he can kiss my palm. "Thank you. I needed that."

"And if it helps to keep you motivated, I'd just like to remind you that I'll be decked out in your jersey tonight."

"Mmm that is incredibly motivating." He shifts us so I'm pressed under him and buries his head into my neck. "Give me one good reason not to rip your clothes off and bury my tongue into your tight little pussy right now?"

The room heats up twenty degrees. "You have to leave for the pregame meeting in like 15 minutes?"

His blue eyes darken. "You think I'll need that long to make you come?"

"No, but I do think the odds of us losing track of time are high and the last thing I want is to be the reason why you get in trouble with your coaches for being late."

"You're right. I am pretty irresistible." He presses a rough kiss to my lips, long enough to leave me breathless, before pulling away. Tracing my bottom lip with his thumb he whispers, "To be continued."

I lay paralyzed in bed as he heads to the bathroom to get ready. My current state of bliss is ruined by the sound of Jake's phone ringing. I lean over to silence it when I recognize the number flashing on his screen. *What the hell was going on?* A pit forms in my stomach as I accept the call. "Mom?"

"Oh, Eliana. I wasn't expecting you to answer. I'll call back later."

I debate just letting it go, but she's met Jake once and

there's no way they magically bonded overnight. I know she'll be annoyed at me for asking about her personal business. Still, I can't help myself.

"Don't hang up. When did you get Jake's number?" My question unintentionally comes out a bit terse.

"We exchanged numbers that day he drove Josie back home following the Christmas trip. I..." She trails off, sounding nervous.

"Oh." This is so confusing. She had basically told me he was a distraction. I know I encouraged her to get to know him more...but something about this whole situation feels super off.

"Yes. You see...I have to admit, I misjudged him. I was just calling to tell him how much I've appreciated his generosity over the last few weeks. It's rare to find a man who's willing to help out a single mother without asking for anything in return. That certainly has never been my experience. I was a bit hesitant to accept the money in the first place, but he insisted the two of you had already discussed it and agreed—"

"Wait, what are you talking about?" She may as well have been speaking in gibberish.

My mom's silence lasts long enough for me to check whether we got disconnected. "Oh no. You didn't know, did you?"

"Know what? What do you mean he sent you money? How much did he send you?" My voice rises with each question.

The room starts spinning, and it feels like my lungs have stopped taking in oxygen. So that's why she didn't need me anymore. Didn't need my money. She had found it elsewhere. I suppose that part wasn't shocking, I had suspected as much. But the fact that it was Jake made my stomach turn.

"Just check in with Jake. And try not to be so hard on him. His heart was in the right place. I have to head to work, but we'll talk more later. Bye, my love."

I can't bring myself to respond, though I am able to pull myself together enough to no longer feel sick and confused. Instead, I just felt angry. Why did Jake go behind my back? Why did he lie and tell my mom that this was also my idea? What was he trying to prove? Did he not think I could handle it on my own?

I had more questions than I could even wrap my brain around, and unfortunately for Jake, by the time he came out of the bathroom, my anger and confusion had only festered.

My emotions must have been written all over my face because he immediately put up his hands in defense, a small smile on his face. "Whatever I did, I would just like to apologize ahead of time and say that you are right about everything and look incredibly beautiful even when you're angry."

Normally, his charms would get me to crack ever so slightly, but now I felt like a wall of steel, nearly impenetrable to whatever would get thrown my way. "So how much money do I owe you now?"

"What are you talking about?" Confusion washes over his face.

"You missed a call when you were in the bathroom. From my mom."

He lets out a sigh. "And what did she say?"

"Oh ya' know. she just wanted to check in and wish you luck on your game," I snap. "What do you *think* she said?"

"I was going to tell you, I promise. I just wanted to find the right time."

"Now seems like as good a time as any. How long has this been going on?"

"It started a few days after we left your home in Providence. I gave her my phone number and told her I'd be willing to help out financially if she needed it, especially if it meant lessening the burden you were putting on yourself and helping Josie out too. It just felt like the right thing to do." He shrugs.

"How much have you given her?"

"20,000 to help pay off the mortgage on her condo. I also offered to pay her a couple thousand dollars monthly for other expenses, but she refused. She just wanted to have her loans paid off and the rest she felt like she could handle." My skin must have turned pale because he immediately jumped to minimize what he'd done. "I promise it's fine. Doesn't even put a dent in my trust fund."

Jake's words of reassurance do anything but. They just remind me how different we are. Twenty thousand dollars was life-changing for my family, but for him, it was nothing. "It's going to take me a really long time to be able to pay you back."

His jaw ticks in irritation. "What do you mean pay me back? I did this so you wouldn't have to worry about working extra to support your family, not so you'd be indebted to me."

"Jake, I'm not just going to let my mom take money from your family."

"I promise they won't care. They know how privileged they are not to have to worry about money. They donate to families in need all the ti—", he stops himself, likely noticing the blind rage in my eyes.

"So we're just another charity case to you!"

"I acknowledge how bad that came out. I didn't mean it that way."

"Well you wouldn't be the first person to think that. Between the Bolton player, and my mom when she first met you, I'm sure everyone on this side of the Charles river thinks I'm only with you because of your money."

"Who cares what people think? I did this because I love you. And when I love someone, I also love all the people that are important to them and will do whatever I can to help."

His words soften some of the tension that's built up in my body, but the rage boiling in my stomach is mixing with my insecurities. Together they're a deadly combination. "I just don't get why you didn't talk to me first. I had the situation under control, and I hate that your solution is to just throw money at the problem.."

I regret the words immediately, especially the way they make him flinch. "That's unfair and you know it." He looks at me, eyes practically begging me to take it back. The silence consuming the room is suffocating. Jake takes a deep breath, eyes shut, until his phone goes off again. "Shit. I need to leave now, or I'm going to be late."

Jake throws his closet door open, slings his gym bag over his shoulder, and walks over to me. "I love you. This isn't over. And we'll talk more after the game."

He presses a soft kiss to the top of my head and my heart tugs at the disappointment on his face that I don't lean into his embrace like I normally would. I know my reaction caught him off guard, but after spending a majority of my life fending for myself and doing whatever I could to keep my family afloat, the last thing I wanted was for someone to view me as incapable of taking care of myself and my family.

Jake never said those exact words, and as I slowly calmed myself down, I knew he would never think that of me. But in the moment that's exactly what I had felt. My relationship with my mom was beyond complicated. And while I constantly wished that I could just have a typical parent-child relationship with her, that wasn't what I knew. Wasn't my normal. Over the years, supporting my family became more than just an obligation, it became a part of my identity. I was dependable and reliable, and you never had to question whether or not I would make sacrifices for my family. But if my family didn't need me anymore, what would I do? Who was I if not a provider? The question was swirling around my head the entire time I was fighting with Jake. And instead of being able to appreciate what he had done for my family, what he had done for *me*, all I could think about was, *who is Eliana Jasper if not the girl who puts everyone else's needs above her own?* I had no idea how to answer that question. And that's what scared me the most.

Chapter 47

Jake

There's nothing I hated more than leaving shit unresolved. Did I have a hunch that Eliana would be annoyed with me once she found out I had given money to her mom? Yes. She always had difficulty asking for help, and would rather run herself into the ground than admit she couldn't handle something on her own. But I never expected my helping her family to turn into this massive thing. While money can be a sensitive topic for most people, evidently for Eliana the issue was nuclear.

Eliana's hurt expression kept replaying in my head, and I know I would never forget it. Never forget that *I* was the one who had caused it. Fuck this sucked. I'm on edge not only from the fight with Eliana but also because I was about to enter one of the biggest games of my career, potentially my last game as a Westchester Wolf. *You're okay, Jake. Hockey is the one place you're in control. You got this.*

"You alright man? You look like you're about to be sick." Ollie leans over and taps me on the knee. We're back inside the locker room after our morning skate, where I missed a lot more shots and opportunities than I ever had.

Hopefully this wasn't foreshadowing for the night because I couldn't live with myself if I let my team down. "Ellie and I had a big fight. We weren't able to figure it out before I had to leave to come here."

"Shit man. I'm sorry to hear it. I know you're going through it, but we need you to have it together tonight."

"I know. I know. I'll be fine once the game starts."

Ollie shoots me a smile, my verbal reassurance being all he needs to restore his faith in me. My coach, however doesn't seem as easily convinced.

"Keeley, let me talk to you for a second." Mason nods his head to the secluded hallway entrance of the locker room. I fidget with my fingers, waiting for him to rail me for my piss-poor performance. He purses his lips. "You okay Jake?"

"Fine, fine."

Mason crosses his arms over his chest, unconvinced. "You weren't playing like yourself earlier."

"I just had a rough morning. Once the game starts, I'll be fine. I promise. The game always helps clear my head."

"What happened this morning?" He probes.

The last thing I wanted was to talk about my relationship problems with my coach. Sure he was only a few years older than me, but he was also someone I used to idolize. And hockey players weren't exactly known for talking about their feelings with each other.

I stand there. Silent.

"I'm not letting you go until you tell me what's up Keeley. I'm your coach, so I have to make sure you're okay, both physically and mentally, before you step out on the ice."

"Eliana and I had a big fight. I fucked up. I just wanted to help her because I love her, and I thought that's what I was doing, but I think she took it as some kinda dig at her. Now all I can think about is how I managed to break things even when all I wanted to do was fix them." I wince at the word vomit and look down at my skates.

"You wouldn't be the first guy who thought he was doing the right thing to protect the woman that he loved, only to have it blow up in his face." Mason's voice is so sincere, matching the look on his face.

The tightness in my stomach loosens "I just hope I can get her to hear me out. Hope she won't hate me for this."

"Do you really love her?" I give him a nod. "And she really loves you?" Another nod. "Then it will work itself out. I promise it will. Love is one of the most impenetrable forces in this world. Even when it feels like the most fragile thing that exists." Mason squeezes my shoulder.

"Damn when did you become such a poet?" I give him a small smile. Of all the conversations I thought I would have with Mason, I never guessed it would've been this.

He rolls his eyes. "When one of my players decided to mope about his love life. You good now?"

"All good coach. I'm glad you decided to stick around and help us. Glad you gave me a second chance."

"So am I. I'm proud of you Jake. You've come a long way."

"I'm not done yet. I won't let you down tonight Coach. You have my word."

* * *

The TD Garden, home of the Boston Bruins, is packed to the brim with Westchester and Bolton fans, including the front row seats I had reserved for Eliana and my family. I give her a smile from the ice, one that she returns, along with a small wave. The tension in my shoulders releases. We were okay. We got in a fight, but we were okay.

"Aye Keeley, looks like your family have the best seats in the house to watch me score." I turn around and see Ryker, the Bolton freshman who seemed determined to make his name by mouthing off to me.

I don't dignify him with a response, though my jaw does tighten as I hear him break out into a laugh. *He's not worth it, Keeley. Don't let him get to you.*

That was much easier said than done, once the game started. Bolton seemed hell-bent on bringing their absolute dirtiest tactics to this game, and I had already taken two "accidental" elbows to the ribs that knocked the breath out of me. My tolerance for bullshit was slowly fading.

I let out a loud curse as Ryker steals the puck from me and starts skating up the ice. Hustling up the ice at full speed still does nothing to stop Ryker as he lifts up his stick and shoots the puck right past Ollie. 0-1 Bolton. Fuck.

"A little too slow there, Keeley. Though I guess I shouldn't be too surprised." Ryker's smirk makes my blood boil.

Head back to the bench. Before I move I feel a sharp pain on the back side of my shin and drop to my knees. I look up and see Ryker holding his stick and looking incredibly smug.

"Ref c'mon open your eyes! He just slashed my alternate captain!" I hear Mason yell from the bench. The ref just looks between me and Ryker confused.

Oh come the fuck on. I inhale sharply and drop my stick. I skate up to Rkyer until I'm eye-to-eye with him. "If you wanna fucking go, you tell me. Don't slash me behind the ref's back."

Ryker drops his gloves and lets his equipment fall to the ice. "Careful Keeley, your girl already saw me score on you. Do you really want her to see me beat your ass too?"

My head snaps to the seats by the Westchester bench at the

mention of Eliana, whose wide eyes are filled with concern. The next thing I know, my head snaps back in pain. *Motherfucker*.

Ryker may have gotten the first punch, but it would cost him the rest of the season. Recovering from the hit, I see red and all I want to do is bash his head in. I can't though. Just because his ass was about to get ejected doesn't mean I would do the same to my teammates.

His face falls as he realizes I'm not taking his bait. The on-ice official pulls him back to his bench, the Bolton coach yelling a stream of profanities in response. The Westchester fans in the crowd go absolutely crazy as Ryker makes his way down the hall into the locker room, and I showboat my way towards my own bench.

My eyes search for Eliana's and she gives me a look of pride, biting her bottom lip in a way that sends a jolt throughout my entire body. Mason quickly yells out the next play to us. Adam skates out first and locks eyes with me as he nods towards center ice. I wait patiently for my opening to come, and charge onto the rink when I get it. Adam launches the puck out of our zone and I'm ready to catch it, skating toward Bolton's goal without anyone around to stop me. Faking left, I sneak the puck in between their goalie's legs and relish the way my bench goes absolutely crazy in response to my breakaway goal. Tie game.

My goal feels like a clean slate for the entire team, as every line starts showing up. Our freshmen are on absolute fire managing to get us the lead in the game, and the vets like me and Adam are more than ready to support them. Five minutes away from the end of the third period we're up two goals, and the championship title is so close I can nearly taste it. My linesmen are covered head to toe in sweat, and we give each other a look that screams this will be the most grueling five minutes of our lives.

Bolton's coach pulls their goalie off the ice and adds another man. A risky move that has helped many teams come back from the chopping block. A move one only makes when they're filled with desperation. To Bolton's credit, they're giving these final fading minutes everything and then some. I swear I see one of their shots slide past Ollie's glove, but he manages to catch it. I don't miss his expression of utter surprise when he realizes he actually stopped the goal.

Try as they might, they can't get past our defense. Every single man on the ice has wanted this moment for years, if not their entire lives. And we weren't about to let this moment be taken from us. The fans in the arena start counting down the remaining seconds...10...9...8...Time passes in slow motion, the crowd goes quiet in my head, and by the time the buzzer sounds, I see gloves flying in the sky and Ollie and Adam charging towards me throwing their arms around me. "Holy shit, we did it! We fucking did it!"

The entire team empties from the bench to the ice, followed by our coaches, and the tournament staff brings the massive Hockey East Championship trophy onto the ice. Adam is the first person that gets to hoist it up to the roaring crowd, handing it to me as I make my lap around the ice. The rest of the team follows and eventually, all our friends and families join us in celebration. My mom, sisters, and Eliana all tackle me at once, with my dad serving as the cameraman, snapping photos of the celebration. Eventually, they let me have some time alone with Eliana, and though there's still a lot left we need to discuss, we decide to let the moment be. She jumps up into my arms, and I wrap my arms around her waist, crushing her to my chest. I lose track of how long we stay embraced in each other's arms. When I eventually have to leave to get cleaned up, I set her down. But I know one thing for certain: I would never let her go.

Chapter 48

Eliana

Hockey House had thrown a massive rager in celebration of their win. The next morning, Adam woke everyone up with the sound of a loud alarm blasting through the speakers. Since everyone's families were coming over tonight for a cookout, he demanded a house-wide deep clean. Jake told me he almost choked Adam after 3 hours of cleaning. My heart squeezed thinking of the man that I love. The man that I had lashed out at for trying to help me. We still hadn't fully talked about why I freaked out earlier, and while I didn't want to bring down the mood, I also knew that avoiding this conversation was weighing down on both of us.

"You all set Dad?" Jake checks in with his father, who was brave enough to take on cooking for a house of hungry college hockey players and their families.

"Sauce is simmering now. Sienna's helping me with the chicken. Dinner should be ready in 30 minutes." His response is met with a round of cheers from the hungry patrons nearby.

Jake takes this moment to grab my hand and lead me upstairs before we get roped into another conversation about game highlights. He shuts the door of his room gently as I take a seat on his bed, toying with the hemline of my jeans. Jake takes a deep breath and lets it out as he sits down next to me.

I stare into his beautiful blue eyes for entirely too long before I get the courage to finally speak. "I'm sorry for how I reacted yesterday. And the hurtful things I said. I didn't mean any of it."

His expression softens as he takes my shaking hand into his. "I appreciate that. I know you've told me that I can't take away your stress, and that you don't expect me to take on your problems. I really just wanted to make your life a little easier. So you wouldn't have to work a ton of odd jobs just to help your mom out."

"I know. Even when I was upset, I knew your heart was in the right place."

"I guess I should've known better. Money is always a sensitive topic, and I know for you it's even more so."

"It is, but honestly I think the reason why I freaked out was even bigger than that. It's hard to explain, but at that moment I just felt so *useless*. Like so much of my identity as a person is being a caretaker for my mom and Josie. I've always been Eliana, the daughter who's reliable and hard working. The daughter that will do anything she can, even sacrifice her own wellbeing, to help her family stay afloat. And when I found out I didn't have to do that anymore...The more I thought about what it meant to no longer be a provider for my family, the more I realized I didn't even know who I was outside of that. Losing a part of yourself is scary. Realizing you've never been able to really be your own self because you were too busy taking care of others...that was terrifying for me."

Saying the words out loud felt both like a relief and a dirty confession. I didn't want to come off as someone who constantly complained about her family and took them for granted. I loved Josie with all my heart, and for all the moments my mom and I argue, I couldn't imagine a world without her in it. But at the same time, I was parentified from an extremely young age. And much as I wished it hadn't impacted me, I couldn't deny that it had.

Jake brings his hand to my cheek, wiping away a stray tear I hadn't even realized had fallen. "I'm so sorry, Ellie. I never meant to hurt you so much. Never meant to make you feel useless."

"It's not your fault. Not in the slightest. I appreciate what you did. Not only for helping my family but also for making me realize that I base my entire self-worth on how much I mean to others. And that maybe it's time for that to change. Time for me to *finally* make space for Eliana, and all of my wants and needs."

Jake presses a series of small kisses to my temple, before pulling back. His expression is a mix of understanding and pride. "The world is better with you in it Eliana. And you won't last long if you try to take on everyone else's burdens without making space for yourself to live. I'm proud of you for finally wanting to focus on yourself and what makes you happy. And I can't wait to be by your side, cheering you on as you do."

I felt a strange feeling of anxiety mixed with excitement at the thought of finally putting myself first. I had no doubts it would be an uphill battle where I'd have to constantly fight the guilty voice in my head that said I was selfish. But it would be worth it.

A knock on the door startles us. "Jake, Eliana, dinner's ready!" Both our stomachs grumble in response.

We rush down the stairs to meet the crowd of people lined up in the kitchen, plates in hand, while Jake's dad serves his homemade pasta and meatballs.

"Ah if it isn't the man of the hour. That breakaway shot was a thing of beauty." Ollie drunkenly slurs, throwing an arm around Jake's shoulder. He turns his attention to me. "I guess I should also thank you too. Jake wouldn't have even been on the ice if you hadn't helped him get his grades back into shape. Do they give out awards for being great tutors? Because they should."

Katherine immediately turns her attention to Jake. *Shit.* I guess the cat's out of the bag. "Ollie, I thought Eliana was your tutor."

Ollie's too drunk to even notice the tension in the room. "Nope. I took it years ago. Still not sure why this guy decided to take PSYCH101 now, but if he hadn't, he never would've met Eliana so I guess it was all worth it in the end."

"Jake, why didn't you tell me you were struggling?" The hurt in Katherine's voice feels like a punch to the gut. I feel Jake stiffen next to me, no doubt feeling even worse than I did.

"Katherine, maybe we should discuss this later." Jake's dad sends me a sheepish smile, as I take in the audience that's watching us. Katherine gives him a small nod before heading into the living room, clearly upset.

"Looks like I'm having two difficult conversations tonight." Jake groans into my neck.

"We'll weather the storms together."

The tension in his shoulders drops. "That's all I needed to hear to know everything will be okay."

Chapter 49

Jake

I'd done everything in my power to stall people from leaving. Of all the ways I had envisioned this night ending, Ollie spilling the beans about Eliana being my tutor, and me having to admit to my family that I am the academic black sheep (which they deep down already knew) was not on my bingo card. The hurt on my mom's face when she realized I had lied to her made me want to crawl into my bed like I had when I was a kid. Much to my dismay, most of my roommates and their parents decided to call it a night after dinner, which left me, Sienna, Charlotte, and Eliana awkwardly cleaning up the kitchen in silence while my dad comforted my mom.

"Maybe if we stall long enough, she'll have enough glasses of wine that she won't even remember what Ollie said," I whisper.

"Unlikely. Mom never forgets anything. Especially when it comes to her kids. You played a dangerous game lying to her." Charlotte's tone is clipped. Wouldn't be surprised if she was also upset that I hadn't come to her for help.

Eliana is standing in the corner, nursing her third glass of wine. "This is it, isn't it? Katherine Fisher hates me. I can kiss away my career and also any chances of my future mother-in-law liking me."

I can't help but break out into a smile. "Future mother-in-law, huh? Glad to know you're not planning on getting rid of me anytime soon."

"Jake. This isn't funny!" she pouts, the alcohol clearly heightening her emotions.

"She doesn't hate you, I promise. If anything, she probably loves you even more now, knowing that you helped me get out of a really rough spot. She's mad at me for not being honest with her, which is fair enough."

"Don't forget you lied to us too. I hate that you didn't trust us enough to tell us you needed help." Sienna stands next to Charlotte, arms crossed. Looks like my apology tour would include multiple stops.

"Alright, I guess I can't avoid this anymore." I give Eliana a kiss on her forehead before walking over to the living room and sitting on the couch across from my mom. My sisters shuffle in behind me and sit next to my parents. Another sign that they were pissed at me. Great.

"I'm sorry that I wasn't honest with you all about how Eliana and I met. It wasn't her idea at all and I take full responsibility for asking her to keep up with my lie. I messed up, and I'm sorry."

"So she was your tutor? Not Ollie's." My mom confirms.

"Yup. I was failing psych. Nearly got benched for the season. Eliana swooped in and saved my ass. And the more we spent time together, the more I started to fall for her, and the rest is history."

My mom's eyes soften, and I mentally pat myself on the back. She was always a softie for a love story, and I would take any advantage I could get to make her less mad at me. "I just don't get why you wouldn't tell us. Why you felt the need to lie. I'm not just your mom; I'm a psychology professor, for God's sake. Don't you think I could've helped you?"

"That's the whole reason why I *didn't* want you involved. I took this class so I could finally relate to you, Char, and Sienna. Finally be able to understand and join in on dinner conversations instead of spending the entire time googling and sitting in silence. You're all out here doing this incredible work that is probably going to change the world some day and I...Sometimes I feel like I'm not one of you because I'm not also an academic."

Hurt flashes over my sisters' faces, while my mom's eyes fill with tears as she speaks. "I have never once viewed you as anything less than my incredible, talented, and compassionate son. And if I've ever done anything to make you think otherwise—"

"That's the thing, you haven't." My head drops to my hands. "Which is why I feel even worse for having these feelings. You, Dad, Sienna, and Char have always supported me in all of my dreams, and I can't explain why I felt like the black sheep of the family, but I did. And when I couldn't even manage to keep my grade up in the class, it felt like I had failed you all in some way."

"You've never once failed us, Jake. Not once. We're proud of all you've accomplished, and we love you so much."

"Thanks, Mom. I love you too, and I'm sorry again for lying."

My mom stands up and wraps her arms around me. Before I know it I'm being crushed into a family group hug, that also includes Eliana as my dad waves her over.

"I'm losing oxygen here," I joke as everyone pulls away.

"Good. Maybe this will help you remember never to doubt

our support and love for you again." Sienna scoffs, mock-punching my arm.

"We can hope. But don't worry, I'll be there to remind him how amazing he is every step of the way." Eliana reassures my family.

I reach out and give her hand a squeeze. "How did I ever get so lucky to have you as my partner?"

"Lots of mocha frappuccinos with extra whipped cream from the Beanery. And breakfast sandwiches. And cooking me dinner. I guess the way to my heart really is through my stomach." She laughs as I wrap my arms around her.

"Lucky for you, I'm an excellent cook."

"Well you certainly have the ego of a chef."

"I prefer the term 'confidence'."

"I'm sure you do." She rolls her eyes, relaxing into my embrace.

My mom lets out a yawn that triggers a domino effect of sleepy expressions, leading to my family giving me one giant goodbye hug before going home. Eliana and I follow suit, heading upstairs to get ready for bed. Most of my post-championship adrenaline has worn off at this point, which means the aches and pains of the game were starting to crawl back in. By the time we're both ready for sleep, I have to grit my teeth just to get into bed.

"You alright?" Eliana worries her lip between her teeth as she joins me, reaching over to the nightstand to turn off the light.

"Much better now that you're here with me," I murmur into her hair. "All I'll ever need is you right here by my side. Nothing else matters."

She lets out a content sound as I wrap my arms around her, closing the small amount of distance between us. "Who knew you were such a romantic, Jake Keeley."

"You bring out the best in me. From the moment we met, I knew I wanted to be better. For myself, for you. I appreciate you taking a chance on me."

"And I appreciate you not letting me push you away in the beginning." She laughs, likely thinking of our less-than-optimal initial encounters.

"I'm nothing if not determined. Especially when it comes to convincing the most incredible person I've ever met to love me."

"It's funny because I was equally determined not to let your charms get to me, and yet here we are."

"Damn. I guess you got outplayed."

"I guess so. It was worth it though. I love you, Jake Keeley."

"I love you with all my heart, Eliana Jasper."

She falls asleep first, with her hand entwined with mine. I get lost in counting the freckles that cover her cheeks, the feel of her body pressed against mine, and the scent of her floral shampoo washing over me. I've never experienced this level of peace before. Never thought I would experience this type of love and contentment. While I couldn't predict the future, I could say with absolute certainty that the time I get to spend with Eliana will be time I cherish from this day until the end of my days.

Epilogue

Three Months Later

Eliana

"In hindsight, we should've left early." Jake gives my knee a squeeze, leaning his head back in frustration as he takes in the never-ending sea of cars in front of us.

"What was that? I thought I heard mention of leaving earlier. But that can't be given how insistent you were that we wouldn't hit traffic. I must be hearing things," I tease.

"Ya know, this is also partially your fault."

I gasp in mock offense. "Oh? How so? Given I told you traffic would be insane and we should leave at 8, but you said 10 would be fine."

"That's my point. We both know you're always right, so you shouldn't have let me convince you to leave at 10. You should've just told me to shut up."

"I would never tell you to shut up. But I do appreciate you acknowledging how I was right."

"Always, love. Always." He presses a kiss to the back of my hand. "Excited for your first time on Martha's Vineyard?" Jake invited me to his family's house on the island to celebrate the end of the school year. His parents and sisters had been there a few days already, and my mom and Josie were driving down tomorrow. After my fight with Jake, I had a long conversation with my mom, who was also apologetic about accepting the money. She had truly believed Jake and I had already discussed it, and mailed him back the check. Jake, of course, refused to accept it and told her she can either cash it, or he'll call her mortgage company and pay it off himself. He insisted on getting paid in home-cooked meals every time we came to visit would make them equal, and my mom rolled her eyes while also thanking him profusely.

Without my mom having to worry about her loans, I also felt free. Speaking about financial matters would likely always be a sour spot for us, my mom did apologize for how much emotional labor she had asked of me all these years. I knew it took a lot for her to acknowledge treating me like a co-parent instead of her daughter. Inviting her on this trip was our first attempt at fixing what had been broken, and attempting to have a normal relationship.

"Yes I can't wait to lay on the beach all day, watch the sunset, and see you man a sailboat."

"The sailboat situation might be a disaster. I haven't gone out on one since high school, but don't worry. I'm an excellent swimmer, so one way or another, I'll get us back to shore." He smirks.

"Mmm maybe you should have Ollie or Adam steer instead." His two best friends would also be joining us this week.

"Not happening. I know I can at least get us out into the ocean. They'd have us capsized in under two minutes."

"Sounds like I should definitely wear a life jacket regardless."

"Hey now. Where's that optimism of yours that I love?"

I look at him like he's grown two heads.

"Alright, fair enough. Optimism was definitely a stretch there. What's the ETA now?"

"Still three hours according to my phone. Which is not surprising given we've moved two feet in the past thirty minutes." I kick my shoes off in the passenger seat. "Might as well get comfy now."

"Three hours?! Well at least it's still early enough that we don't need to worry about missing the ferry to Martha's Vineyard."

"True. Though we still have three hours of time to kill. And I'm on a strict 'no working' policy." I look at Jake from the side of my eye.

"That's right. You have two weeks before you start your summer internship, which means you should be doing nothing but recovering from the spring semester and enjoying the summer until then."

"I don't think I've ever gone two weeks without working. My body feels on edge without direct access to my laptop." I'm partially joking, knowing I had a small nightmare last night that I forgot to turn my final papers in and failed the semester. Clearly, I had some lingering post-exam anxiety to work through.

"Hmm sounds like I need to do a better job at helping you relax then." Jake loosens his grip on my knee to draw idle circles up and down my thigh, drawing out goosebumps.

"And how do you plan on doing that?" I pry.

"I have a few ideas." A wicked glint appears in his eyes. One that sends a rush of heat through my body.

"Like wh—" I gasp as he pushes the top of my skirt up to

my stomach, completely exposing me. He traces the top of my panties before dragging his index finger, adding pressure to my clit.

My eyes start to close, letting the pleasure come over me, when I remember where we are. I move to cover myself. "We can't do this here. Someone could see."

"No one's going to notice us."

"We're in standstill traffic. Someone will notice," I counter.

Despite the words leaving my mouth, the look of determination on Jake's face has me silently screaming at myself to throw caution to the wind. I feel something fall on my lap a second later.

"Use that towel to keep yourself covered. I want your panties off and legs spread in the next two minutes." His voice drops three octaves sending a chill down my spine.

A moment later, my panties are at my ankles, a towel covering my legs, and Jake is moving his hand back onto my thigh. "Such a good girl. Are you wet for me already?"

My eyes shut, and I give him a small nod, unable to form words.

He clicks his tongue. "That won't work for me, Ellie. I need your eyes on me, while you answer me out loud."

I still hadn't gotten used to how dirty Jake's mouth could be. From the smirk on his face, I could tell he was enjoying every moment of leaving me speechless. "I—"

"Take your time, babe. We're not going anywhere anytime soon." He nods at the traffic in front of us.

"You're such a— Oh god...*yes*." He cuts me off by pressing his thumb firmly on my clit, drawing small circles.

"Fuck I love seeing you like this. Legs spread just for me, dripping wet." He quickens the pace of his thumb, all while teasing my entrance with his index finger. "Such a good girl letting me play with this pussy."

My nails dig into the car door in pleasure as he sinks his finger inside of me, adjusting his hand so the base of his palm rubs on my clit. I moan so loud I swear it shakes the car as he continues to move his finger in and out, all while applying the perfect amount of pressure to my sensitive bundle of nerves. "More Jake. I need more."

He adds in another finger, groaning at how easy it is for me to take him. Leaning my head against the car seat, I start moving my hips against him. "God I love you. You're dripping all over me, baby. You look so damn beautiful taking my fingers. It's taking all my restraint right now not to drag you into the back seat, throw your legs over my shoulders and make you come on my cock over and over again."

The pleasure building in my body takes control over the rational part of me. "Yes. Do it. Do whatever you want, just don't stop. I'm so close, so, so clo—" In an instant the feeling of fullness is lost as is the orgasm that was seconds away from coming.

Breathless, confused, and incredibly irritated, my head snaps to Jake, who's licking his fingers clean, moaning as he tastes me on him.

"Why did you stop?" I nearly growl.

His eyes are filled with mischief. "The traffic is moving. I had to drive."

I look ahead at the two extra two feet of space ahead of us. "We barely moved!"

"We just have so much time to kill, it would be a shame if we finished so quickly and had nothing else to do, wouldn't it? Plus, I've never gotten the chance to edge you before. Would you be willing to give it a try?" His tone shifts from teasing to sincere, and I'm reminded that despite all of Jake's joking, he would never do anything I was uncomfortable with.

It's his never-wavering dedication to making me feel as safe and loved as possible that has me reaching over for his hand and placing it back between my legs. The next hour is a delicious mix of torment and bliss. Jake does everything in his power to avoid my clit, burying his fingers in me and mercilessly rubbing against my g-spot over and over again but never letting me come.

I'm a shaking mess covered head to toe in sweat and somehow, I have never felt so cherished and taken care of. I bring my hand to brush through his hair and turn his face so he's looking at me. "I'm not sure I can hold off much longer."

"Show me what you need. Use me." My mouth drops open as I follow his command, adjusting his hand in between my legs so that he has two fingers buried deep inside of me while his thumb hovers over my swollen clit.

"Good?" Jake asks, waiting for me to nod before giving me everything I needed and more. His thumb on my clit is relentless as is the movement of his fingers as he brushes against a spot inside of me that makes me clench around him. "Fuck that's right. Squeeze my fingers babe. God you're so damn wet for me. Such a good girl. All for me."

My peaked nipples hardened even more at his words as I move my hips to match his pace. I wrap my hand around his wrist, making sure he can't stop, as I finally, *finally*, am able to let my orgasm come. I nearly sob as I feel the pleasure take over and also build again. Though Jake's rough movements on my core have slowed down ever so slightly, I've been so pent up for the last hour that I can't help but come on his hand again.

"You're so beautiful, Ellie. So fucking beautiful." Jake murmurs as I let the exhaustion take over.

* * *

Jake woke me up when we were about thirty minutes away from the ferry, likely knowing I'd need a little more time than normal to get myself together. We'd spent most of the time on the roof of the boat, staring at the beautiful blue water surrounding us. Once we docked, the drive to his family's summer home was fairly quick, allowing us to arrive just as Jake's dad was finishing up grilling.

"Food smells great, Dad," Jake calls from the kitchen through the open patio door.

"I hope you kids came hungry because I made enough to feed a small village

"Don't you worry Dad. Ollie and Adam are coming over so we'll definitely put a large dent in whatever you got cooking up."

Sienna tenses up next to me as she rummages through the kitchen drawers. "Oliver's coming?"

Jake's eyes narrow. "Yeah why?"

"Just want to make sure we have enough steak knives. I'll add one for him...and Adam." She runs out to the patio to set the table before either of us can say anything.

"Do you think that was weird?" Jake grabs the plates from my hands, stopping me before we walk outside.

Did I think Sienna was acting weird? Sure. But I wasn't about to tell Jake that, especially since I didn't want to trigger Jake's overprotective older-brother senses. For now I would stay out of it. "Nah I don't think so. She was probably just tired from laying out in the sun all day. I wouldn't read into it."

Jake decides to let it go, giving me a shrug before leading me outside where I'm engulfed in a hug by his mom. "Ellie, it's so good to see you. I just received an email that all your paperwork has been approved for your internship. I can't wait to have you in my lab this summer."

"Me too! I'm so excited. I've already started thinking of a

few ideas we could analyze with the dataset you shared with me—"

"As much as I love seeing you both nerd out over your work, may I remind you both that we are on *vacation*, so I'm going to have to cut this conversation short." Jake interrupts, pulling me toward the table and placing a massive steak in front of me.

"This is bigger than my head." I laugh.

He leans down, pressing his lips next to my ear. "You spent a lot of energy today. Need to make sure you refuel."

My face feels like I'm standing next to a bonfire and I'm eternally grateful for Adam and Ollie arriving right then to distract Jake's family from my sudden embarrassment. "I'm gonna get you back for that."

Jake's eyes widened. "Is that a promise?"

I roll my eyes as I watch Ollie's gaze linger a little too long on Sienna. Jake is thankfully distracted by whatever Adam is saying to him to notice. The rest of dinner is fairly uneventful sans the gorgeous sunset we all took in from the shoreline right outside Jake's house. Ollie and Adam bailed after that, followed by Sienna and Charlotte, who decided to have an early night.

"C'mon, our night's not over yet." Jake walks over to his car and drives us to the local ice cream store downtown. While we finish our sweet treats, he tells me about the time when he and his sisters ordered the ice cream tower, consisting of a dozen scoops and every sundae topping known to man, and were sick for three days after. Jake threw up all over Charlotte's stuffed teddy bear when they got home, and she still hasn't let him forget it.

Jake drives us along the shore of the island until we reach the top of a hiking trail littered with families, friends, and couples counting the stars above them. He helps me up onto the hood of his car and wraps an arm around me as we look up at the night sky.

"I know my history with identifying constellations is a bit shaky…" He trails off as I chuckle into his chest. "But I've been studying up for this very moment."

"Wow. Voluntarily studying? Your tutor would be so proud," I tease.

"As she should be."

"So tell me, what did you learn?"

"Those stars right there represent Andromeda and right underneath her is Perseus." His long arm points to the stars to our right.

"And what's their story?"

"They both went through many trials and tribulations in their lives. Fought like hell to be together, and had a love so great that when they died their love was immortalized in the sky as stars, to represent their never-ending love and loyalty to each other."

"That's beautiful." I press a small kiss to his cheek, taking in the stars.

"It is, though I know one love story that's even greater than theirs."

"Oh? Which one?"

He moves from looking at the stars to my face. It's hard to see in the dark, but I swear his eyes start to tear up as he declares, "Ours."

My eyes flicker from the man in front of me and the stars in the sky. We may not have a constellation dedicated to us, but one thing was for certain. He was my entire universe. And I was his.

THE END

Acknowledgments

For Monna, my personal Josie. When you discovered my secret author identity I was mortified (largely due to the spicy scenes I've written), but when you told me how proud you were of me it was a moment I'll always cherish. I love you to the moon and back, and then some.

To Kelly. My real-life Nicole — at least Eliana and Nicole got to live close to each other in the bookish universe! I promise one day we won't have thousands, or even hundreds of miles in between us. Love you loads.

Alexa thank you for always being ready to eat all my books up even when they're half written (or sometimes a mere few sentences of a plot rolling around in my head distracting me from editing other books that exist). Thank you for always supporting me and all my crazy plans (and reminding me to take care of myself).

Sammy for always understanding me and my Type-A over dramatic ways. I always feel safe coming to you.

Erin, for always listening to my (not always coherent) post-real-job rants, being the best roommate, having the kindest heart...and storing all my copies of *The Ice Out* when we had to evacuate from the fires (do you remember fire-nado? Wild).

Belinda, for being such an incredible rock for me this past year and half. You bring so much light and inspiration into my life, and I hope you know how much I appreciate you.

Gloria, for being a massive support for me this year. I see you. I hear you. You're going to change the world one day.

Jericha, for showing me that I don't need to set aside my dreams for the hopes that I'll get to them eventually. I deserve to live now, and you have shown me that.

Alexis for being an amazing friend and ongoing inspiration. I wouldn't be the person that I am or the author that I am without you.

Lauren, my incredible editor, who has now been handed two surprise books written by me without batting an eye. Thank you for making sure my character's voices are always heard.

And lastly, to you, my lovely reader for welcoming Jake and Eliana into your homes, believing in me, and asking me for more. You're the reason I continue to do this.

With Love,
Mina

Behind the Book

Eliana and Jake were never supposed to have their own book. In fact Eliana was never a character I even imagined until I was about 70% done with writing *The Ice Out*. This book is the first of its own interconnected standalone series, but (for those of you who don't know) it does broadly exist in the same universe as my *Castle Harbor* series. Jake Keeley was initially created as plot fodder *The Ice Out*, which follows Violet and Mason (if you haven't read their story yet....I highly recommend you do! And if you have read their story, I hope it was fun 1. seeing the same scenes you have seen before in a different perspective and 2. getting some new scenes of them as well). Long story short I needed a reason for V&M to have to work together and thus the asshole-hockey-player-problem-child that is Jake Keeley was born. For reasons unbeknownst to me I thought it would be absolutely necessary to have a scene in *The Ice Out* where Violet and Mason interact with Jake and his tutor...and thus Eliana was created. At the time she was *also* just supposed to be plot fodder but, the second I put Jake and Eliana together I couldn't deny their chemistry and before you know it I started to write *Outplayed.*

While Jake and Eliana caught me off guard, in some respect having a book was bound to happen — one thing about me is I will always fall for the side characters (in shows, movies, books that are not my own). Though Eliana was a blank canvas initially, once I decided to give her a book I knew her inside and out. She was the eldest daughter, parentified from a young age, struggling to balance living her own life and dreams with her family's. That on its own is a lot to deal with. Adding the layers of Eliana being a woman of color, and the child of an immigrant makes her relationship with her mom, and the duty she feels towards her family, makes the situation exceptionally complex to navigate.

How can you tell a person that sacrificed everything and left the only home that they knew to ensure that *you* could live a better life that you can't help them anymore? And how can you live your own life when you're taking on someone else's burdens as your own? The answer to both questions is you can't. Much of the dynamic of Eliana and her mother was pulled from my own personal experiences, thus writing Eliana's struggle with telling her mom no and setting boundaries in their relationship was fairly easy (living it out in real life however...that was much harder). Eliana's relationship with her mother is a complicated one, that will likely be a work in progress for a while. But one thing I hope was clear was that they both do love each other in their own way, even if their definitions of love differ.

Eliana is also her own person. As a reader you're probably like "...well duh" but something about spending two paragraphs talking about her relationship with her mom made me want to highlight her. She's a researcher, a friend, a woman of color, someone who is strong headed, loyal, dependable, not afraid to speak her mind, and often overexerts herself for the things and the people that she loves. The issue is when a majority of your identity has been spent taking care of others...it can be hard to take care of yourself. It can also feel foreign when you no longer are responsible for the people you spent a majority of your life caring for. Eliana is someone who is so used to picking up everyone else's broken pieces that she doesn't have time to focus on her own. But she should. She deserves it. Deserves to have time to herself, time to lick her own wounds, and time to celebrate all the things she's accomplished.

Now we have Jake Keeley. While he was a bit of a selfish dick in the beginning (which even he will admit he was), for some reason I couldn't ignore the voice in my head that told me Jake was so much more. I knew I could do the classic trope (which I love for the record) of 'hockey player took a class because he thought it was easy...jokes on him'), but I wanted to do something different. Wanted to add some layers to the classic hockey playboy we know and love. I also wanted to flip the classic arc of "Academic kid in a family of jocks feels misunderstood." And thus we have Jake Keeley, who loves and feels supported by his family of Psychologists so much that he wishes he could also join in on the fun. Naturally he also falls for his tutor who is also a super brainy researcher.

What was also interesting to explore was Jake's dynamic with his family and his related insecurities. Despite the fact that they were so supportive of him, and Jake himself knowing his family was proud of him...he still couldn't shake the feeling of being different from them. Couldn't shake the feeling that he wasn't good enough. That is a feeling I know all too well, and I think many people can relate to. Sometimes, no matter how much someone else tries to convince you that you are good enough, it's hard to internalize it until you yourself believe it.

Though Jake and Eliana's upbringing vastly differed, one

thing they have in common is their dedication to supporting and helping the people that they care about. Some of my favorite moments of this book were Jake taking care of Eliana without her even having to ask, bringing her food, giving her space to vent, and taking care of her when she got sick. His relationship with his parents and sisters also stand out to me as moments where you get to see how much he cares about others.

Another thing they have in common (that I can also relate to) is difficulty asking for help, even when you know you need it. If I can leave readers with any message from this book it's 'You can do anything, but not everything'. Asking for help isn't a sign of weakness and while it can be scary to open yourself up into trusting someone to help you, trying to take on the entire world on your own leads to burnout, frustration, and can result in a sense of loneliness. Asking for help is not only brave, but it allows you some space to sustain yourself, so you can continue to be the incredible human being that you are. It's a lesson that may be hard for many (like myself) to fully embrace at moments, but through writing this book I reminded myself that it's okay to take time for you. I learned that it's okay to not fight every battle in my life alone. And I hope that you, my lovely reader, learn that as well.

Author's note addendum April 7th, 2025

The entirety of this book including the authors note above was written in prior to November 2024. Given so much as changed in the world from then until now, I find it important to highlight that my books will always be a safe space for immigrants, children of immigrants, BIPOC, queer, neurodivergent readers. I am outraged by the world we live in and will continue to showcase characters from diverse backgrounds hoping that this serves as a place for my readers to feel seen and represented.

If you're in need of support or resources please check out: https://www.aclu.org/know-your-rights

From the bottom of my heart, thank you for your continuous support now and always. You, my reader, are the reason why I'm able to do this and that means the world to me.

Mina Myles

About the Author

Mina Myles is a romance author by night and PhD student by day. Her home base is Southern California, but if you've read one of Mina's books then you know her heart is still in Boston.

Mina's characters will have you kicking your feet, but don't move the tissue box too far because pain and angst are never too far behind. After all, what's the sweet without a dash of salt and a little spice?

To be the first to know about future releases sign up to her newsletter: minamylesbooks.com/newsletter

You can also find her on
Instgram: @minamylesbooks
TikTok: @minamylesauthor

Also by Mina Myles

The Ice Out (Castle Harbor Book 1)

Troped (By Mina Myles & Sierra Spencer)

www.ingramcontent.com/pod-product-compliance
Lightning Source LLC
Chambersburg PA
CBHW032342310726
48973CB00007B/1817